PRAISE FOR T.R. RAGAN

Her Last Day

"Intricately plotted . . . The tense plot builds to a startling and satisfying resolution."

—*Publishers Weekly* (starred review)

"Ragan's newest novel is exciting and intriguing from the very beginning . . . Readers will race to finish the book, wanting to know the outcome and see justice served."

—*RT Book Reviews*

"Readers will obsess over T.R. Ragan's new tenacious heroine. I can't wait for the next in the series!"

—Kendra Elliot, author of the *Wall Street Journal* bestsellers *Spiraled* and *Targeted*

"With action-packed twists and turns and a pace that doesn't let up until the thrilling conclusion, *Her Last Day* is a brilliant start to a gripping new series from T.R. Ragan."

—Robert Bryndza, #1 international bestselling author of *The Girl in the Ice*

T0058672

BURIED
DEEP

OTHER TITLES BY
T.R. RAGAN

JESSIE COLE SERIES

Her Last Day
Deadly Recall
Deranged

FAITH MCMANN TRILOGY

Furious
Outrage
Wrath

LIZZY GARDNER SERIES

Abducted
Dead Weight
A Dark Mind
Obsessed
Almost Dead
Evil Never Dies

WRITING AS THERESA RAGAN

Return of the Rose
A Knight in Central Park
Taming Mad Max
Finding Kate Huntley
Having My Baby
An Offer He Can't Refuse
Here Comes the Bride
I Will Wait for You: A Novella
Dead Man Running

BURIED DEEP

A
JESSIE COLE
THRILLER

T.R. RAGAN

THOMAS & MERCER

Published by Thomas & Mercer, Seattle

www.apub.com

Amazon, the Amazon logo, and Thomas & Mercer are trademarks of Amazon.com, Inc., or its affiliates.

ISBN-13: 9781542091480
ISBN-10: 1542091489

Cover design by Kirk DouPonce, DogEared Design

Printed in the United States of America

Listen to the voices in your head.

ONE

Jason Geiger slid into the back seat next to his wife and shut the door.

He exhaled.

He shouldn't be doing this. Sitting here now. Celebrating. It was all wrong. But he hadn't found the courage to tell Lacey he wanted to call it quits.

"Where to?" the driver asked.

"The Firehouse," Jason said.

Lacey leaned forward as if the driver wouldn't be able to hear her otherwise, a ridiculous notion considering she wasn't exactly soft-spoken. "It's a very special night," she told him.

The driver didn't flinch. Nor did he say a word.

"It's our eighth anniversary," Lacey went on. "Well, I mean, the actual day is a few days from now, but Jason would never be able to get a weeknight off. He works too hard." She turned his way.

Jason forced a smile as he reached for the bottle of champagne in the ice bucket. Nice touch, considering the price for a ride to the restaurant and back was more than fair, and the car was definitely not a limo. He lifted the bottle as he looked at the driver in the rearview mirror. "Thanks."

No reaction.

Something about the man looked familiar. Jason stared at him, trying to place where he might have seen him before. He finally gave up and instead concentrated on opening the bottle of champagne. A shot of whiskey sounded pretty good, but champagne would have to do.

The foil and wire had been removed from the bottle, and all he had to do was pop the cork. Jason poured a few inches of bubbly into the plastic cups provided and handed one to his wife. She hesitated, then took a tiny sip and made a toast. "To the best life," she said.

"To the best life," he repeated.

He gulped down the champagne and refilled his glass.

He was thirty-two years old. He had his whole life in front of him. The prospect of spending another eight years with Lacey just didn't sound appealing any longer. He used to see her as cute and quirky. Now he saw her as overly talkative, always hovering over him. She did go out of her way to do things for him and make him comfortable, which was nice, but it just wasn't the same.

Basically, they were friends. Nothing more.

He'd never questioned her love for him. But still. He'd spent so many nights in bed, tossing and turning, unsure of how to tell her what he was feeling. But the time was never right. It didn't matter how late he came home, she always had a smile on her face. She was perky and positive, for the most part. Sure, she had her moments, but her bad days weren't like most people's. Any momentary lapses in her always-sunny disposition were more like blips on a radar screen. Fleeting.

Every morning he woke up thinking, *This is the day I'll tell her*, and every night he climbed into bed beside her and kissed her good night.

He might not be able to pinpoint the exact problem he was having with Lacey, but that didn't change anything. He knew without a doubt that, for him, she just wasn't enough.

Lacey could hardly contain her excitement. Lately, it seemed as if she and Jason never had time for each other, which was why she'd been saving her big news for tonight.

She was pregnant.

Finally.

Jason had no idea of the extreme measures she'd taken to make it happen. After they had sex in the morning, which wasn't nearly often enough, he would run off to work, and she would stay in bed and keep her legs raised high, her heels resting against the wall for hours. This was only one of the tricks of the trade she'd gotten from kindhearted people on the internet. She had tried the Espresso, Nutella, and Wine Diet. The No-Dairy Diet. Headstands and yoga.

Nothing worked until one day, she simply gave up trying.

Voilà! And now they would be having a baby.

She couldn't wait to see the look on Jason's face when she told him.

Tonight would be a turning point in their marriage. She knew that for certain because Jason had seemed so far away lately. Sometimes she would catch him staring off at nothing for minutes on end. When she asked him what he was thinking about, he usually looked surprised or guilty, as if she'd caught him with his pants down. Then he'd smile and say he was simply tired or he was thinking about a business meeting coming up.

Lacey had talked to Jason's parents and his brother, but they all shrugged off her concerns, suggesting it might be time to find a hobby. Even though she worked part time at a fitness center and volunteered at the local animal shelter, they told her she had way too much time on her hands.

Jason grabbed her arm, pulling her from her thoughts. "Do you smell that?"

She sniffed the air. She couldn't smell anything, really. But that was probably because all her senses seemed off-kilter since she'd learned she was pregnant. Nothing tasted the same. She sniffed again, and this time she thought she caught a hint of something minty. No. No. It smelled like the bathroom cleaner her mother-in-law used.

"I don't feel good," Jason told her.

When she looked at him, she was surprised to see how pale his face had become. He was leaning back against the seat, and his face was pasty white. She took his empty cup and put her full one inside of it before placing it in the bucket. Then she loosened her husband's tie.

He closed his eyes.

Air. They needed air.

She turned to her right and pushed down on the button to lower the window, but nothing happened. When she looked at the driver, she frowned. He had a plastic apparatus over his mouth and nose. "Is that a gas mask?" she asked.

There was no answer.

For the first time since she'd climbed into the car, the driver met her gaze in the rearview mirror. His eyes were flat, expressionless. And she didn't like it one bit. "Please open the window. It's stuffy back here, and my husband isn't feeling well." Panic didn't fully set in until she realized he meant to do nothing about the situation. It was then that she looked straight ahead through the windshield and saw nothing but trees and grassy fields for miles. *Where are we?*

Her breath caught in her throat. Her skin felt tingly and strange.

She turned back to her husband and said, "Jason. Something's not right." But Jason was out cold. She grabbed his shoulders and shook him. "Jason!"

Leaning over and gagging as if she were going to be sick, she searched through her purse for the pepper spray she always carried. She reached for it, then grabbed hold of her iPhone and tried to activate the emergency SOS by pressing the side button and the "Volume" button. But the car swerved, and her right side slammed into the car door. Her phone dropped to the floor and disappeared under the passenger seat.

With the pepper spray still in her hand, she used her thumb to swipe the lever to the left as she leaned over the front seat and sprayed the driver. He gasped. The car swerved.

Everything was hazy. Her throat constricted. She needed fresh air.

The driver slammed on the brakes, and they skidded to a stop.

The side of her head hit the back of the headrest on the passenger side. She grunted and grabbed the door handle, trying to get out.

The door wouldn't open.

She had to do something.

Thinking fast, she reached over the seat for the device covering the driver's nose and mouth and yanked hard. The strap broke, and the mask fell to his lap.

It sounded as if he snarled at her before he opened his door and jumped out. Her heart skipped a beat when she saw him coming around to her side.

This was her chance!

She scrambled over the seats to get behind the steering wheel, clicked down on the lock, and let out a triumphant laugh when she saw the keys still in the ignition. She started the engine and felt a thump above her head as she drove off.

She couldn't see him in the rearview mirror. Where was he?

Thump. Thump. Thump.

He was on top of the car.

Cursing under her breath, she slammed on the brakes.

Jason hit the back of her seat, and she jerked forward. The lunatic driver had fallen from the roof and was now hanging on to the windshield wipers. He pulled himself up, a few inches at a time, his body sliding against the hood of the car until his face was pressed against the glass. He stared at her through the window, daring her to make her next move.

The strange fumes floating around the interior of the car were making her dizzy. She put the car in reverse and slammed her foot against the gas pedal. The car shot backward, and the man flew off.

But her reactions were slow, and before her foot hit the brake, the car swerved off the road and hit a tree. Her head jerked to the side, taking her breath away. She shoved the stick into "Drive" and hit the gas pedal again. The tires spun but couldn't get a grip.

He was charging her way.

Before she could move to the passenger seat, his fist shot through the window, shattering the glass and making contact with her jaw, leaving her in the dark.

Two

PI Jessie Cole looked down the sight of the gun, took aim, exhaled, and pulled the trigger.

Her heart rate picked up a notch.

Her license to carry had been revoked after shooting a man in self-defense nearly six months ago. Thanks to friend and lawyer Andriana Iudice, the revocation was successfully appealed. This was Jessie's third trip to the indoor range in Rocklin to practice shooting since the review board voted in her favor. She had a healthy respect for guns, which meant it was critical that she practice as often as possible in order to get to know her gun again.

When Jessie was done shooting, she made sure her pistol was empty before packing it away in her bag. A quick slap of her palm against the button on the wall to her right caused the target to whir toward her. After removing the paper target from the cardboard backing, she folded it and slipped it inside her bag along with her ammo, safety glasses, and earmuffs. She grabbed her coat from a hook to her left and put it on, then found a broom and swept the spent brass out of the walkway. "Leave your bay cleaner than you found it" was one of the range's many rules.

As she headed toward the door, she saw Colin Grayson packing up in aisle twelve. Not only was Colin a detective with the Sacramento Police Department, he was also her boyfriend, her lover. The thought made her smile. A mere glance his way made her heart kick up a notch. Their relationship had been long and complicated, with lots of ups and downs, and was stronger for it. He joined her outside a few minutes later, and they walked across the parking lot together. "How did you do?" he asked.

They stopped at the back of her car. She opened the trunk and put her things inside, then pulled out her target and unfolded it. "You tell me."

He examined it closely. "Looks like you're still shooting low and to the left."

"I raised the muzzle and flexed my wrist to the right, but it didn't help."

"I was watching you shoot in there. You need to relax. If that doesn't work, you probably aren't taking the slack off the trigger before pressing it."

She frowned.

"It'll just take some time."

She nodded.

"Speaking of time, I was hoping we could take a little drive."

"Now?"

He laughed. "I take it 'now' is a bad time."

Before she could answer, both of their phones buzzed simultaneously. Colin glanced at his phone. "Gotta get this."

"Wait," she said. "Where were you going to take me?"

He leaned her way, brushed his lips over hers. Straightening, he said, "It was no big deal. I'll call you later."

She waved him off and had to stifle the urge to say "Stay safe" as she watched him jog toward his car. He was a grown man, perfectly capable of taking care of himself. Yes, his work as a detective could be dangerous at times, but she didn't like to think about that. She'd learned early on that worrying was a draining and futile emotion. Before she could ponder why he wanted to take her for a drive, she saw that it was her assistant, Zee Gatley, who was calling. "Hi, Zee. What's going on?"

"I just wanted to know if you would be returning to the office soon. It's insane over here. The phones are ringing like crazy. In the past two hours we've gotten calls from two more prospective clients."

"Hang tight. I'll be there soon."

"Ten-four."

Although it felt as if she and Zee had been friends for much longer, they'd met under less-than-desirable circumstances five months ago. Their bond was strong because of it.

Zee was twenty-eight. She'd been diagnosed with schizophrenia when she was a young girl. She didn't talk a lot about her illness, but Jessie knew that Zee often heard three distinct voices in her head. As long as Zee took her medication, she did okay. Better than okay. When it came to investigative work, she was a natural.

Thirty minutes later, Jessie walked into her office on J Street in Sacramento and was surprised to find a woman she didn't recognize sitting in the chair in front of her desk. Zee was nowhere to be seen.

The woman looked over her shoulder, her brows lifting in surprise. Midthirties, Jessie guessed. She sported a pixie haircut and long blonde bangs swept to one side of her forehead.

She was about to stand when Jessie stopped her. "No need to get up. I'm Jessie Cole."

"Penny Snyder."

They shook hands. Jessie walked around the desk and took a seat across from her.

"Your assistant went for tea. She said she'd be right back."

"Great." Jessie pulled pen and paper from her top drawer. "What can we do for you, Penny?"

"I need help finding out what happened to my mother."

"Okay. Why don't you start from the beginning?"

"The beginning?"

Jessie nodded. "When was the last time you saw your mother? Maybe you could start there."

"Oh. I was only five," Penny said, "but I remember the day vividly. Mom took me shopping for a summer dress to wear on my first day of kindergarten." Penny exhaled. "That same evening, she made a big fuss over laying out my dress and shoes next to the flowery blue backpack filled with bright-colored crayons. She tucked me into bed, told me she loved me, and walked out of the room. I never saw her again." She paused before saying, "That was thirty years ago."

Jessie waited as Penny reached into the leather bag at her side and pulled out a slightly smashed shoebox that she set on the desk. The box was held together with duct tape and rubber bands. "I found this a few weeks ago in my dad's closet. I didn't mean to snoop," she added. "Dad was . . . is . . . much older than my mom. He had a heart attack, and he's in the hospital."

"I'm sorry."

"Thanks. I went to his house to feed the cat and water the plants—"

She stopped midsentence. "I'm rambling. Bottom line, I found the cat and the box in his bedroom closet, and I haven't been able to sleep since." She removed the rubber bands and took the lid off. Inside were pictures and old newspaper articles. Maybe a letter or two. The first thing Penny reached for was a news article. The paper had yellowed but was still readable. "This is an article that was printed in a local paper after my mom's sudden disappearance. While I was growing up, Dad refused to talk about her. He always said he had been punished for *her* wrongs, but it was over and therefore time to let it go."

"Punished for her wrongs?" Jessie asked.

Penny unfolded the paper and handed it to Jessie. The headline read, ARLENE SNYDER VANISHES WITHOUT A TRACE. "Possessive and controlling husband, Nathaniel Snyder, was ordered to spend eighteen years in prison for killing mother-of-one Arlene Snyder, whose body has not been found." It went on to say that Nathaniel spent his time in jail denying he murdered his wife. Ten years into his eighteen-year sentence, because of new and better technology, a retrial was granted. Further DNA testing revealed that the bloodstain found in the trunk of Nathaniel's car belonged to his daughter, Penny, not his wife. Nathanial had said all along that his daughter cut herself at the park, and he used the first-aid kit in his trunk to take care of her wound. This time, the prosecution was unable to prove guilt beyond a reasonable doubt, and Nathaniel was released.

"I was fifteen when he got out," Penny said.

Jessie finished reading the article and handed it back to her. "So, you believe your mother is still alive?"

"It's complicated," she said. "I lived with my grandparents on my mother's side until Dad was released. I was nearly an adult by then. For ten years I had been told over and over that my father was an evil and violent man. I believed them."

"That must have been a very difficult time."

"It was bad. My grandparents tried to get custody of me but failed, since Dad was exonerated. I wasn't horribly upset because a part of me wanted to get to know my dad, and he wanted to get to know me. I made things difficult for him, though. I didn't fully trust him, and he knew it."

Her eyes brimmed with tears. "He tried hard to prove his love. He would make jokes while I remained stone-faced. He attempted to help me with my homework. I pushed him away. I refused to have friends over, figuring they wouldn't be allowed to go to an ex-convict's house anyway." She paused to think before adding, "I was athletic. I played soccer and basketball, and Dad didn't miss a game. He spent most of his free time watching and analyzing playbacks of his recordings of my games. Sometimes I sat in the living room and watched, but I never said much."

"And your grandparents? Did they visit?"

"No. They despised my father. They thought it was ridiculous that he was let off on what they called 'some hokeypokey DNA test.' Convinced that he killed my mother, they sent me a birthday card each year, and I talked to them a couple of times on the phone, but mostly, they kept their distance until I was old enough to drive and come visit them."

The door opened and Zee entered, holding two to-go cups—a hot tea for Penny and a coffee for Jessie. Zee placed the cups in front of them. "If you've got this covered, I'm going to go finish up the workers' comp case."

"Sounds good," Jessie told her. "Thanks for the coffee. We'll talk later."

After Zee left, Penny straightened in her chair. This time when she reached into the box, she pulled out five three-by-five pictures and laid them neatly in front of Jessie. "Look at how happy my dad and mom look."

Jessie examined the pictures: Penny's mom and dad dancing in the living room, looking into each other's eyes, wearing matching aprons and waving at the camera, playing in the pool, and so on. Both of them bright-eyed and smiling. *Definitely happy,* Jessie thought. *No denying it.* And yet Jessie wasn't exactly sure where Penny was going with this.

"There are more pictures in the box," Penny went on. "And love letters, too, written to each other before and after they were married. Dad never showed me any of this. Doesn't that strike you as odd?"

Jessie looked up from the pictures. "How so?"

"He knew how badly I wanted to know more about Mom. But he wouldn't talk about her. All these years," Penny said, her voice quivering, "all he had to do was hand me this box."

"Maybe it was too painful for him to look at the pictures or to read the letters," Jessie offered.

Penny shook her head. "Look at the wear and tear on this stuff. Everything inside this box has obviously been handled so many times you can see thumbprints around the edges of the paper where the ink is wearing off."

She made a good point. No thin layer of dust or mold coated the letters and pictures, or even the inside of the box for that matter. "Have you ever looked for your mom before?"

"No."

"Why not?"

"Well, for starters, I don't know anything about her, not really. I couldn't even tell you where she went to school since nobody would ever talk about her. I don't have any information to give you other than her name."

"What about your grandparents? Didn't they tell you about your mother?"

She shook her head. "They don't have any pictures of her on the wall or bookshelves. Grandpa once told me that seeing her image every day brought them too much pain."

Jessie knew from experience that everyone handled grief and loss in their own way, so she kept her opinion to herself.

"Mom disappeared thirty years ago. Over the years, I've searched for information online but have never found much." Penny sighed as she met Jessie's gaze. "To tell you the truth, those are all just excuses. The real reason I didn't look for Mom was because up until recently, I truly believed my dad had killed her."

"But the contents of this box changed everything?"

"Yes. Sort of silly, I know, that a box of pictures could change the way I saw the past, but I guess it made me look at my dad in a new light, made me see that there could be more to the story. In my heart, I know he didn't do it." Penny picked up one of the pictures and turned it so that the image of her mom and dad smiling at each other faced Jessie. "He loved her. He's maintained his innocence from the beginning. She's out there somewhere, and I'm hoping you can help me find her."

Jessie frowned. "Even if your dad didn't kill your mom, that doesn't mean she's alive and well."

"I understand." Penny rested a hand on her chest. "My heart is telling me she's alive. I know that might sound silly, but it's enough for me. I need to do whatever I can to learn the truth."

"Okay," Jessie said. "I'll do my best to find out what happened."

THREE

Lacey opened her eyes and saw nothing but darkness. Sweat dripped off her face and down her neck. The air was stuffy and thick.

Her heart rate spiraled as she tried to lift her head. Something was pressed against her forehead. She reached upward and wrapped her fingers around the object. It felt like some sort of pipe. It jiggled when she tried to move it. Fine dirt fell onto her face, just missing her eyes.

Where was she?

She and Jason had been on their way to dinner to celebrate their anniversary. A crazed man's face flashed within her mind. He'd been wearing a mask. She'd tried to get away, but the gases he'd released into the vehicle had made her woozy. Broken glass, a fist connecting with her jaw . . . that's the last thing she recalled.

She was panting now, hyperventilating. She needed air.

The pipe.

It must be plastic PVC piping. She slid her finger between the bottom of the pipe and her forehead, careful not to move it too much so that dirt wouldn't pour in. The tip of her finger slid into the pipe.

Desperate for air, she held the pipe in place as she scooted her body upward, her back scraping against wood until the tubing was above her mouth. She drew in a breath.

Oxygen filled her lungs.

Thank God.

She took a bigger, deeper breath and then another.

She was about to call out Jason's name when she heard him. He was close by, muttering gibberish, his arms flailing in the darkness, banging against the contraption they were trapped in. He grabbed for her, his fingernails clawing into her skin. "Help me!"

"Jason! Stop!" She could hear dirt falling in around him.

"I can't breathe," he said.

"Above your head," she told him. "See if you can find a pipe. You have to be careful not to move it around too much or—"

He sputtered and coughed. A few seconds later, he was gulping in air.

She put her mouth to her own pipe and drew in another deep breath. "That man," she said to Jason, her voice quivering. "The driver. I think he's put us inside a box of some sort."

No answer. Was Jason crying?

Her body trembled as she continued to take slow, deliberate breaths through the pipe. Sweat dripped down the side of her face. This couldn't be happening. Who would do this to them? Was it some sort of sick prank? Would they be let out soon in front of bright lights and studio cameras?

Panic threatened to take hold.

She went back to breathing. It was a while before she dared to stretch and move her legs, using her feet to feel the boundaries, if any. She did the same with her left hand. There was less than six inches of space in every direction. If she reached to her left, she felt wood. If she lifted her hands and feet above her, she hit wood. If she scooted upward or downward on her back, more wood.

They were definitely inside a wooden box.

The dirt told her that she and Jason had been buried alive.

And yet whoever had done this to them had also given them access to oxygen. Why?

Psychological torture?

She felt around again, hoping he'd left them with a flashlight. Anything at all.

Wanting to explore, she slid to her left, away from Jason. As soon as she let go of the pipe, though, it began to slip downward. Dirt rained down around her.

Shit.

She grabbed the pipe, holding it upward again. Whoever had done this must have propped the pipe against their foreheads before burying them.

Was he playing with them? "Jason? Are you okay?"

Again, no answer.

She was claustrophobic. Since she was small, she'd had an excessive fear of being trapped in small places. There had been times when she would walk eighteen flights of stairs while Jason took the elevator. When they were first married, Jason would tease her about her phobia. Later, he'd made it clear that her fear annoyed him. He would force her onto an elevator, telling her it was all in her mind. And every time that happened, she would freeze in place, a visible sheen of sweat on her face.

At the moment, it took every single ounce of energy she had to not panic. "Jason," she said, trying to sound calm, "it's going to be okay, right? We're going to find a way out of here?" She didn't care if he lied to her, she just needed some sort of reassurance. She needed him to talk to her.

No response.

She closed her eyes, tried to imagine she was on a beach in Hawaii. It wouldn't do either of them any good if she gave in to his fear.

"Where are we?" Jason asked in a high-pitched voice that sounded like a child.

He didn't sound at all like himself. Why did she get the feeling he might not be able to handle the truth? Sooner or later, once he grew curious enough to stretch out an arm or a leg, he would discover what she already knew.

They were trapped.

Buried alive.

A pool of sweat had gathered on the curve of her lower back. She had no idea how long the air would last. "Jason, if we're going to have any chance of getting out of here, we'll need to work together to figure out how to get out of this box."

No answer.

Beads of sweat rolled off her forehead. She needed to stay strong for their baby. "It seems we've been buried underground," she went on, since talking soothed her. "We're in a box that I'm guessing is about six feet by six feet." As she talked, she brushed her hand over the wood above her face, to the right of the pipe.

She had an idea.

Holding on to the pipe to make sure it didn't move, she bent her left leg toward her left hand and removed her high heel from her foot. Just that small movement was a tight squeeze, but she'd done it. She straightened her leg again as she rested the shoe on top of her stomach.

She sucked in more air through the pipe.

"What are you doing?" Jason asked.

She took hold of the shoe with her right hand. "Hold on to your PVC pipe."

"Why?"

"I'm going to use the heel of my shoe to hammer at the wood above us."

She didn't wait for an answer. She had bought the Valentino Mary Jane pumps with stiletto heels and metallic-capped toes two months ago. Jason had balked when he'd discovered how much she'd spent. He hadn't cared that she'd found the shoes used on eBay and had gotten them for half the usual retail price. Besides, she'd bought them the day after her birthday to cheer herself up since the entire day had passed without festivity.

She banged the shoe hard against the wood above her head, again and again. Breaking the wood, if possible, and then digging through dirt, might be their only chance of escape. She stopped when she heard Jason call her name. "What is it?"

"All that noise. My head's pounding. I need water."

He had to be joking. "Are you serious? I'm thirsty, too, Jason. We can't just lie here and do nothing."

"I'm going to be sick."

She took long, deep breaths from the pipe, closed her eyes.

"I don't know how much longer I can stand being trapped like this."

His voice sounded distant as she concentrated on her breathing, in and out. She couldn't allow his fear to paralyze her. Panicking would take too much energy and use more oxygen than necessary. If they had any chance at all of getting out of here, she needed to relax. *Think of the baby,* she told herself. In hopes of tuning Jason out, she considered their relationship. They hardly talked anymore—about anything. For months now, he'd been so quiet it had made her feel as if she were living alone. And yet she'd figured things would change after she told him they were expecting. If they could get out of here alive, maybe they could find a way to make their marriage stronger than ever and become the family they were meant to be.

Hoping her eyes would adjust to the dark, she waved a hand in front of her face. Although she had the sensation of seeing a moving image, no light reached her eyes. Blindly, she reached her hand upward above her head and felt around. To her right was the spot where she'd struck the wood with her shoe; she was surprised to realize she'd already made a dent. Judging by the fine sawdust beneath her fingertips, it was particleboard.

Her adrenaline spiked. Particleboard was a soft wood. They could do this. "I think it's working, Jason. I can't stop hammering. If we give up, we'll never get out of here."

No response.

"If you get sick, please turn your head the other way." She started up again, using the metal toe of the shoe to smack against the wood.

The noise was deafening. It wasn't long before she was soaked in sweat. She wasn't sure how much time passed before she stopped. Her arm ached as she reached for the spot she'd been hitting. The divot in the wood was bigger, deeper. She had no idea how long it would take to break through. If and when that happened, she worried about dirt spilling through and suffocating them both before they could dig their way out.

"Is it really working?" Jason asked.

"Yes. But it could take a while, maybe days before the area is big enough for one of us to try and push through."

"We're going to die in here, aren't we?"

Between the two of them, her husband was usually the optimist in the family. He'd never had a defeatist outlook. One of the things that had drawn her to him straightaway was his strength and confidence. He was a leader. A doer.

Despite her own fears and doubts, she was determined to stay positive. "No," she said. "We're not going to die, but I will need your help." When she tried to bend her right leg upward so she could remove her other shoe, she realized she couldn't get her foot past Jason's knee. "I need you to bend to your left and reach for my shoe."

"I can't!"

She heard a rising panic in his voice. His breathing was rapid and uneven. "Yes, you can," she told him. "Use your right hand to hold on to the pipe and keep it from slipping downward while you use your left arm to grab hold of my shoe."

"Let me out!" He was hitting his fist against the wood above him.

"Knock it off!" she shouted back at him. "You're using up valuable oxygen. Grow up and start hammering, damn it!"

Heat flushed through Lacey's body. She held tightly to the shoe and continued to bang the shoe hard against the wood.

It wasn't long before Jason was hammering, too.

He'd been sitting in front of his computer for nearly an hour. Just as he'd planned, the Rohypnol had finally worn off, and Jason and Lacey Geiger were now awake and fully aware of their perilous predicament.

Jason's wife was a feisty one. She'd almost gotten the best of him in the car. He still had scratches and bruises from the encounter.

The screen was black, but with the volume turned all the way up, he could hear every word.

Jason Geiger was even more pathetic than he'd thought.

Hearing the man shout for help and bang on the wood had been music to his ears.

How does it feel to be powerless, Jason?

He laughed.

Who's in charge now?

Once the hammering became too much, he shut his laptop and walked away. In the kitchen, he propped his hands on his hips and thought about making dinner. He was hungry, but his insides felt jittery.

He'd never killed anyone before. It was much more intense than he'd thought it would be. All these years of planning, and now it was finally happening.

Wow. What a rush.

His stomach rolled. No longer hungry, he began to pace.

Jason Geiger was a little bitch. He deserved everything he was getting. The man with everything, the man who coveted power above all else, was going to see what it felt like to have no control. *Where are your attorneys when you need them, Jason?*

The hate he'd felt for so long now was burning a hole through his heart. He flexed his fingers as he walked back and forth.

A rustling sound caught his attention. He stopped walking, held his breath while he listened. It was nothing. Probably a gust of wind stirring the trees outside. His nerves were shot, making him overreact to every little noise. He didn't like feeling so jittery. One minute he found himself wanting to flee, and in the next, he would inwardly celebrate getting to this point.

He thought about all the years he'd spent preparing for this day, this moment. The plans he'd drawn up had taken a year to complete. Then came the excavation. Covering the roof with soil was not a good idea under normal circumstances, since it would eventually biodegrade and settle, but since he planned to destroy the room along with its occupants, that wouldn't be a problem. Forming the walls and framing for the ceiling and air vent had been time consuming but easy overall. He'd poured the floors, three walls, and the ceiling, leaving one wall open until after he'd dragged his victims inside the room and into the box.

Another dose of Rohypnol had kept the couple sedated long enough to get everything done with time to spare. Once they were set up in their makeshift graves covered with particleboard and dirt, he'd positioned and nailed thick plywood in place of the tunnel opening before using a bulldozer to fill the hole and pack it tight.

In a few weeks, Jason Geiger would be dead.

Incredible warmth ran through his body. He wasn't sure what he was feeling . . . freedom, relief, satisfaction? He couldn't remember the last time he'd felt any one of those emotions.

The idea of it all coming to an end sounded like a dream, a fantasy.

Once this was all over, it would be time to think about what came next.

He went back to the refrigerator, rolled open the freezer drawer, and pulled out a ham-and-cheese Hot Pockets sandwich from the freezer.

Suddenly he was hungry again.

FOUR

Ben Morrison, crime reporter for the *Sacramento Tribune*, was standing in the kitchen making a fresh pot of coffee when Melony came up behind him and circled her arms around his middle, resting her cheek against his shoulder.

He stopped what he was doing. "Did I wake you?"

"No. Gloria just texted me. Roger Willis was released on bail yesterday. She's upset."

Gloria was the mother of the girl Roger Willis had touched inappropriately in a movie theater two months ago. Ben pivoted so he could wrap his arms around Melony. He knew she'd been dreading something like this happening. He held her close and said, "His trial will be held in a month. Let's hope the system will work for us and they'll put him behind bars where he belongs."

Melony drew away from him. "The bail wasn't set high enough. They never should have released him. According to Gloria, the Sacramento PD has identified two more victims who allegedly suffered from his abuse."

Roger Willis had been their daughter, Abigail's, soccer coach. Ben's skin prickled at the thought of the monster touching his little girl. An adult she'd been told to listen to, a man she'd thought she could trust, had taken advantage of his position. It made Ben sick to his stomach. Roger Willis deserved to be locked up and subjected to the sort of unwarranted sexual abuse he seemed intent on dishing out to young girls.

"Did you hear what I said?" Melony asked.

Ben nodded. "I'll look into it."

"What do I say to Abigail? How am I supposed to drop her off at school as if nothing has changed?"

"I'll take the kids to school today. I'll talk to the principal to make sure he's aware of the situation."

"I thought you needed to get to work early today?"

"It can wait."

She released a heavy sigh. "I think I'll go lie down until it's time to wake the kids."

Ben kissed her on the forehead. "Good idea." When she got as far as the arched doorway leading into the living room, he said, "Don't worry about Willis. I promise you that man will never get within twenty feet of our daughter."

FIVE

Jessie gulped down the rest of her coffee, shouldered her purse, then crossed the room and poked her head inside Olivia's bedroom. Her niece was sitting on the edge of her bed, slipping on shoes. Cecil, the one-eyed cat, was on the dresser, staring at the hamster on his wheel as he went 'round and 'round. Considering how much exercise the critter got, he was amazingly pudgy. "Ready to go?"

Shoes were on. Now Olivia was shoving books and papers into her backpack. "Five more minutes."

"Two minutes," Jessie said firmly. "We're going to be late."

The engine was warmed up by the time Olivia slid into the passenger seat. Jessie headed west on J Street toward Alhambra.

"I start my driver's education course in two weeks."

Jessie frowned. "That can't be right . . . already?"

"Yep. Fourteen days. It's all I ever think about," Olivia said. "You've been too busy making moon eyes at Colin to notice much of anything else."

"Moon eyes?"

"Yeah. Googly eyes, whatever you want to call them. Zee said the same thing—that all this lovey-dovey business has taken you off your game."

Jessie chuckled. "Taken me off my game?"

Olivia nodded. "Zee told me that you arrive late and leave early and that you've been forgetful."

Jessie had no words. She was being reprimanded by a fifteen-year-old kid. Before she could remind Olivia to do her chores after she returned from school later today, Olivia asked her what case she was working on.

"Well, after spending weeks sitting at my computer handling pre-employment background checks for one client and the legitimacy of potential investments for another, I got a visit from a woman who's looking for her mother."

"An adoption case?"

"No. Her name is Penny. She was only five when her mother disappeared. Although no body was ever found, her father was convicted of the murder when Penny was small."

"Without a body?"

Jessie nodded. "It happens. My research shows that he was found guilty in part due to evidence given by Penny's grandparents, who told the jury that Arlene had said she was afraid her husband might kill her. They also found a bloodstain in his car, and the neighbors testified to hearing a disturbance the night before she disappeared."

Olivia sighed. "I don't think that's right. I mean, what if someone said Grandpa or even you killed your mom after she disappeared?"

"That's different. My mother made it clear she wasn't happy with her life. She packed up her things and left. There are limited reasons why people disappear. Once you eliminate the most obvious explanations, the jury is sometimes left with murder."

"But if the woman really did leave, isn't that Penny lady angry that she might have been abandoned?"

Jessie wished she hadn't said as much as she had about the case. It was too close to home. After Olivia's mom disappeared, Jessie had become her niece's legal guardian. For ten years Olivia had struggled with the idea that her mother might have left her. As it turned out,

Jessie's sister, Sophie, had been thrown from a car after a tragic accident, buried in a ravine covered with thorny brush. Her body hadn't been found until recently.

Jessie stopped at the light.

"Maybe I don't want to be a private investigator, after all," Olivia said, saving Jessie from having to answer her last question.

"Why not?"

"Sitting behind a computer all day sounds sort of boring."

"At the moment, boring is sort of nice. I think we've had enough excitement over the past few years, don't you think?"

"I live for danger," Olivia teased. "Speaking of which, I've been looking at used cars. I found a 1998 Honda Accord for nine hundred and ninety-nine dollars. By the time I get my license, I'll probably have closer to fifteen hundred."

"How many miles does the car have?"

Olivia reached into the front pocket of her backpack and whipped out a piece of paper. "Let's see . . . here it is . . . only three hundred eighty-two miles."

"You mean three hundred eighty-two *thousand* miles?"

She scanned her paper again. "Yes. That's what I meant. I called the person selling the car. He was super nice. He said the car would easily last another five to ten years, at least."

"He has no way of knowing that. Keep looking. That's too many miles. Colin will help you look for a car. Once we find one, we'll have to take it in to be inspected."

Olivia fell back against her seat. "I'll never get a car."

"Not with that attitude."

"Will you at least take me driving this weekend?"

"Not until you have your permit." Jessie pulled up to the curb in front of the school. "I'll see you tonight. I'm going to try out a new recipe."

"Whatever it is, I'm sure Colin will love it," Olivia said flatly before she shut the door and walked off.

"You little brat," Jessie said under her breath. It dawned on her as she watched Olivia meld with a crowd of teenagers that Olivia was nearly the same age Sophie had been when she'd given birth to her.

They were a lot alike, those two.

Jessie had spent the ten years after her sister went missing trying hard to be a good parent. It wasn't always easy. Saying no and being consistent when it came to disciplining Olivia could be challenging at times. When Olivia was only five, Jessie's days seemed to be filled with meal preparation, going to the park, running errands. None of it sounded too bad, but it was the exhaustion, the loss of sanity, and the constant doubts that nearly did her in back then.

Jessie smiled as she pulled away from the curb. Thankfully, Olivia was a good kid. She was smart. She had a good head on her shoulders. But that didn't mean Jessie could let her guard down. She was pretty sure parenting never ended. Jessie remembered what she was like at Olivia's age, and *mature* wasn't an adjective she would use to describe herself or any other kid she'd known. Maybe twenty-five or thirty was the magic age when she could stop worrying?

Maybe never.

After working in the office for a few hours, Jessie was back behind the wheel. She arrived at the house on Thirty-Eighth Street just as Penny Snyder pulled up to the curb behind her.

The home was a Craftsman bungalow, a style common in the Sacramento area. It had a low-pitched roofline, wide eaves, and decorative trim. The place belonged to Dorothy and Ellis Kash, Penny Snyder's grandparents.

By the time she and Penny said hello and were headed up the walkway, Penny's grandparents were waiting to greet them at the door.

Her grandmother stood at about four foot eleven. She wore beige slacks and a button-down silk shirt that matched her short steel-gray hair. Her husband towered over her. The wobble in his step and the multiple age spots on his face and hands made him appear much older than his wife.

Jessie followed Penny and her grandparents inside. Their home had an open living space with lots of natural light. She could see the kitchen with a large white-marble island centered beneath high ceilings with wood beams. Lots of cabinetry and granite counters that went on forever. There were floor-to-ceiling built-in bookshelves on the back wall of the living room where they ended up. Lit candles left a subtle rose scent lingering about. The place was immaculate.

Dorothy insisted they take a seat on the upholstered couch while she and her husband put together a tray of finger foods: pickle slices, olives, cheese, and crackers. Once everyone had a tall glass of ice water, the elderly couple found a seat.

"You two are old friends?" Dorothy asked.

"Not exactly," Penny said. "I didn't want to tell you everything over the phone because I wasn't sure how you would react, but this is Jessie Cole. She's an investigator in Sacramento. She specializes in finding missing persons."

Dorothy's expression changed from friendly to suspicious in an instant. "Ellis," she said to her husband, "I thought you said she was bringing an old friend from school with her?"

His face reddened. "That's what Penny told me. How was I to know? Have you ever known me to be psychic?"

Dorothy was not happy. She refused to make eye contact with Jessie.

"Grandma, there's no reason to be upset. Jessie has agreed to help me look for Mom."

Penny's explanation didn't seem to help. Dorothy's spine was as straight as a flagpole.

"What if Mom is alive?" Penny said before turning toward Ellis. "Wouldn't it be wonderful to see your daughter again?"

"If she were alive, that would mean she abandoned us all." Dorothy reached for a tissue and dabbed at her eyes. "I refuse to listen to any more of your . . ." She stopped, pointed a finger at Penny. "Did your father put you up to this?"

"Dad is in the hospital," Penny said, her tone lined with exasperation. "He's very sick. After all this time, why do you still insist on blaming him for everything?"

"Watch your tone," Ellis warned.

Penny sighed. "I found a box of letters Mom and Dad exchanged over many years." Her face brightened, and it was obvious she still held on to the hope that her grandparents might help her search for answers. "They were in love. I truly believe Dad still loves my mom. All I am asking is that you allow Jessie to ask you a few questions about Mom. It won't take long, I promise."

"No," Dorothy said. "We've been put through enough. Your mother is never coming back. It's over."

"Dad," Penny continued, "spent ten years of his life locked behind bars, in large part due to your testimony."

"Thank the Lord," Dorothy said, sweeping a hand through the air as she stood and walked away, leaving her husband to fend for himself.

"He's innocent," Penny told her grandfather after Dorothy disappeared.

"I'm sorry, Penny," he said. "We can't help you. I'm going to have to ask you both to leave."

As they all stood, Penny stared at her grandfather. "I'm sure it'll make you both feel better to know that Dad is in the hospital, fighting for his life."

Jessie watched Ellis Kash closely. He didn't look like he cared one way or the other. She followed Penny back the way they'd come. What she'd just witnessed was sad. Before leaving the house, she turned to face Penny's grandfather. "You really don't want to help your granddaughter find her mother?"

He pointed a finger at the door, his hand shaking. "Get out."

Jessie did as he asked. She had dealt with her fair share of family drama over the years, but as far as she was concerned, Dorothy and Ellis Kash took selfishness to another level. They hadn't spent two seconds taking Penny's feelings into consideration.

Jessie caught up to Penny. "Are you okay?"

"I'm fine." Penny gestured toward the house. "Sorry about what happened in there. I had an inkling that one or both of them would blame my father for my visit, but I really did think they would at least consider talking to you about Mom."

Jessie agreed. What harm would it have done them to tell Jessie about Penny's mother, their only child, if only to appease their granddaughter?

"I don't know what I was thinking," Penny said. "To this day they blame Dad for every little thing that goes wrong in my life. As long as I don't mention him, we usually get along." She shook her head. "Why can't they just throw me a bone? What's wrong with hoping and wishing Mom were alive?"

"Absolutely nothing." Jessie thought of her sister, Sophie. For years, she'd fantasized about finding her sister alive. She knew what it was like to hang on to the tiniest sliver of hope.

Penny opened her car door and tossed her purse onto the passenger seat. Turning back to Jessie, she asked, "What now?"

"I was able to find some of your mother's friends on Facebook. Karen Cosso was your mom's good friend throughout high school. She lives in Cameron Park. I'm going to pay her a visit, ask her a few questions about who your mom used to be. What did she like to do in her spare time? Did she have dreams and goals?" Jessie paused. "According to the court documents I read from your father's first trial, there were no signs of mental health issues and no ransom demand after her disappearance. Those things eliminate suicide and kidnapping."

Penny gave her a halfhearted smile. "Thank you for agreeing to help me. I need to know what happened. I have to know the truth."

Jessie nodded.

"If I didn't have to get back to work," Penny added, "I'd go with you."

"It's okay. Most people don't like to talk to investigators, no matter what the reason. It's better I go alone."

"You'll let me know if you learn anything new?"

"Of course. Hopefully, we can meet up again next week to talk about how the investigation is going. At that point, you'll be able to decide how far you want to take this."

"All the way."

"We could hit a dead end," Jessie warned. "That happens."

Penny smiled. "You're going to find her. I feel it in my bones."

As Jessie watched her drive off, she ignored the sinking feeling that Penny Snyder was being overly optimistic.

Whether or not Penny's father had anything to do with her mother's disappearance, statistics showed that the odds of finding Arlene Snyder after all these years were not good. If her mother was indeed alive, wouldn't she have made contact with her daughter or her parents?

But maybe the notion that Jessie held little hope of finding Arlene Snyder said more about Jessie than it did about her client. Ever since Olivia had been kidnapped while babysitting Ben's two young children, Jessie had been feeling out of whack. It had happened two months ago, but it felt as if it had happened last week. Every problem seemed bigger. She wasn't sleeping well, and she often felt on edge. That moment when she'd learned Olivia had been taken replayed over and over in her mind in a constant loop.

Jessie climbed behind the wheel of her car, turned on the engine, and cranked the music, hoping some tunes would cheer her up.

Six

Ben tapped on the door to Ian Savage's office at the *Tribune*, entering after his boss told him to come on in.

"You wanted to see me?"

Ian nodded. "It's come to my attention that we need to breathe a little life into our paper. Of course, there has been declining circulation in this new digital age we're living in, but it's nothing the paper can't handle. Sizable audiences continue to buy and value our newspaper." He paused.

Ben said nothing.

"In my opinion, the newspaper industry needs to change the doom-and-gloom narrative that surrounds it. We need to explore opportunities and experiment with content. No cookie-cutter model for us. We need more stories like the series you did regarding Sophie Cole."

Ben was surprised to hear it. At the time, the stories he'd written about Jessie Cole's missing sister really hadn't garnered him much notice in the way of awards, let alone attention from Ian.

"So, what do you think?"

Ben scratched his chin. "What do you have in mind?"

"Glad you asked." Ian scooted his chair forward, his eyes piercing Ben's as if the ideas swirling around in his head were going to burst through his skull. "Cold cases."

Ben had no idea where, exactly, Ian was going with this, but he nodded just the same.

Ian pointed at Ben. "Remember the slew of unsolved murder cases you worked on before your accident . . ." Ian slapped the flat of his palm on his desk. "Of course you wouldn't remember, unless you've regained past memories?"

"Unfortunately, that hasn't happened." Over ten years ago, a car accident had left Ben with retrograde amnesia, unable to recall memories from his past.

"Just as I thought." Ian seemed no less enthusiastic. "Well, then, what I would like you to do is search the archives and find one of the murders you covered. It has to be an unsolved case. I want you to talk to past witnesses, if possible, see how their views on the situation have changed, if at all." Ian looked thoughtful before he added, "People are curious creatures. They want to know how things turned out in the end, good or bad. I want you to work on finding a cold case that might resonate and connect with the reader."

"A story with a universal message," Ben said.

"Sure, as long as it hits an emotional chord. And do your best to put a positive spin on it."

"A positive spin on murder," Ben murmured.

"Crime is a part of life. If Bruce Wayne's parents were never killed, would there be a Batman?"

"We're talking about real life," Ben said, wondering about Ian's frame of mind. His boss wasn't usually the type of man to get too excited. At the moment, though, his eyes looked overly bright, his face beaming. "The physical and emotional impact of any crime," he reminded Ian, "is devastating for families."

Ian wagged a crooked finger at him, a habit he couldn't seem to kick as he seemingly ignored what Ben had just told him. "One of the cases you covered that really had an effect on me," he said, "was the murder of Jon Eberling. He was in his early forties at the time of his death. Found in a trash bin in an alleyway in Midtown. Strangled. If my memory serves me, you interviewed his mother. Three days before her son's murder, an intruder had broken into her home. Your account of what happened to her cat broke readers' hearts. Broke my heart, too."

"I wouldn't call that a positive spin."

"No," Ian agreed. "Which is why you need to go out there and meet with her again and let the readers, and me, know that she's okay. Maybe she has a new cat. Hell, I don't know. You've got the experience. Make it work."

After leaving Ian's office, Ben spent most of the day scouring files and notes from a stack of cold cases he'd covered over a decade ago before driving to see Gina Eberling, the cat lady.

Apparently, Ian's mind was like a well-oiled cog that was working just fine. Gina Eberling's son, Jon, had been murdered twelve years ago. She lived in a mobile home in Roseville and was more than happy to allow Ben inside to have a chat.

Ben sat across from Gina, now seventy-one years old, in a cramped living room that smelled faintly of laundry detergent. A lightweight tube split into two prongs was attached to her nasal area, giving her supplemental oxygen from a nearby tank. After taking a seat, she'd told her caretaker to leave them be. The sound of rattling pans in the kitchen was nearly deafening.

Gina rolled her eyes at all the racket coming from the other room.

Ben smiled as he pulled out pen and paper.

"I went to high school with your boss," Gina said, catching him off guard.

"Ian Savage?"

Her blue eyes brightened. "He was my first kiss."

Ben's attempt to hold back a chuckle caused his throat to tickle. He coughed more than once.

"Margot. Could you please bring Mr. Morrison some water?"

He heard a ponderous sigh followed by the opening of a cupboard and running water. Margot was tall and thickly built. She plopped the glass of water down on the coffee table in front of him and left the room with her nose in the air.

"Don't mind her," Gina told him. "She's doing Weight Watchers again. Never turns out well for the poor girl. She just gains the weight right back."

"I can hear you," came a voice from the other room.

"Did I say you couldn't?" Gina looked at Ben. "Where were we?"

"You were talking about dating Ian Savage."

She giggled like a schoolgirl. "Oh, no. We weren't dating. Although he did write me a few poems and begged me to be his girlfriend." She waved her hand through the air. "Enough about my love life. You're here to do a story about the thief who broke into my house all those years ago."

"That's right," he said.

"I would think you would have more recent crimes to write about."

"Your story spoke to people. An intruder broke into your home, and only days later you lost your son. Our readers want to know how you're getting along."

"I see."

"Do you mind telling me again what happened, in your own words?"

Her clasped hands settled in her lap. "I'll do my best. I remember waking to a screechy sound, like a mouse scurrying around in the crawl space. Margot wasn't with me back then. Even if she had been here, I don't think I would have called out for her. I remember staring up at the ceiling until the noise stopped. I had just drifted off to sleep again when I heard a crash." Her eyes widened as she told the story, making it feel as if it had happened last night.

"It sounded like glass breaking." Gina put a hand to her chest.

Worried about her heart, Ben was about to ask her if there was anything he could do for her, but she continued.

"I sat up and flipped off the covers," she said. "Although I was much younger at the time, I was still unsteady on my feet. It took me a minute to turn on the light and find my cane."

Oftentimes, when Ben interviewed victims of crimes, no matter how big or small the tragedy, they had a difficult time remembering the chain of events and usually offered one- or two-word answers to his questions. But that wasn't the case with Gina Eberling. It all happened twelve years ago, and yet he could hardly keep up. "Is that when you noticed an intruder?"

She shook her head. "I didn't see him until I made it to the end of the hallway, where I could see right into the kitchen. His face was covered with a black stocking, and he was going through drawers and stuffing things into his pockets. He looked up suddenly and froze at the sight of me."

"What did you do?"

"Well, for a good twenty seconds, we stared at one another. He probably thought I looked old, or maybe he thought he could easily disable me. He might have been able to do just that if I hadn't seen Harry."

"Harry?"

"My cat. Harry and I had been together for thirteen years. The young man, the thief," she amended, "killed Harry. I realized later that he'd taken my wedding ring that I often left in a dish by the kitchen sink."

Ben scribbled in his notebook.

"After my husband died," she said after a short pause, "Harry was my sole companion for years. Why would he do that? Why would he kill my cat?"

Ben had no good answer.

Gina said, "I figured he was on drugs."

"Were you scared?"

"Maybe at first, but not after seeing Harry's unmoving and bloody body. That made me mad. And when the man walked toward me and I saw the bloody knife in his hand, I shook with fury. I waited until he was close enough to make my move."

Ben sat motionless, waiting for her to finish.

"When he got close enough, I picked up my cane and swung hard, hit him across the chest and shoulder and whatever else I could reach. The adrenaline running through my body was incredible. His knife dropped to the floor, and when he tried to grab it, I used the cane to whack him across the knuckles. He cried out in pain and begged me to stop. I hit him two more times before grabbing a can of ant spray I had brought out earlier and using it to spray him in the eyes."

Ben hadn't read the write-up he'd done twelve years ago because he'd wanted to hear it all straight from Gina. "Did he get away?"

She nodded. "Unfortunately, yes. He stumbled to the door. By the time he got the chain unfastened, I was on the phone in the kitchen, dialing 9-1-1. It was too late. The police arrived ten minutes later, and he was long gone."

The silence settled around them before Ben asked, "So how are you doing now, Gina, twelve years later?"

"I don't sleep well, and I suffer from panic attacks. I've been to the doctor many times. It doesn't take much to set me off—constant worry, shortness of breath. Sometimes my reactions are unprovoked."

She shook her head. "He killed Harry. Why in the name of God would he kill a poor defenseless animal?"

Gina seemed so frail and agitated by the remembrance that he didn't have the heart to ask her about the death of her son. Instead, he sat with her for a while longer and talked to her about happier times. When he left Gina Eberling, she was giving her caretaker flack about what she was cooking for her next meal.

As Ben drove back to the office, though, Gina's question about how anyone could kill her poor cat, Harry, wouldn't leave him.

And he knew why.

Six months ago, Ben had begun to see visions of bloodshed and carnage. Unsure as to whether the images had anything to do with his life prior to his accident, he'd decided to look into his past, which included a visit with his sister, Nancy. That visit occurred ten weeks ago, and yet his conversation with his sister had stayed with him, haunting his dreams.

Nancy had always made it clear she wanted nothing to do with him, but Ben needed answers, and he couldn't see the harm in asking her to help him fill in the gaping black hole that was his childhood.

But forcing Nancy to see him had been a mistake.

Her fear of him had been downright palpable. Her trembling lips and the way her gaze kept darting around the room made him feel as if she might flee at any moment. But she remained seated, and when she finally mustered the courage to look him in the eye, she'd told him he used to collect dead animals and bones. She said he was a frightening person to be around. The only reason his sister had agreed to talk to him was because he'd promised never to return to Florida to see her.

For months, he'd been looking for answers to his past but had only ended up with more questions.

Would his memories never return? And if they did, what then?

"Be careful what you wish for" was a phrase that often crept through his mind. Had he ever been, or could he still be, some sort of monster?

Ben held tightly to the wheel as he released a heavy sigh.

Perhaps it would be best if he simply listened to his wife, who repeatedly reminded him that the past no longer mattered. He was no longer plagued by grisly images of death. His sister was out of his life forever, and his father was dead.

Let it go.

SEVEN

Lacey had no idea how much time had passed. Hours? Days? There was no way to tell. No tiny crevices of light. It was the sort of darkness found under a bed in the middle of the night. If she allowed herself to think about it for too long, her imagination got the best of her, and she would become numb with fear, waiting for a sharp-clawed hand to cover her mouth and nose and smother her.

Her head throbbed. She felt weak as she reached up and slid her fingers against the particleboard.

The dent was much larger, deeper. They were getting close, but it would take a while. She tried to remember how long someone could survive without water. Three days? Four? She'd read stories of people lasting more than eight. They had been indoors. No sun or heat.

Her left leg was cramping. She needed to stretch, move, and bend. Holding on to the pipe, she stretched her arm as far as it would go to the right. The tip of her finger brushed against Jason's hand. She scooted that way and slipped her hand into his.

She remembered the first time they'd held hands. He'd brought her to one of his construction sites, a large office building in Folsom. After placing a hard hat on top of her head, he took hold of her hand and gave her a tour. The place was busy. Knowing Jason was in charge of something so grand made her feel proud. His employees showed him the utmost respect as they walked by.

Jason had started his construction business from nothing. He was a hard worker, determined to be successful. He believed quality was king. He refused to cut corners to reduce costs. He often said that his company's reputation was only as good as his last project. Over the years she'd learned that some of his workers considered Jason to be a hardhead, a stickler for perfection. He hired only the best people. And he expected a lot from them. It wasn't long before he began to act the same way at home, refusing to accept anything less than perfection. She didn't mind. She liked working hard and being the best she could be.

But now, lying here in the dark, her eyes were being pried open, and she was beginning to see Jason in a whole new light.

Her thoughts shifted to the day of their abduction. She'd spent hours getting ready for their anniversary dinner at the Firehouse. It had been so long since they had spent quality time together. Her pulse had raced every time she'd thought about telling him the big news.

Swallowing the knot lodged in her throat, she decided to make the announcement. He was her husband. For better or for worse, he needed to know the truth. "I'm pregnant," she said.

He let go of her hand, his movement jerky. "I need water. I don't have any saliva."

Stunned by his self-centeredness, she went back to her pipe and took in some air. Did he not hear what she just said? Did he think he was the only one who was thirsty and afraid? Was his fear causing him to shut down to all else? Too confused and angry to speak, she used her feet to push herself the other way. As she did so, she stretched out her left arm, surprised when her hand brushed against something crinkly. She inched her body that way until she could feel something that seemed like a paper bag in her grasp. She then scooted back for air, bringing the bag along with her.

"What are you doing?" Jason asked. "Have you been hiding something from me?"

She cringed. How could he think so little of her? Being angry or annoyed with him wouldn't accomplish anything, so she ignored him instead.

The bag was the size of a standard grocery bag. It had been folded closed. Keeping the pipe in her mouth to breathe, she held the bag on her stomach and used both hands to open it and reach inside. There were two items: an apple and a water bottle. Her heart soared. Her mouth watered. She was so hungry and thirsty.

"What is it?" Jason asked, his voice panicked. "What are you doing over there?"

"I think it's a water bottle and an apple," she said. "Reach to your right and see if there is another bag over there on your side."

"I can't do it. The pipe will fall, and more dirt will come in. I need water. Please give me some water, Lacey. Don't be selfish."

Stiffening, she did what she always did when it came to Jason. She did what he asked. Reaching out, she placed the plastic bottle into his outstretched hand that she couldn't see but knew would be there.

While he drank up, she pulled the apple from the bag and brought it to her nose, inhaling its sweet scent before taking a bite. Juice trickled down her throat. It was the most delicious piece of fruit she'd ever tasted.

Her stomach gurgled and grumbled as she chewed.

"Don't eat all the apple," he told her.

She took another bite.

"Here's the water," he said. "Let's trade."

She handed him the apple. For a fleeting second she thought he might not give her the water bottle. She was wrong, but it wasn't until she unscrewed the lid and drank that she realized he'd only left her a few sips.

Nothing productive would come from getting angry, so she bit her tongue. *Stay calm. You can do this,* she repeated over and over in her mind as she picked up the shoe by her side. After taking a series of deep breaths from the pipe, she lodged the shoe between the wood floor and the pipe, to hold the pipe up, then inched her way to the upper-left corner of the box, making her way slowly around what little room there was, her fingers brushing over every bit of space, hoping to find more food.

"What are you doing?"

"Trying to see if there is another bag."

She was near his feet. She began to feel hot and clammy. Her chest tightened. Her throat burned. She wriggled her way back to her original spot. Panicked, she used her feet to give herself a push. Her shoulder hit the shoe. The end of the pipe clunked against wood, and dirt leaked in.

"What's going on?" Jason asked. "What's happening? I don't like you being so secretive over there."

Her heart rate spiked. She needed air. She felt around until she found the pipe and tried to shove it back through the hole. Dirt blocked its path.

Panic set in as she sucked in dry, hot air. It wasn't enough. Her lungs burned. She jiggled the pipe around, pushing harder, desperate to get it back into place, relieved when the dirt finally gave way and the pipe was back in its original place.

Dizzy, she was afraid she might pass out.

After the dirt stopped falling through the pipe, she brushed the mound of dirt to the side and put her mouth at the end of the cylinder so she could breathe again. As the air filled her lungs, relief settled over her and she was able to think again. Since the pipe hadn't come all the way through, she couldn't be sure how deep they were buried.

"Lacey?"

She closed her eyes, took slow, deep breaths. It was a while before she said, "I'm okay. It's not getting enough oxygen that we need to worry about. If we don't get out of here, there's a chance we could be poisoned by carbon dioxide."

"How do you know that?"

"I saw a show on how to get out of sticky situations, like being trapped in a small space or if you find yourself in a car that's sinking into a lake or—"

"What about the other bag?" he asked, cutting her off.

He wasn't listening to her. He didn't seem to care that she'd just risked her life to find water and food for both of them. The thought that kept running through her mind was *This is not my husband.*

"What about food and water?" he asked again.

Reining in her frustration, she said, "If you're still hungry and thirsty after drinking the entire water bottle and eating three-quarters of an apple that was meant for both of us, maybe you should take a look around, Jason."

"I can't do that."

She'd never been confrontational. In fact, she went out of her way to avoid conflict, but at the moment all she wanted to do was scream at the top of her lungs. "Jason," she said in a stern voice, "are you kidding me?"

"What?"

"This isn't just about you. I'm freaking out over here because I'm trying to do whatever I can to survive. Moments ago, I told you I was pregnant. You've made it perfectly clear that you don't care one way or another." Venting felt good, so she kept it up. "Even before we got shoved in a fucking box, you were quiet and distant. I need you to grow a pair and help us out of this situation."

Once again, he remained quiet.

It was dark and cold. She'd never felt so alone. Shivers snaked up her legs and arms.

As she rested a hand on her stomach, praying the baby would be all right, she thought about the apple and the water she'd found. Was their captor testing them? Why would he leave food and water if he wanted them to die? Nothing made any sense. But for some reason, it gave her hope.

Reaching around in the dark, she found her shoe. With it firmly in her grasp, she began hammering at the wood again.

She wasn't ready to die. She would get out of here, with or without Jason's help.

EIGHT

Cool air pressed against Jessie's face as she followed the brick path that curved along lush green grass all the way to the front entry. Pausing at the doormat, she rang the bell and waited.

The sprawling estate where Arlene's friend Karen Cosso lived was set among majestic oaks, mossy rocks, and cleared meadows. Beautiful.

The man who answered the door was tall and distinguished, with thick gray hair that was swept neatly over one eye. He wore light-colored slacks and a crisp white-collared shirt peeking out above a light-yellow cashmere sweater.

"Hi. I'm Jessie Cole, private investigator. I tried to call first, but I wasn't able to get through. I hope I'm not catching you at a bad time." None of that was true, but the white lie worked more times than not. It was easier for people to give excuses over the phone rather than face-to-face.

"Bill," he said. "What can I do for you?"

"I was hoping I could talk to Karen Cosso about the disappearance of her good friend Arlene Snyder."

A woman came forward, sliding easily between the doorframe and Bill. If she was Arlene's friend, Jessie deduced that she would be around the same age, which would be late fifties to early sixties. She looked much younger.

"I'm Karen," she said. "Did I hear you say Arlene Snyder's name?"

"This is Jessie Cole," Bill cut in. "She's an investigator."

Jessie nodded, smiled, and said, "Arlene's daughter, Penny, hired me."

Karen raised a brow. "Whatever for?"

"She wants to know the truth about what happened to her mother all those years ago."

"Gosh, what do you want to know?"

"Anything you can tell me about Arlene would be a great start."

"Have you talked to her parents, Dorothy and Ellis Kash?" Karen asked.

"I was there an hour ago," Jessie said. "It's too painful for them to talk about their daughter. They are firm in their belief that she was murdered by her husband and therefore see no reason to go back in time and relive everything that happened."

Karen looked at her husband. "I don't see any reason why I shouldn't talk to her, do you, Bill?"

"It's your call, honey."

Karen touched her necklace as if unsure, but finally gestured for Jessie to come inside.

"Thank you," Jessie said. "I appreciate it."

Karen and Bill were attentive hosts. Once they were certain Jessie was settled in a comfortable seat in the living room, they both disappeared.

Bill was the first to reappear with tea for two and a plate of cheeses and bite-size pieces of sourdough bread he'd made himself. When Karen returned with a stack of photo albums, Bill left them alone.

"I see Bill brought you something to snack on."

Jessie nodded as she chewed and swallowed. "It's delicious."

"He retired a few months ago," Karen whispered. "Thank God he likes to make bread."

Jessie smiled as Karen took a seat next to Jessie and opened one of the albums.

Karen flipped through a few pages before pointing at a woman sitting under an umbrella at the beach. "That's her. That's Arlene." Karen examined the photo for a long moment. "Five of us girls took a trip to Puerto Vallarta, Mexico, after graduating from UC Davis." She turned the page. Every third or fourth picture included Arlene at one party or another.

Karen set the first album aside and grabbed another from the pile and peeked inside. "Ah, this is what I was looking for." She handed the album to Jessie.

"Arlene and Nathaniel's wedding day," Karen said, pointing. "I was the maid of honor. I forget the name of the best man." She pondered on it a bit before blurting, "Rhett! The best man's name was Rhett. I remember teasing him and calling him Rhett Butler." She rolled her eyes.

"Did it surprise you when you heard the news about Arlene's disappearance?"

"Yes and no," Karen said. "Yes, because Arlene adored being a mother to little Penny. And no, because she often expressed her regret about marrying too soon."

"So she was unhappy in her marriage?"

"Nathaniel was fifteen years older than Arlene. Not that that matters . . . I mean, I don't think that was the reason she was unhappy. In fact, I think she loved her husband, but she just wasn't ready to be tied down. It was little things that bothered Arlene."

"What sort of things?"

"Arlene wanted to go to nice dinners and travel the world. Nathaniel wanted to save for their future."

"When did Arlene first start showing signs of unhappiness? Was it right after they were married, or was it after Penny was born?"

Karen clicked her tongue. "Let's see. I recall Arlene using Erica, another friend of ours, and me as examples of the life she wanted. We were both single. We would take weekend trips to San Diego or Santa

Barbara. Erica and I also traveled to Bali once and spent a couple of weeks there." She paused to think. "So, Penny was probably three and a half the first time Arlene said anything to me about wishing she'd waited to marry and have children."

Karen tapped her head lightly. "What am I thinking? No, the first time Arlene expressed regret was during Penny's second birthday party. She and Nathaniel invited everyone over for a barbecue. Her parents were there, and so was Nathaniel's mom. Yes, that was the first time I remember Arlene expressing her unhappiness and doubt about the life she'd chosen for herself."

"Do you think maybe she was just having a bad day?"

"Possibly. I didn't think much of it at first, but after I traveled to Bali, her complaints increased. I still might not have thought too much of it all if she hadn't gotten so upset when I told her I was going to marry Bill. I thought she'd be excited. Instead, she read off a long list of reasons why I should think twice before saying 'I do.'"

"Obviously you didn't listen to your friend's advice."

"Oh, no," Karen said. "Bill's the best thing that's ever happened to me. We have three wonderful boys. All two years apart. Raising those boys could be trying at times, but I wouldn't change a thing."

Jessie sipped her tea. "Did the police interview you after Arlene disappeared?"

"Yes. They did. More than once. I heard through the grapevine that Nathaniel thought I knew more than I was telling them." She frowned. "To this day I have a hard time wrapping my head around everything that happened. I liked Nathaniel. When Arlene grumbled about being tied down, I told her she was being foolish. Nathaniel was a wonderful and supportive man. He promised to take her to Paris someday. When she talked about going back to college for her master's, he was all for it. In my opinion, he never tried to stop her from doing whatever it was she wanted to do."

"What about abuse?"

"Physical abuse?"

Jessie nodded.

"I never once saw any signs that Arlene had been verbally or physically abused." She lifted both hands for emphasis and said, "I never witnessed one fight between Arlene and Nathaniel."

"So what did you think when the jury found Nathaniel guilty?"

"I thought it was absolutely insane. I always thought of myself as being a good judge of character. If Nathaniel killed Arlene, then all bets were off."

"Meaning?"

"Meaning I could no longer trust my instincts, let alone anyone I knew. If that man could hurt someone, then everyone I knew was suspect. For years after, I gave everyone in my family the side-eye."

Jessie inwardly smiled. "If Arlene wasn't murdered or kidnapped, my first thought would be that she ran away."

"For years I've been telling Bill that I think she ran off and started a new life in some exotic location."

Jessie lifted an eyebrow. "Where would that be?"

"That's the million-dollar question. Mexico? Hawaii? Bali? Who the heck knows?"

"Why would Arlene do something so drastic? Why run off, leaving everything behind, instead of simply divorcing the man?"

"I've thought about that, too," Karen said. "I think she was a coward."

"Could you elaborate?"

"Certainly. Plainly put, Arlene was a chickenshit. She was obsessed with caring what people thought about her. How could she leave her daughter and husband for no other reason than wanting to be free, wanting something new, for wanting more?"

Jessie shook her head. "You would have to be downright evil to let the father of your child go to jail, knowing he was innocent."

Karen shrugged. "Maybe she didn't know. Or maybe something happened to her after she ran off." She made a tsking noise. "You've got your work cut out for you, don't you?"

"It seems so," Jessie said. "Any other friends or acquaintances of Arlene's that you think might be helpful to my investigation?"

"Hmm. It's been so long, but maybe Pam Carr could help you. Pam and Arlene were very close at one time."

Jessie jotted down the name. "Does she live around here?"

"She used to live in Sacramento, but we lost touch soon after Arlene disappeared. I really have no idea where she's living or what she's doing these days."

"Were you and Pam close at one time?"

"Truthfully, I always considered her to be an odd duck, but she and Arlene always seemed to get along fabulously. Though without Arlene around, there was no longer anything to keep Pam and me connected."

Bill stepped into the room holding a cell phone. "It's Callan," he said to his wife.

Karen's face lit up. She jumped to her feet. "I need to talk to my son," she told Jessie. "Callan is my youngest, and he met a girl recently. We think she might be 'the one'!"

After Karen grabbed the phone from her husband, chatting excitedly as she walked off, Bill looked at Jessie and shrugged. "If I could help you, I would."

Jessie stacked the photo books on the coffee table and began to gather her things. "You never met Arlene?"

"Once, a few weeks before our wedding. She asked me where Karen and I were going for our honeymoon. When I told her Kauai, she looked absolutely devastated, said she'd always wanted to visit the islands. I hardly knew the woman, but I do remember feeling bad for mentioning it."

"Was she in your wedding?" Jessie asked as he walked her through the house, back the way she'd come in.

"She was supposed to be a bridesmaid, but she disappeared a few weeks before our big day."

Jessie frowned. "That must have been a difficult time."

"Karen was very upset with Arlene, convinced she'd run off."

"After a jury found him guilty, did Karen change her mind about Nathaniel?"

"No," he said, shaking his head. "She always thought he was innocent. After reading about Nathaniel's release, I recall Karen feeling vindicated, knowing she'd been right about the man."

Bill opened the door for Jessie. "Hold on," he said. "I'll be right back."

By the time Jessie had stepped outside, he returned with a bag in his hand. "Here," he said, handing it to her. "A loaf of bread to enjoy with dinner."

"Thank you so much for everything." As she started toward her car, she tried to absorb what she'd just heard. Karen seemed to think Arlene had simply packed up and run off to start a new life, possibly in some exotic land.

It sounded outlandish . . . downright inconceivable. Jessie didn't know Arlene, but she knew it wouldn't be easy to leave a child. If Arlene Snyder did pack up and leave, did she know her husband might end up being a suspect in her disappearance?

Nobody could be that selfish. Or could they? She thought of Dorothy and Ellis Kash and found herself reconsidering. Yeah, there were a lot of selfish assholes out there, and maybe Arlene was willing to push everyone else aside for her own benefit.

After Penny Snyder had first paid her a visit, Jessie put Arlene's name and date of birth into more than a few databases. Not unexpectedly, she found close to a thousand people by that name. She then did a search using Arlene's social security number. Many investigators considered that to be a slam dunk when it came to finding someone.

Unfortunately, when she typed in the number, Arlene showed up as being deceased in the same year she disappeared.

If Arlene were alive, she most likely would have needed a job, in which case she would also need a social security number.

Or maybe not?

Arlene might not have been suicidal, but she could have been suffering from a mental illness that caused her to wander. Worse, she could have been a victim of abduction or kidnapping.

Jessie unlocked her car and slid into the driver's seat.

It might be time to pull Zee onto the case. They would need to check mortuaries and hospitals and continue to question people who knew Arlene Snyder.

Like working an archeological dig or piecing together a puzzle, investigative work was tedious at times. Searching and assembling the evidence took days, months, sometimes years. Nothing would be solved until she dug up that one important clue or found that last squiggly piece of the puzzle that would ultimately bring it all together to a satisfying conclusion.

NINE

Ben was watching his daughter practice soccer in an indoor facility in Rocklin when his phone buzzed. It was Melony. "Hey," he said, "what's going on?"

"I'm running late," his wife told him. "Do you think you could pick up Sean at the Cranstons' on your way home?"

"Not a problem. Everything okay?"

"Just the usual emergency room chaos."

"I'll pick up dinner, too."

"You're a saint."

"I don't know about that, but I love you, and I'll see you at home." Ben ended the call in time to watch Abigail score a goal. A few months ago, he and his wife had separated for a few weeks. It had been rough on the kids, on all of them. He was glad to be home. Having a routine gave him a sense of normalcy despite the chaos inside his head. "Way to go!" he cheered when Abigail glanced his way.

Practice ended ten minutes later. One of the girls' mothers had played college soccer and volunteered to coach the team. She made the game fun and knew how to keep the kids engaged. While the team talked things over, Ben gestured to Abigail, letting her know he would wait for her outside.

The facility, partitioned off by a half wall, was big enough to allow for two practices at once. As he made his way to the door, he recognized

Paige Willis, Roger Willis's oldest daughter, playing on the indoor field at the far corner. He stopped to let his gaze roam slowly over the people sitting on the bleachers. He didn't see either of her parents.

As soon as Ben stepped outside, he heard shouting. Across the parking lot, he saw Paden White, the father of the girl who'd been molested in the theater by Roger, waving his arms and yelling.

Ben jogged toward the commotion.

"Get in your car and *go!*" Paden shouted, pointing toward the parking lot exit. "Get out of here before I call the police!"

As Ben approached, the person Paden was yelling at got out of the car.

Ben recognized the man at once. Roger Willis had balls. Wasn't it just yesterday that he'd gotten out on bail?

Willis shut his car door, making sure to bump Paden with his shoulder as he walked by.

Paden wasn't having it. He took a swing, his fist connecting with the middle of Willis's face. Blood spurted from Willis's nose, but Paden wasn't finished with him. He lunged at the man, taking Willis to the ground.

"Stop this!" a woman pleaded from her car across the way.

"Come on," Ben said, pulling Paden to his feet. "This isn't the time or the place."

Paden was on his feet, hovering over the man, Willis's shirt clutched in his fist. "I gave him a chance to get out of here, but he thinks he's above the law. Thinks he can do whatever he wants."

Blood oozed from the corner of Willis's mouth. "I didn't go inside," he said, knocking Paden's hand off him before pushing himself to his feet. "I'm following the rules," he told Ben. "This isn't a goddamn school."

"Paden," Ben tried again when he saw the man's hands curl into fists, "don't do anything foolish and mess with his upcoming trial.

Justice will prevail. We have plenty of witnesses, and two more victims have come forward. Let him go."

Paden hesitated long enough to prompt Ben to decide that now was a good time to lead Paden away.

A large group of people had gathered. Ben glanced around. He saw Abigail standing next to Paden's daughter just outside the facility. He headed that way, leading Paden through the crowd.

"Come on, Jane," Paden said to his daughter.

Jane's bottom lip trembled when she met her dad's gaze.

"Let's go home." Paden turned toward Ben before walking off and said low enough so the girls wouldn't hear, "He's lucky I didn't kill him."

Behind the wheel of his van, Ben waited for Abigail to buckle up before driving off. Everything that had just happened replayed in his mind. Paden had every right to be angry. Ben had told Paden that justice would be served if they took a back seat to the legal system. He was beginning to wonder if that were true. What if Roger Willis was found innocent? What then?

Ben drew in a slow, steady breath, but it didn't stop the adrenaline from racing through his body. There was a pounding in his ears. He didn't like the edgy, twitchy sensation coming over him, making him feel as if he might lose control. And then what? He wasn't sure. And that bothered him most of all.

"I thought you said Coach Willis was in jail," Abigail said.

Ben pulled the van over to the side of the road.

"What are you doing, Dad?" She touched his arm. "Are you all right?"

Raking his hands through his hair, he nodded, took a deep breath, and did his best to compose himself. But he felt anything but calm. He looked at Abigail, forced a smile. "Roger Willis was let out on bail, which means someone paid a lot of money to guarantee that he'll show up to court when it's time for his trial."

"But why? What if he hurts someone else? Jane is scared. She told me she's having nightmares and has to sleep with the light on. How is she going to be able to pay attention at school when she knows he might be right outside, waiting for her?"

"I talked to the principal at your school. He and the rest of the teachers and staff are aware of the situation. There will be extra security posted outside to make sure he doesn't come anywhere near the school."

She sucked in a shaky breath.

He could see the fear in the tightness of her shoulders. She'd been through so much in the past few months. He couldn't bear to see her like this. Kids her age had enough to deal with—schoolwork and peer pressure. "Coach Willis will be back behind bars very soon, and you'll never have to see him again."

"What about Jane?"

"She won't have to see him, either."

"You promise?"

"Cross my heart."

TEN

In order to get Jason to stop whining and help the two of them escape, Lacey had made a deal with her husband. Whenever they were both too exhausted to work, they would try to sleep. After some rest, they would hammer away. They had been working for hours, doing their best to stay within a one-foot-by-one-foot area.

But when it came time to rest, Lacey never slept. Instead, she lay in silence listening to Jason breathe, hoping and praying she would free-fall into oblivion . . . just for an hour or two. This went on for hours, maybe days. She'd completely lost any ability to keep track of time. Without light to help her tell the time of day, without enough sleep, without the ability to move more than a few inches at a time, she was beginning to lose hope. Being in the dark, surrounded by quiet, had also given her too much time to think about and analyze her relationship with Jason, because she didn't like where her thoughts were taking her. She was coming to the cold, hard realization that their marriage was a farce. And it was as much her fault as it was his. She'd missed all the signs, and she had a feeling it all stemmed from the life she'd escaped as a teenager. With Jason, she'd seen so much potential . . . so many possibilities. She had a house of her own, a car, food on the table. His shitty behavior was nothing compared to the life she'd run away from at the age of—

"Are you awake?" Jason asked, interrupting her thoughts.

"Yes."

"I don't want to die," he said. "I'm scared. Why did you have to make such a big deal about our anniversary? We should have—"

Of course. She should have known. He was blaming her for their predicament. She picked up the shoe and slammed it against the wood. Every time he tried to speak, she did it again. Laughter bubbled up inside of her. Was she going insane? She felt so far removed from the woman she was only days ago.

Dirt fell through the spot where she'd been beating her shoe. "I did it!" Excitement thrummed through her body. Her last swing had broken through the very center of the square. Grains of dirt fell through. The hole wasn't big enough to worry about the two of them being suffocated. Not yet.

"Now what?" Jason asked.

"We—I mean, *I* need to make sure the entire area is weak enough for me to break through."

Jason made a tsking noise with his tongue. It was a familiar habit of his. Something he did when he disagreed with her. Funny how it had never irritated her before this moment.

"I don't think this is a good idea," he said.

"It's our only option, Jason. Why don't you understand that? If we stay here and do nothing, we might have hours to live. There's no way of knowing for sure." But her instincts told her it was true. She'd been feeling dizzy and light-headed. They needed to get out of here fast.

"What about the dirt?" Jason asked, his voice quivery. "Once you try to dig your way out of here, it will cave in, and I'll be suffocated, buried alive."

He didn't care about anyone but himself. "Just keep your mouth on the pipe," she told him. "That's all you have to do. You'll be fine. I'll be the one to suffocate if I can't break through."

It was quiet for a moment before he said, "Okay. You're right."

"You don't care about our baby, do you?"

"I never wanted to have children. That was all you."

Her pulse quickened. "You never once told me you didn't want children. I talked about having a family since the day we met. You never said a word—"

He said nothing. He didn't have to. The truth smacked her in the head. Whenever she'd talked about having children over the years, he'd clammed up.

She swallowed.

"Are you okay?" he asked.

"No. I'm not okay."

Nothing.

She wanted to laugh out loud. Yep, she was definitely losing it. She'd never been an angry person, but at the moment, she hated him more than she'd hated anyone. Or, at least, as much. She wasn't fucking okay. She was hungry and thirsty, her head was pounding, and they were probably going to die in here. But she kept it all to herself.

"We're going to have to keep hammering," she said in a controlled tone of voice. "When the hole becomes large enough, I'll need you to put your hand through the opening and pull down on the wood, bringing it toward you. It's the only way to give me enough space to try and push through."

After a long pause, she said, "Did you hear me?"

She heard a noise. It sounded as if he was crying.

"I heard you," he finally said. "Are you ready? Are you going to try to break through the wood now?"

No "I love you," when this could very well be their last conversation. The past six months flashed through her mind. Jason had been working long hours. When he did have time off, he spent it with his brother and his friends. And he never invited her along. She'd spent most of her free time making his favorite dishes for dinner, and yet he might as well have been eating soup from a can, judging by his reaction when he sat down to eat. The few conversations they'd had were stilted

and awkward. He would pick fights for no reason, and she couldn't
. remember the last time he'd appeared happy to see her.

It bothered her to know that it took being buried alive with the
man to see everything so clearly. Yes, their marriage was a farce, but
had it always been that way? Jason might never have been the amazing
husband she'd thought he was, but had he ever been happy?

Had she been so obsessed with getting pregnant that she'd ignored
all the signs of being in a dysfunctional relationship?

"I'm ready," he said.

Tired of overthinking everything, she picked up the shoe and
started banging.

It wasn't long after that when the hole was big enough. Jason didn't
have to be reminded of what to do. She could hear the wood cracking
as he pulled. A large chunk of particleboard dropped to his side.

Dirt came in through the hole as she scooted to the right. Holding
her breath, she reached upward, got a good grip on the other side of
the hole, and pulled.

The board broke. As quickly as humanly possible, she twisted
around, contorting her body so that she was on bent knees, her back
against the dirt coming through the hole.

Dizziness washed over her.

Her insides burned. Time was running out.

Using every bit of strength she could summon, she thought about
living to raise her child. Jason might not want children, but she did.
She wanted to be free. She wanted to survive. Screaming, she pushed
upward, digging furiously through soil on both sides of her, shocked
when her head popped out of the dirt.

She sucked in a breath. And then another as she shoved away splin-
ters of broken wood until she stood on wobbly legs. Excitement turned
to confusion when her head smacked against a low ceiling. *What the fuck?*

Bits of light came through a vent nearby, enough light to throw eerie shadows around. They had been buried inside a small room with three cement walls. The fourth wall was made of wood.

A lump caught in her throat. No. No. No. It couldn't be.

This was insane!

She wasn't outside.

This couldn't be happening. Covered to her waist in dirt, she estimated there to be two feet of earth above the box they'd been buried in. She pulled herself out. At five feet, two inches tall, she had to stoop to walk around.

There wasn't much to see. Her eyes watered. "You will not cry," she scolded herself.

No food or water anywhere in sight. She went to the wall made of wood and pushed her weight against it, pounding her fists all the way across, up and down, desperate to find a door or a weak spot. It was solid. Nothing like the particleboard she'd just broken through. Her stomach churned.

Glancing back at the pipe sticking out of the particleboard, she knew it was time to save Jason. She stepped into the box and began breaking off pieces of wood and tossing them aside. It wasn't until she'd removed the dirt from around Jason's face and chest that he finally opened his eyes. Jerking upright, his eyes wide and filled with panic, he sucked air into his lungs.

"What happened?" he asked. "Where are we?"

"Well," she said without humor, "it looks like we're in another box. Only this one is bigger and made mostly of cement."

He crawled out on all fours, then looked back at her. "What the hell is going on?"

"We're fucked, Jason. We are completely and totally fucked."

ELEVEN

Wednesday morning Jessie was at her desk when she picked up a call.

It was Colin. He started the conversation with "I miss you."

"Can you meet me for breakfast at the Cornerstone Café in the morning?"

"Sounds good. What's the catch?"

Jessie laughed. "How did you know there was a catch?"

"It's all in the tone."

"I was hoping you could look up an old case and let me know if you find anything interesting."

"What's the name?"

"Arlene Snyder."

"Got it," Colin said. "How are you holding up?"

"I'm fine. How about you?"

"The same." He laughed.

"What's so funny?"

"I was just thinking we could record one of our conversations and just hit 'Play' every morning."

"That's not funny," Jessie said. "It's sort of sad."

"Maybe we should take a look at the calendar and schedule a getaway."

"With the kids?"

"Of course. If it were just the two of us, I wouldn't know what to do with myself," he teased.

It was Jessie's turn to laugh.

"Time's up. Gotta go."

"I love you."

"Love you, too."

Two seconds after the call ended, Jessie's cell phone buzzed as Zee walked through the office door. "I'm going to pick up this call," Jessie told her. "Don't run off until we've had a chance to talk."

"I'll head upstairs and get our usual."

"Great." Jessie picked up the call. "Jessie Cole. How can I help you?"

"Good morning. Grant Taylor here, with Taylor and Fitch Investigations in beautiful Phoenix, Arizona."

A scuffling noise and murmuring sounded in the background. "Sorry about the noise," the man said. "We're doing a little remodeling over here."

"Not a problem."

"I've heard a lot about you and the work you do, and I was hoping you might be interested in working with me on an unusual case."

This wasn't the first time an investigative firm in another area had called for help. It wasn't a common practice, but it happened. "What's it about?"

"I'm basically looking for a missing person, which I've been told you specialize in. Her name is Anne Elizabeth Corrigan. In a nutshell, Anne has a very large inheritance coming her way. Over a million dollars left to her by her grandmother, who passed away recently. We've run all the usual searches but have come up empty-handed."

A loud crash sounded, prompting Jessie to hold the phone away from her ear.

"Damn. Are you still there?"

Jessie inwardly sighed. "I'm here."

"So, what do you think? Interested?"

"I charge seventy-five dollars an hour." She was about to add that she had a full schedule and wasn't sure if she had the time to look for Anne Corrigan.

"I'm willing to pay you double that."

She perked up a bit. *It must be a difficult case,* she thought. Otherwise they would have located the woman already. "I would need a five-thousand-dollar, nonrefundable deposit for any possible costs accrued."

"Done."

This was way too easy. What was he hiding? "How old is Anne Corrigan?"

"Thirty-three."

That ruled out a runaway teenager. "Do you know where she was born?"

"New Jersey."

"Social security number?" Jessie asked.

"Yes—"

"But it leads nowhere," Jessie finished for him.

"Correct. We know she left home at the age of sixteen because her mother filed a missing person's report at the time."

"Did anyone follow up? Was there an investigation?"

"Not as far as I can tell. Her biological father passed away when Anne was ten. Her mother remarried a man by the name of Everett Miller. Looks like the mom still lives in New Jersey. Not sure about the stepdad. Nobody has returned my calls."

"Was the girl abused? Is that why she ran off?"

"No idea."

"Since you're calling me, I assume Anne Corrigan is connected to Sacramento in some way."

"Correct. It's a long shot, but it's all we have to go on," Mr. Taylor said. "In the files that I'll send you if you agree to take the case, you'll see two pictures. One is of a ten-year-old Anne Elizabeth Corrigan with her grandmother. The other is a photo of a young couple announcing their marriage in the *Sacramento Tribune*: Lacey Page just married Jason Geiger. The woman in the photo resembles Anne Elizabeth Corrigan."

"How in the world did you make the connection between a ten-year old girl and a woman in a wedding announcement?"

"It was a damn miracle. We spent a lot of money on ads, asking if anyone had seen Anne Corrigan. Lo and behold, we got a call from a woman in Sacramento who said she used to be in charge of archiving articles, including announcements. Told us she never forgets a face."

Jessie held back a snort. The odds of Lacey Page and Anne Corrigan being the same person had to be astronomical. "Did you use age-progression software on the ten-year-old?"

He cleared his throat. "Well, uh, no. It's complicated."

"How did you get involved in the case?" Jessie wanted to know.

"Friend of a friend." He laughed. "It's all about who you know in this business."

The guy sounded friendly enough, Jessie thought, but shady, too.

"I'll make the check out to the Jessie Cole Agency and send it to the address listed. Or would you rather give me banking information so I can make a direct deposit?"

"A check is fine." She gave him the information he requested so he could send copies of the information in his file.

"There is one more thing," he said.

Jessie waited.

"This particular case needs to be settled right away."

"There's a deadline?"

"Afraid so. It was brought to my attention recently that the heir needs to be found on or before the end of this month, or the money goes to charity."

"That's two weeks away."

"Correct."

"I'm sorry. There's no possible way I can—"

"There's a twenty-five-thousand-dollar bonus, no strings attached, if you succeed in finding her."

"Seriously?"

"Seriously."

"I would need that in writing, along with proof of funds."

"Not a problem."

"Forget sending a check for the five thousand dollars," she told him. "I think it would be best, after all, if you made the direct deposit."

More information was exchanged before Jessie ended the call. She was still thinking about the conversation when the door came open and Zee appeared with paper cups in hand. Her timing was impeccable.

Zee placed Jessie's coffee on her desk in front of her. "What's wrong? Did something happen?"

"I just got off the phone with an investigator in Arizona. He wants me to help him find someone."

"Another missing person's case?"

"I'm not exactly sure what it is. He's sending me copies of his case files, but it sounds like it might be a situation where this particular someone doesn't want to be found."

"So why not leave her be?" Zee asked.

"Because her grandmother died and left her a whole lot of money."

"Interesting."

"Definitely. But we just got a whole lot busier, and I'm going to need your help."

"Finally!"

"When can you finish with the workers' comp case?"

"By the end of the day. The man said he injured himself in the company parking lot. And then yesterday, he posted on social media for all the world to see that he actually fell outside his home. He was quite proud of himself since he'd already collected over a thousand dollars in benefits."

"Not the brightest crayon in the box."

"Nope."

"Okay, you finish that up. I have other things to work on. I'm meeting with Colin in the morning after he's had a chance to look into the Arlene Snyder case. Let's check back here at ten thirty and discuss what needs to be done."

"Ten-four. I'll be ready to roll."

TWELVE

Ben glanced at his watch: 8:15 p.m. He and Melony were at the Sullivan home, a few miles from their house. Gretchen Sullivan had set up a neighborhood meeting to talk about bullying at the kids' school. For an hour they'd discussed the importance of being observant about any changes in a child's demeanor, since victims are reluctant to speak up because they often feel ashamed. It was helpful if parents knew the signs and symptoms of the victim and the bully. After the discussion died down, a few of the men, Ben included, sat in front of the TV, mindlessly watching a football game as their wives caught up with each other.

Ben was tired, ready to go home. A few feet away, Melony was in a huddle with three women. He waited fifteen minutes before giving her the eye and gesturing at his watch.

Melony said something to Gretchen Sullivan, who was standing beside her. A single mother, Gretchen was raising two daughters while working full time. As if that wasn't enough, she somehow found the time to be an active member of the PTA and host elaborate fund-raisers. He'd heard Melony complain that Gretchen's children were always immaculately dressed and well behaved. Melony wanted to know how she found the time to pack organic lunches, jog every day, and arrange meetings like the one tonight.

Ben didn't know how Gretchen managed, nor did he care. It was getting late, and they still needed to pick up the kids and get them to bed.

"Okay, people," Gretchen said, clapping her hands together.

One of the men sitting next to Ben picked up the remote and shut off the television.

"Before everyone runs off, I wanted to let you know that it has been brought to my attention that Roger Willis was let out on bail."

Murmurs erupted around the room.

"Yesterday, Roger Willis was seen by some of you, sitting in his car in the parking lot of an indoor sporting facility. He was in plain view and only a few feet away from the entrance to the building where dozens of young girls were practicing soccer. As you may or may not be aware, there are multiple victims who have come forward to say they were abused by Mr. Willis."

Ben kept his eyes on Melony. She stood tall, nodding her head at everything Gretchen was saying. Ben felt uneasy. He didn't like the idea of Roger Willis being discussed in any manner that might jeopardize the case. He'd once covered a story about a group of vigilantes who attempted to take matters into their own hands concerning a pedophile. In that case, significant resources had to be diverted to protect the suspect. In the end, nobody won.

"I would like to ask all of you to come to the next city council meeting to protest Roger Willis's release. At the very least, he should be ordered to wear an ankle bracelet so we know where he is at all times."

A woman whose name Ben didn't know said, "I read about a pedophile recently jailed thanks to a group of concerned citizens who duped him into meeting a young girl at the mall. He was caught red-handed on video."

"Wouldn't that be considered illegal entrapment?" someone asked.

"Even worse news," Gretchen said, ignoring the question about entrapment, "is that I have it on good authority that Roger has been abusing his daughter, Paige. She confided as much to a friend." She paused to collect herself. "How can we stand by and do nothing?"

Everyone started talking at once.

Ben took that opportunity to get up and make his way over to Melony. "We've been here for over an hour. It's past the kids' bedtime."

"Give me two minutes to let Gretchen know we're leaving."

Ben let himself out and waited for Melony outside. She appeared a few minutes later, and they walked to the car.

"What's wrong?" she asked Ben as they drove off.

"Between Paden White throwing Willis to the ground and getting in a couple of good hits and now this—a group of wannabe vigilantes talking about illegally ensnaring the guy—I'm worried Willis will be let go on some crazy technicality."

"You were so fired up about Willis," Melony said. "Ready to beat the crap out of him on the soccer field only months ago. But now, suddenly, you want everyone to keep his or her distance and hope the system takes care of him? You know what happened to Jane in the theater. It could have been Abigail." Silence had no chance to settle before she added, "What if you hadn't been there to pick up Abigail yesterday? What if you weren't able to get there until five or ten minutes after practice and she waited outside for you—alone? Would Roger Willis have tried to talk to her? Anything could have happened, and it chills me to the bone."

If Melony had any idea of the turmoil caused by the mere mention of Roger's name, she would let it go. But he didn't want her to know about the uncontrollable tremors he experienced or how his pulse elevated whenever he thought about the man. "Trust me, Melony. It chills me, too. Roger will be tried before a judge and jury. I just think it would be best if we stayed calm until then."

"Didn't you hear what Gretchen said about Roger abusing his own child?"

"It's hearsay. We have no proof," Ben answered. "As you've said many times, Gretchen tends to exaggerate and can be overly dramatic."

"It sounds as if you're defending the man."

"No," Ben said. "I would never defend him." The truth was, Ben wasn't comfortable talking about Roger Willis these days. Just hearing his name clouded his vision and made it difficult to think straight. For the past twenty-four hours he'd felt as if he were hanging on by a thread, trying hard to at least appear unruffled.

"Well, Gretchen has good reason to be upset at the moment. She was a victim of sexual abuse herself when she was young. The whole Roger Willis situation has obviously hit too close to home."

"Are you going to attend the city council meeting?" Ben asked.

"Definitely."

Ben pulled into the driveway and shut off the engine. The kids were just across the street. It wasn't easy balancing his inner hostility toward Willis with his desire to protect his family. He turned toward Melony. "I want that man behind bars just as much as anyone else. I don't want the two of us arguing over anything that has to do with Roger Willis. I'll go to the city council meeting. If it'll make you feel better, I will also go to Roger's house and talk to him in the flesh."

"And say what?"

"I would tell him if he ever so much as talks to Abigail, I will—"

"No more talk of Roger Willis," she said softly. "You're a good man, and our kids are lucky to have you to protect them. Please don't go near that man's house." She exhaled. "You're right. I say we forget about going to the city council meeting, stay clear of the whole thing until the trial."

Ben felt some of the tension leave his shoulders. "Are you sure that's what you want to do?"

"I'm sure."

Thirteen

His hatred for Jason Geiger had been like a cancer, dividing and spreading, damaging tissues and organs. But listening to the man lose his shit down there in the hole made everything better, despite the occasional bout of paranoia, and especially now that he'd gotten his nerves under control.

The first time he'd met Jason was when he was twenty years old. Jason had seemed like a good guy, fair and even-tempered. Years later, he realized he couldn't have been more wrong.

Jason had turned out to be the exact opposite of the man he pretended to be. He was a narcissist, a pathological liar, and a sneaky asshole who cared only about himself.

Yeah, sure, the world was filled with assholes. Everybody had run into at least one in their lifetime. But Jason was different. He was truly evil. Nobody knew that better than he did. He'd been watching Jason long enough to know that the man thoroughly enjoyed others' misfortunes. He wanted others to like him so that he could gain their trust. That was why he went out of his way to be polite, bordering on charming. Control was everything to a man like Jason.

If he couldn't control every aspect of his life, he felt powerless.

He knew all of this because he'd worked closely with Jason for over a year.

Short but not sweet.

In the end, he'd lost everything.

As his life had crumbled around him, fueled by revenge, he'd become obsessed with learning everything he could about Jason Geiger, spending much of his time gathering information on the man. Never before had he been so obsessed with anything or anyone. He spent a lot of time watching Jason from afar, taking endless videos of him walking to and from his car or hanging out at a bar with his friends. If he wasn't following Jason, he was usually on the phone talking to one of Jason's clients. He'd tell them he was considering working with Jason on a project and wanted to know if they had any information that might help him make an informed decision.

Turned out they had plenty to say.

He'd learned that Jason was afraid of his own shadow. One guy he had a long conversation with told him how surprised he'd been to learn of Jason's fear of insects, especially red ants, and how Jason wore tall rubber boots whenever he visited a construction site. Apparently, Jason was also terrified of the dark.

A fucking pansy-ass.

Jason was not the respected businessman that he pretended to be. He lived a double life, never revealing his true self to those closest to him.

Once he realized Jason felt no remorse for the lives he'd ruined by refusing to pay people money owed and filing frivolous lawsuits, that was when the real work began. He'd drawn up plans for a house of horrors, custom-made for Jason. Unsure as to whether or not he would be able to get Jason alone, he made sure he had enough room for two people. When he discovered Jason was having an affair, he got excited about the idea of burying Jason with his wife, figuring that would only add to his discomfort.

He did the work himself—the excavation, the air vent, forming and pouring concrete walls and ceiling. And then there was the key and the box filled with red ants. Water bottles and food. So many details that Jason had yet to discover.

At first he considered leaving the couple with flashlights and instructions, teasing Jason by giving him false hope that they'd make it out of there. But that would have been too easy. Instead, he decided to leave just enough food and water to keep two people alive for a week or two. At the last minute, he also decided to leave Lacey a picture of Jason with his mistress. The more drama, the better.

Ultimately, he wanted Jason to sit in a small cramped space, day in and day out, knowing he was going to die. He wanted to listen to him whine and moan. Mostly, he wanted Jason to suffer.

After completing the underground room, he'd spent months working on a plan to get Jason into his car. It was during that time that he discovered Jason and his wife had an anniversary coming up.

Obviously Jason wasn't happily married, but he hadn't left his wife, so it was worth a shot. He promptly began sending Lacey Geiger fraudulent emails from the best restaurants in town, even went so far as to suggest dinner at the Firehouse for half price. He'd taken a few graphic design classes in his day, even built his own website, and he knew how to make a decent-looking coupon.

Lacey didn't waste any time calling the number on the coupon he sent her, and he did the rest, even called the restaurant and made reservations just in case she called the Firehouse to verify. Then came the offer of transportation. He'd left postcards on both their cars and in their mailbox. For a ridiculous price, his transportation company would drive them to and from the restaurant.

Too good to be true?

He laughed. Never. Jason liked a good deal as much as his wife did. They ended up being putty in his hands.

The best part, after his underground room was finished, had been going to bed at night, dreaming of the day when Jason Geiger would wake up in the dark only to realize he'd been buried alive.

The idea of the biggest asshole on the planet being eight feet under and having absolutely no control over his dilemma was just too damn good.

FOURTEEN

Jessie met Colin for breakfast at the Cornerstone Café & Bar downtown. When she walked through the door, Colin waved her over. For years their relationship had been moving forward at a snail's pace, which suited them both. Neither of them was worried about taking it to the next level. Jessie appreciated their similarities: they were both workaholics, and yet they were respectful in that they didn't check emails or multitask on the phone when they were together.

Jessie had dated two men before Colin. Both times she'd felt suffocated. She didn't like having someone breathing down her neck all the time. Colin was the exact opposite. He wasn't needy, compliant, or dull.

He stood, greeted her with a kiss.

They slipped into the booth across from each other. When the waitress came, they didn't waste any time. Colin ordered a breakfast burrito stuffed with scrambled eggs, sausage, ham, onions, bell peppers, and cheese. Jessie didn't usually get hungry until later in the day, but the smell of maple syrup prompted her to order French toast and coffee.

"Busy day ahead?" he asked once they were alone again.

"Always. What about you?"

"Same."

"You look beautiful this morning," he said.

She smiled, taking in his rugged good looks. He wore an old, faded Ramones T-shirt and jeans. He was thirty-nine, but he could easily pass for ten years younger. Not fair. "Going undercover, I see."

Nodding, he looked down at his shirt. "Piper picked it out for me."

"Your daughter has good taste. How is she?"

"She's an eleven-year-old girl obsessed with Katy Perry. I'm completely out of my element."

"Wait until she's a teenager. Puberty, peer pressure, and demands for more freedom."

"Sounds fun." Colin reached across the table to take her hand in his. "Still on for Friday night?"

It took Jessie a minute to recall what he was referring to. And then she remembered Olivia's plans to spend the night at her friend Bella's house.

"Did you forget?"

She winced. "Sorry. The good news is Friday night is a go. The bad news is, it's your turn to make dinner."

He laughed. "Not a problem."

The waitress brought their food, and they both dove in. Jessie was hungrier than she thought. After a few bites, she asked, "Were you able to find anything on Arlene Snyder?"

He nodded, chewed, swallowed. "No reports of domestic abuse were ever filed."

"Who filed the missing person's report?"

"Her parents, Dorothy and Ellis Kash."

"You would think her husband would have been the one to call the police and file the report."

After taking a few more bites, Colin said, "The lead detective on the case at the time passed away a few years ago. I skimmed the file, and it was clear that no one spent a great deal of time looking for Arlene Snyder."

"Why not?"

He shrugged. "Investigators believed foul play was involved. The case did receive some national coverage in the beginning, but most of their resources and time was spent examining Mr. Snyder, and you know how that played out. Bloodstain in the trunk, Arlene's parents testifying that their daughter was afraid for her life, and the neighbors heard a disturbance. Mostly circumstantial, but it was enough to satisfy investigators."

"And nobody bothered to look for her after his release?"

"I have two good reasons for that: time and money. The department didn't—and doesn't—have the funding to spend on cold cases. The media was no longer interested. Arlene Snyder wasn't a young child when she disappeared. Nathaniel Snyder's lawyer was able to show that Arlene was taking Xanax at the time she disappeared, which led some to speculate she wasn't happy. If someone wants to disappear, they have the right to do so."

"She was taking medication?"

He nodded. "There was a note in the file."

"Hmm. What about the neighbors who heard a commotion coming from the Snyders' home?"

"When they were questioned again, they told investigators they regretted testifying, since the raised voices they heard could have come from any number of homes within their densely populated neighborhood." Colin took a bite of his burrito.

Jessie said, "I met Arlene's parents. They didn't want to talk about their daughter, and they definitely weren't interested in searching for her. Don't you find that odd?"

"I did read in the report that they were outspoken in their criticism of the police after Nathaniel Snyder was released, certain that he was responsible for her death. For five days afterward they sat on the steps outside the police department, waving signs and threatening to sue."

"Did they make good on the threat?"

"No. Five days of protests and then poof, they were gone."

"Why would they do that—go to all that trouble and then just let it go as if it had never happened?"

"One more mystery to untangle."

"Think of all the unsolved cases out there just waiting to be unraveled."

"Most never will be," he said before digging into the last of his breakfast.

Jessie thought of every parent who had ever experienced that awful split-second nightmare when they turn around and see their child gone in a grocery store—the panic and nausea that followed only to find the child in the next aisle.

But some parents had to live that nightmare throughout their lives. Too many families were ripped apart by grief, left to wonder what happened to the missing family member. And Jessie knew firsthand how difficult it was to let go of that one tiny glimmer of hope that they were out there somewhere and were alive.

FIFTEEN

As Lacey used a piece of wood to dig through the dirt, hoping to find another bag with food and water, Jason sat on the ground, his back propped against the cement wall. Ever since she'd helped pull him from the box that was now half filled with dirt, he'd been a little whiny brat—he was cold, hungry, thirsty. He couldn't stand up. He had a cramp. His head hurt.

"Who did this?" he asked for the umpteenth time. "That's what I want to know. Look around. This took somebody a lot of time to build."

Lacey stepped out of the hole where they'd been buried, then jumped on top of the wood where she knew it would break with a little pressure. It cracked down the middle of the left side. Little by little she removed the pieces of particleboard and piled it in one corner of the room. She'd been right about the size of the box. Six by six, with two feet of dirt covering the top. Lacey looked at Jason and said, "Maybe you could help me out here or use some of that frustration of yours to help us find a way out."

"Who was that driver who picked us up?" he asked.

As usual, he wasn't listening. "I have no idea."

"But you arranged everything."

She got a good grip on the wood and grunted as she pulled, dislodging another large section of wood. She tossed it aside, then fell to her knees and dug through the fresh dirt. "I made plans for our celebration dinner at least three weeks ago," she said.

Lacey stopped what she was doing and pointed a finger at him. "I remember where I got that number. You came in from work with a flyer. It was for a transportation service that was offering a fifty percent discount for first-time users." She frowned. "You're not insinuating this is all my fault, are you?"

"Well, if you didn't have to make a big deal out of every birthday, holiday, and anniversary, you have to admit, we wouldn't be here."

Continuing her search, she jabbed her hands into the soil and reached around, fingers digging. She felt paper. Another bag. "Yes!"

Her lips curved upward as she pulled the bag from the dirt. It was heavier than the last one. She held it close to her chest as she climbed out of the box, crawled to the side of the room opposite Jason, and took a seat, her back propped against the wall.

She peeked inside. Four water bottles, four granola bars, and four apples. She reached inside and pulled out a water bottle, untwisted the cap, and took a long gulp before putting the lid back in place.

"What else is in there?"

"I'm not going to tell you until we've talked."

"About what?"

"About our relationship and what went wrong." She knew it was silly or maybe even crazy for her to ask, considering their circumstances, but for the first time she was seeing their relationship clearly. He had nowhere to go. And she wanted answers.

"Do you really think this is the time or the place?"

"Yes. I do."

"We've been kidnapped and buried alive, but you want to talk about my unhappiness." He shook his head. "You're just a little spoiled princess who has always gotten everything she asked for, aren't you, Lacey?"

"You don't know anything about me, so fuck off."

"We've been married for eight years. I know everything about you."

She shrugged. He knew nothing about her life before she'd met him, about all she'd been through.

"I'm hungry and thirsty," he said, sounding like the overindulged princess he'd just accused her of being.

"You get nothing until you open up and tell me why you've been so disengaged. You haven't been happy for a while."

"Who told you?"

Her heart sank. She might not like this other man she'd discovered down here in the bowels of hell, but she couldn't just shut off her feelings and emotions in a matter of days. It pained her to think that everybody but his wife might have known that he wasn't invested in their marriage. "Nobody told me anything. I should have known."

"How could you have?"

She snorted. "It was right there in front of my face. You've been distant, you nitpick everything I do, you've completely shut down when it comes to our relationship. We stopped having long conversations about future plans a while ago. And you don't make any effort whatsoever to spend time with me." She swallowed. "But I didn't see the signs because I was focused on starting a family."

He shrugged.

"How long have you been feeling this way?" she asked.

"Why does it even matter?"

Ever since she'd awakened in the dark, her emotions had run hot and cold. One minute she hated him, and the next she wanted to hold his hand. She didn't know why it mattered, but it did. "We've been together for eight years. You're my husband. Tell me, Jason. You owe me that much."

"Six months," he said. "Maybe longer."

Her mind flickered back to all those mornings and nights she'd tried to seduce him, hoping to get pregnant, praying for a baby. She remembered the times she'd succeeded—he wouldn't kiss her or gaze into her eyes when they had sex. "Why did you fuck me if you wanted nothing to do with me?"

"You shouldn't curse. It's unbecoming."

"Fuck you."

Silence.

"Why didn't you tell me how you felt?"

"I was going to get around to it. You have no idea how difficult it is to run a business. Do you know the financial risk I took to start that business?"

"With my money!" she reminded him.

"All those long hours while you were doing yoga and baking cookies for the neighbors. Hiring and firing is not a pleasant task. I can't even remember the last time I took a vacation."

It was all about Jason. What a fool she'd been. "So, as far as me and you, there was no endgame planned?"

"I wanted to tell you. Every morning I would wake up and say to myself, 'This is the day I will come clean and tell Lacey how I feel.' But then I would come home, eat dinner, and I don't know, just not do it."

She didn't believe it for a minute. "You knew exactly what you were doing. Do you have any idea the work and the love I put into those dinners? I was working, too, you know? And yet you never asked about my day. You never once thanked me for spending hours making your favorite food, doing your laundry, and catering to your every need."

"You're too nice. I've said it a million times."

She stiffened. "I cleaned the house and took out the garbage. I mowed the damn lawn. You never lifted a finger around the house."

"I figured you liked doing it."

Feeling twitchy and on edge, she took another gulp of water. Glaring at him, she grabbed a granola bar, tore off more of the wrapper, and took a bite. She closed her eyes and moaned in ecstasy while she chewed. It tasted wonderful, and she wanted him to know how much she was enjoying it.

She was angry—at Jason, at herself for being blind for so long, at the person who had shoved them in a dark hole. After she swallowed, she said, "Is there someone else? Is that it?"

"No."

"Hmm. I see. It's just me you don't like."

He cleared his throat. "Yes."

"Thank you for your brutal honesty."

Fuck him. She was done asking him to explain himself. Instead, she decided to focus on figuring out who had done this to them. "Do you remember where you found the flyer you brought into the house? The one offering a discount on transportation?"

He raked a hand through his hair, glanced at his dirty hand, and grimaced. Jason was a two-shower-a-day man.

"The flyer was sticking out from the welcome mat by the front door."

She tried to recall what the flyer had looked like. It was likely sitting inside the kitchen drawer. It frustrated her that she couldn't remember the name of the company or the person she'd talked to on the phone when she'd called. Years ago, she'd been the only witness to a fatal car accident and had been unable to describe or identify the person who had run from the scene. After that event, she'd gone out of her way to take lessons on witness identification. The downside was that she now examined everyone she met.

She summoned a vision of the driver when she saw him climb out of the vehicle and walk around the front of the car. She estimated his height to be five foot nine. His head was as round as a bowling ball. His hair was dark—a buzz cut that revealed small, nondescript ears. His biceps strained against the leather jacket he was wearing.

"What was the name of the company?" Jason asked.

"I don't remember."

"Are you going to share whatever it is you found in that bag?" he asked.

"Until we find a way out of here, we're going to need to ration what's here." When she pulled out two water bottles and bars, something fell to the ground. She unfolded the paper and examined it under the shadowy light filtering in through the vent. It was a picture of Jason with their neighbor Chaya Cohen. They were in bed—the bed Lacey shared with her husband, the bed where their son or daughter had been conceived. She ripped the photo to pieces, crawled to the hole, and tossed it in the dirt.

"What are you doing?"

"Nothing." For a long moment, she merely stared at him. His elbows were propped on his knees, and his head was bent forward. She knew she shouldn't be hurt by his betrayal, not after the way he'd treated her since their abduction, but that didn't stop a sharp pain from ripping through her chest.

A picture was worth a thousand words. Everything made a little more sense. A part of her wanted to confront him about Chaya, but another part wasn't ready to hear any more lies.

If Jason wanted to know what she was doing, all he had to do was crawl over to the hole and figure it out.

She needed to stay focused on finding a way out of here and saving her baby. Stooped over, she brought Jason his share of granola bars and bottled waters. "This needs to last you for as many days as possible," she told him. "I kept the same amount for myself."

"Look around you, Lacey. There's no way out."

"So, you're just going to give up, is that it?"

He muttered something under his breath as she made her way to the vent in the ceiling. The vent cover was made of thick metal. It looked a lot like the vents in her house, but much bigger—approximately two feet by two feet. There were dozens of tiny slits in the cover, which was the only reason they were getting enough oxygen. She peeked straight up through the narrow spaces. All she could see was aluminum framing. The slits weren't wide enough to fit her finger through. The cover had been nailed to the cement ceiling.

She left the vent, stepped into the box, and got down on her knees for another look around, convinced they were missing something. She slid her fingers around the bottom edge and found a spot where she could wedge her finger between the side of the wooden box and . . . *Damn. More cement.* She'd hoped it was dirt because then maybe they could have removed the wood flooring, piece by piece, and dug their way out of here.

After a moment she climbed out again, grabbed one of her shoes, and went back to the vent.

"They used masonry nails," Jason said in a gloomy voice. "We would need a pry bar to remove them. Even then it probably wouldn't work."

As she examined the vent cover, she brushed her fingers over the nails, hoping they might be loose. No such luck. "I'm going to try and use my shoes as a hammer to chisel around each nail."

"There are too many. The metal on the toe and heel of both shoes is already wearing down."

"You are just full of optimism, aren't you?"

"That's right, Pollyanna."

She plunked a hand on her hip. "Wow. So I guess my positivity has been one more thorn in your side all these years."

"You could say that."

"What did I ever do to you? You could have left at any time."

The look on his face unnerved her, a cross between anger and defeat. "Do you have any idea what it's like to be married to Mrs. Perfect? All my friends call you June Cleaver without the pearls. What they would do for one home-cooked meal. I never brought them the cookies and cakes you baked because it only made their wives look a little tired and sad. How do you tell your friends and family that you're leaving a woman because she's just too damn perfect?"

Her stomach roiled. "You don't tell them anything. You just walk out the door and leave." Lacey lifted the shoe and started hammering around one of the nails. Right away, bits and pieces of cement fell to the ground.

Sixteen

After breakfast, Jessie spent the rest of the day in the office with Zee, searching the internet and sifting through information on two cases. Zee would continue the investigation on Arlene Snyder, while Jessie focused on locating Lacey Geiger.

"Be careful what you wish for," Zee said.

Jessie looked up from her computer screen. "What are you talking about?"

"I've been begging you to give me a *real* case, something meaty like a missing person's investigation. But now, as I look at all the contradicting statements made by people you interviewed, I'm wondering what the heck I was thinking."

Jessie smiled. "Just think of it as a puzzle. Gather the pieces and go from there. One step at a time."

"But we don't even know if this Snyder woman is dead or alive."

"No," Jessie said, thinking of her sister. "No, we don't."

"Was Arlene content or unhappy?" Zee asked as her fingers clacked away on the keyboard, taking multitasking to a whole new level. "According to your notes, Karen Cosso didn't believe Arlene was happily married, which she never understood because she considered Arlene's husband, Nathaniel, to be a great guy. Arlene's parents, on the other hand," Zee continued, "are convinced Nathaniel killed their only daughter. And yet not one report of domestic violence was ever filed by neighbors or friends, or by Arlene herself."

Zee shook her head. "I can't believe Arlene's parents wouldn't want to at least try to find their daughter. If there was any chance at all of finding their only daughter alive, why wouldn't they latch on to that?"

"Your guess is as good as mine," Jessie said.

"I think Arlene's parents are hiding something. Maybe they had something to do with her disappearance."

Jessie couldn't deny that the same thought had entered her mind.

"Or maybe her parents had no idea their daughter was unhappy and on medication."

Jessie looked at Zee. "I think the odds are against Arlene's parents ever opening up to either one of us."

"Never say never," Zee said cheerfully. "I just found an interesting tidbit on Arlene's father, Ellis Kash."

Jessie waited for her to elaborate.

"He was arrested twice for drunk and disorderly conduct."

"When?"

"Let's see." Long pause. "Both arrests occurred within the first year after Arlene's disappearance."

"Which tells me he took the news pretty hard."

"What was he like when you met him?" Zee asked. "Was he sober?"

"His wife did most of the talking, and we didn't stay long, but he looked and acted normal. I would say he was sober. He was a quiet man. As far as looks go, he's tall with bent shoulders. I thought he looked much older than his wife. How old is he?"

"Eighty-seven. His wife, Dorothy, is eighty."

Sounded about right. "What about Pam Carr, the woman Karen Cosso mentioned as being one of Arlene's closest friends when she vanished—did you find an address?"

"Yes. And a phone number for a Pam Carr in El Dorado Hills. She's the right age, and she used to live in the Sacramento area. I'll give her a call to see if she's willing to talk."

"Great."

"I'm also checking hospitals within a thirty-mile radius of the house Penny grew up in to see if there was ever an Arlene Snyder brought in around the time she disappeared. After that, I'll check jails in the area, too."

Jessie lifted a questioning brow.

"Maybe Arlene committed a crime," Zee said. "You know, maybe she was thrown in jail but never contacted anyone."

"Highly unlikely."

"Stranger things have happened."

Jessie couldn't argue with that.

After Zee put on her headphones and began clacking away at the keyboard again, Jessie read over the information she'd received from the lawyer in Arizona.

Just as Grant Taylor had said, there were two photos: the picture of Lacey Page, announcing her marriage to Jason Geiger, and one of a young Anne Corrigan, sitting next to her grandmother. The resemblance between Lacey and Anne was striking.

As far as where to start, Jessie figured she had two options: head for New Jersey to talk to Anne Corrigan's parents, or drive a few miles away, knock on Lacey Geiger's front door, and show her the picture of the little girl with her grandmother. She glanced at her watch. It was just past four. She stood, gathered her coat and bag.

Zee removed the headphones and gave her a questioning look.

"I'm heading off to question Lacey Geiger, the woman who resembles Anne Corrigan. After that, I'm going straight home. Mind locking up?"

"Not a problem," Zee said. "See you tomorrow. Oh. Wait. One more thing."

Jessie turned.

"Did you read your horoscope for the month?" Zee wanted to know.

"No," she said, holding back a smile. "Should I have?"

"Always," Zee said. "An unpleasant occurrence is going to throw you off guard."

"When?"

Zee lifted her shoulders. "Not sure, but I was worried, so I did a tarot card reading for you."

Jessie smiled. Even though she wasn't into tarot cards or horoscopes, she appreciated Zee's passion for both. "And?"

"You need to be prepared," Zee said. "As in carry your gun at all times. Don't let this scare you, though. Just know that you can choose to act, and your future isn't set in stone. Okay?"

"Okay. Thanks."

"Not a problem." Zee put on her headphones and went back to work.

SEVENTEEN

At four fifteen, Ben stopped at the grocery store to pick up something for dinner. Melony was working late again.

As he stepped out of his van, grabbed a cart, and made his way into the store, he found himself thinking about the first time he'd gone shopping for food after the accident that had left him with retrograde amnesia. When it came to his taste buds, he'd no longer had any idea what he liked or disliked. He and Melony had gotten more than a few laughs when his eyes lit up at the taste of spaghetti or chocolate cake and ice cream. Everything he'd eaten had been "new" to him.

He grabbed a ready-to-eat chicken at the front of the store and found the tortillas on an end rack. He had just added a gallon of milk to his cart when he spotted Roger Willis.

Ben stiffened. Seeing the man twice in the past forty-eight hours set him on edge. Why would Willis continue to leave his house as if nothing had changed? Did he want to be seen by neighbors and old friends? Let everyone know he wasn't a threat?

Or was there more to it?

Willis was a pedophile, a sex offender, which meant he was likely to repeat the crime because he had little control over his impulses. It was a fact. And here he was again. Was he stupid, or seriously cocky enough to believe he could go about his business without suffering any consequence?

As Ben drew closer, he saw that Willis and his daughter, Paige, were examining the grocery list. Willis had one arm slung casually over the girl's shoulders. Ben recalled what Gretchen had said about Paige being sexually abused by her father. It upset him that the man was allowed to see his daughter, much less be left alone with her unsupervised. But Roger's wife trusted him and had been able to convince Child Protective Services to allow him to remain home until the hearing.

"Can I get ice cream?" Paige asked.

"Absolutely. This is a celebration, honey."

Willis stared after his daughter as she ran off, his head tilting as if for a better look. Ben had no idea Willis had seen him until he looked at Ben and said matter-of-factly, "They grow up so quickly, don't they?"

Ben maintained eye contact, his pulse elevating. "I think it would be wise for you to stay indoors until you get your day in court," he said.

"Why would I do that?"

"For your own safety," Ben said calmly.

"Is that a threat?"

"I'm just worried about your well-being. There are far worse things that could happen to you outside a prison cell than inside."

"You Morrisons tend to be overdramatic." Willis chuckled. "My lawyer and I are confident I won't be spending any time at all behind bars, so you might want to get used to seeing me around town."

Ben's jaw hardened. "I wouldn't bank on that."

"Are you kidding me? A young, hysterical little girl whose father attacked me in public on the witness stand? It'll be a matter of 'he said, she said.' I'm not too worried."

Ben drew in a slow, steady breath.

Roger feigned concern. "You don't look well, pal. Is it your heart? Should I call for help?"

The heat swooshing through Ben's body was nearly unbearable. Without another word, he walked off, pushing his cart down the closest aisle and heading for the checkout stand. For the first time since

Willis was arrested, Ben considered the real possibility of him getting off scot-free.

A fresh swell of rage rose within him. For the first time in months, darkness pulsed within his veins, clouding his vision. He concentrated on his breathing until he was outside, groceries in hand.

He spotted Willis two parking spaces away from where Ben had parked his van. As his daughter climbed into the back of his car, Willis planted his hand on her buttocks as if to help her inside, giving a squeeze as he looked over his shoulder at Ben, letting him know he could do whatever he damn well pleased.

There were no uncontrollable tremors passing through Ben's body. No pounding in his ears or elevated pulse. Instead, a clear vision of Willis taking his last breath enveloped him. The overwhelming disgust consuming Ben only minutes ago floated away, leaving him with a sense of peace.

He could breathe again.

Eighteen

Before leaving the office, Jessie dialed the number for Anne Corrigan's mother in New Jersey and left another message. Since that was turning out to be a dead end, she gathered her things and jumped in the car.

It was time to pay Lacey Geiger a visit.

The drive was a short seven minutes across town. Jessie pulled her car up to the curb outside the house belonging to the Geigers. It was a classic Tudor in the heart of Curtis Park. Beautifully landscaped with vintage charm.

Jessie's shoes clapped against the stone walkway as she admired the newly mowed lawn and perfectly trimmed hedges. She stepped onto a large covered porch and knocked on the apple-red door. After a minute, she rang the bell.

"Hello!" someone called out from behind her. She turned and watched the man approach from the house directly across the street.

He was short and round with a buzz cut and a bad case of acne. By the time he crossed the road and caught up to her, his breathing was labored.

"Derek McDowell," he managed. "I live across the street." He took a couple of breaths. "Are you a friend of the Geigers?"

"No. I have business I need to take care of with Lacey Geiger and was hoping to talk to her. Do you know when she'll be back?"

"I haven't seen either one of them in nearly a week." He gestured toward the small pile of newspapers gathered at the end of the driveway. "I have their mail since the postman couldn't fit it all in their box. I was afraid somebody would come by and steal it."

"Do they usually tell you if they're going to be gone?" Jessie asked.

He scratched his chin. "No, but they have gone away before, and they usually stop their mail."

"Maybe they just forget to alert the post office," she said.

He scratched the top of his head. "That's possible."

"When was the last time you saw them?"

"I was washing the dishes and happened to be looking outside when I saw them get into a car with a driver. They were all dressed up."

"And you haven't seen them coming or going since that time?"

"No."

"You're absolutely sure they never returned home?"

"Like I said, nobody has been picking up the mail. I would think they would grab their mail if they came home, don't you?"

"I do," Jessie said. "What day was it that you saw them leaving the house?"

"Are you with the police?"

She shook her head. "My name is Jessie Cole. I'm a private investigator. It's very important that I talk to Lacey as soon as possible."

"Is she in trouble?"

"No," Jessie assured him. "It's nothing like that."

"Oh. That's good."

The odds were Jason and Lacey Geiger had gone somewhere and forgotten to stop the mail, Jessie thought. But she was here, and the neighbor seemed more than willing to talk, so she decided to find out what she could. "Derek, do you remember what day you saw them leave in the car?"

"It was Friday night."

Jessie pointed to the Camry parked in the driveway. "Is that their car?"

"That's Lacey's car. Jason drives a shiny new Mercedes that he parks in the garage." He pointed that way. "It's in there now."

"Are you sure? Did you look through the window?"

His face turned red. He obviously felt guilty for snooping around.

"Lacey Geiger is a very nice lady," he said. "I was concerned. The only person I've seen over here recently is the kid who mows their lawn."

"Did you talk to the kid?"

"Yeah. He didn't know where they had gone off to, either."

"Do you know the kid's name?"

"I forget, but he lives in the yellow house on the corner." Again, he pointed.

Jessie pulled out her cell phone and made notes.

"What do you think we should do?" he asked.

We? "I'm going to visit the fitness center where Lacey works and see what I can find out. Did you and Lacey ever exchange emails and telephone numbers?"

"No," he said. "It would have been a smart thing to do. You know, in cases like this. Would you mind keeping me in the loop so I know what to do with their mail?"

"Sure." She grabbed a pen and the small notebook she kept in her purse and handed it to him. "If you could write down your contact information for me, that would be great."

He did as she asked.

"If I think of any other questions, do you mind if I call you?"

He shook his head. "Not at all. You don't think I should call the police?"

"I have a friend at the Sacramento Police Department. Let me see what I can find out. I'll be in touch."

That night, back at home after Jessie and Olivia had eaten dinner and taken Higgins for a walk, Olivia worked on her homework while Jessie organized her notes. Lacey had been scheduled to work at the fitness center three days this week, including today. She hadn't shown up.

The manager had been calling Lacey on her cell and home phones but had yet to hear from Lacey. Since she was worried about Lacey, she'd shared both numbers with Jessie.

When Jessie mentioned the neighbor seeing Lacey and Jason dressed up on Friday night, one of Lacey's coworkers recalled Lacey mentioning that she and her husband were going to the Firehouse to celebrate their anniversary.

Jessie looked up the number to the Firehouse, a restaurant known for its steak and seafood, and made the call. After explaining that she was a private investigator looking for Lacey and Jason Geiger, who'd had reservations for dinner the previous Friday night, she asked if there was any way of checking to see if the couple had arrived as scheduled.

Jessie was put on hold.

A few minutes later, the manager picked up and told Jessie that Lacey Geiger had made reservations for Friday, January 12, at 6:30 p.m. but had never shown up. He told her that they'd held the table for an hour and tried to contact Lacey, but their calls had not been returned.

Strange days indeed, Jessie thought after the call ended.

Things were getting weird. This was one of the craziest cases she'd ever taken on. She wasn't even 100 percent sure that Anne Corrigan, the person she was looking for, was actually Lacey Geiger.

Talk about falling down a rabbit hole.

Two weeks to find a woman who had run away at a young age and somewhere along the way had changed her name. A woman with secrets. Jessie thought about the bonus money. She needed a new water heater. The car needed to be tuned. A few shingles had fallen from the roof. Twenty-five thousand dollars would come in handy. Her next call was to Colin.

"Bad news," she blurted out when he picked up.

"Damn. I had high hopes that we were actually going to spend twenty-four hours together."

"I know. I'm sorry. I have to go to New Jersey."

"What for?"

"It's a long story, but it involves a missing person and a big bonus if I can find her before the end of the month."

"I'm in the car on my way to the gym to get a quick workout in. I'm all ears."

"I'm trying to locate a woman who ran away from home when she was sixteen. Her social security number is a black hole. But I have a picture of a woman in Sacramento who goes by the name of Lacey Geiger who happens to hold a striking resemblance to the sixteen-year-old missing girl. This is where things get really strange."

"Go on."

"I thought the easiest route would be to talk to Lacey Geiger, see if she could possibly be Anne Corrigan."

"But she might not want to be found," Colin said.

"That's what I was thinking, too. But when I went to her house, nobody answered the door. Of course, I didn't think too much of it until the neighbor appeared and told me he hadn't seen Lacey or her husband since Friday night. Both Lacey and her husband's vehicles are parked at their house. Newspapers are piling up in the driveway, and the neighbor has been collecting their mail."

"And you think they might be in New Jersey?"

"No. New Jersey is where Anne Corrigan was born and raised. Her mother and stepfather live in Newark. They aren't answering the phone or returning my calls. Before I continue my search for Lacey, I need to know if Anne Corrigan and Lacey Geiger are one and the same."

"And if they are?" Colin asked.

"Then I have my work cut out for me. I went to 9Round, a fitness center in Midtown where Lacey works. One of her coworkers recalls Lacey mentioning that she and her husband were going to celebrate their anniversary at the Firehouse, a nice restaurant in East Sacramento. I talked to the manager there. Apparently the Geigers never showed up."

"Has anyone reported her or her husband as missing?"

"No. Their neighbor was thinking about calling the police, but I told him I would look into it."

"Why don't you give me the address so I can stop by on my way home? I'll take a look around the property, see what I can find out on my end."

"That would be great. Thank you. I'm going to make flight arrangements, find out where Lacey's husband works, and make a few more calls."

"Call me when you get to New Jersey so I know you made it there safely."

"Will do. Love you."

"Love you, too."

NINETEEN

It was getting dark by the time Colin knocked on Lacey and Jason Geiger's house. "Police," he announced, followed by, "Detective Colin Grayson with the Sacramento Police Department. Please open the door."

No answer.

His phone buzzed. He unhooked it from his belt and picked up the call when he saw that it was his daughter, Piper. "Hey, sweetheart. What's going on?"

"Did you tell Jessie the plan? Was she excited? What did she say?"

"Sorry, honey. We've both been sort of busy."

"But you said you were going to talk to her tonight."

"I did say that—it's true. Jessie had to go out of town for a day or two. I'll talk to her as soon as she gets back, I promise."

"Mom is bugging me to do my homework. I better go."

"I'll call you tomorrow."

"Bye, Dad."

"Love you," he said before he heard a click on the other end.

As Colin walked to the front of the house, he realized he'd been putting off showing Jessie the house he'd found. It was a three bedroom, two bath in Sacramento, not too far from the Golden 1 Center. Last week he'd put an offer on the home. The minute he'd gotten the call from his Realtor telling him his offer had been accepted, he'd panicked.

What if Jessie didn't like the place? What if she rejected his suggestion that they move in together and take their relationship to the next level?

He'd planned on showing her the house after their last outing at the gun range. When that didn't work out, he'd decided to broach the subject tonight.

But now he was beginning to wonder if he was chickening out. Every time he thought about talking to Jessie about moving in together, he felt a wave of anxiety travel down his arms. His ego didn't like the uncertainty of it all.

Their relationship had a rocky start. He'd met Jessie more than ten years ago when her sister, Sophie, went missing. He'd been a shoulder for her to cry on. There had been a spark between them that had quickly ignited into something more. Things had progressed quickly from there—too quickly. Although he'd been separated from his ex-wife at the time, they were still legally married when his ex showed up at Jessie's house to let him know she was pregnant with his child.

Understandably, Jessie dropped him like a hot potato.

But fate was fickle, and it wasn't done with them. Years later, years after his marriage had dissolved for good, he'd run into Jessie downtown. They'd had coffee. Jessie Cole did something to him, made him feel things he'd never felt with another woman. She was the one for him. And that was too damn bad, because she didn't trust him. All she could offer him was friendship.

So he'd taken what he could get.

His perseverance had paid off. She loved him and he loved her. But they were both busy people and seldom had time for one another.

He used to think that two busy people didn't stand a chance. Until suddenly it dawned on him that all those preconceived ideas about how a relationship needed to be were silly. Their connection was special. They didn't have a lot of time, which was a good thing because it meant they didn't have time for any bullshit. Dating someone who was just as busy as he was made for a pretty interesting relationship. It wasn't often that they had dinner together, followed by a movie and sex before bed. What they had was better than that.

No time for dillydallying. They had limited time, which meant sex in the kitchen, in the car, in the bathroom. Conversations were usually short, but they were also meaningful. When they did have dinner together, they unplugged and focused on each other.

They were good together, almost perfect.

Now he just needed to find time to convince Jessie to move in with him.

Piper was all in. She and Olivia would have their own rooms. The house had a big yard for Higgins. This was their chance to be one big happy family.

He sighed, looked around, and got back to work.

Just as Jessie had said, there was a Camry parked in the driveway and a pile of unread newspapers collecting near the mailbox. Overall, it was a quiet neighborhood, the streets lined with trees.

Police were often asked by concerned citizens to check on a neighbor or a friend they hadn't seen for several days. If nobody answered the door, decisions had to be made whether or not to force entry into the home. The first thing he would check for were any foul odors. Suicide or foul play would be his first concern. But the couple could be on vacation, or maybe they left town to get away for a while. There were many reasons why someone might not answer the phone or door.

All of this needed to be taken into account.

He walked around to the side of the house, reached over the fence, and was able to easily unlatch the gate. He tried the door to the garage. It was locked. Peering into the garage window, he could see a black Mercedes. The wall behind the car was covered with industrial steel shelving, coolers, sleeping bags, and plastic bins neatly stacked. Everything you'd expect to see inside a garage.

In the backyard there was a covered grill, a small patch of green grass and brick decking with wood chairs and planters filled with flowers. There was a string of lights overhead and a mini storage shed set in the far corner.

Colin walked up to the patio door. The shades were pulled tight, making it impossible to see inside. He knocked again, announced who he was, listened and waited.

Nothing. No foul smells of decomposition.

He checked every window and door; everything was locked up tight. Next, he looked under planters and doormats for a key. No luck there, either. He finally decided to force entry into the garage. Inside, he flipped on the switch, looked around. No funny smells coming out of the car. Nothing unusual. From there he was able to unlatch the door leading from the garage to the kitchen.

"Police!" he announced for the third time before he stepped inside the residence. The interior of the house was as neat and clean as the outside. No furniture out of place. No food left in pans on the stove. No dishes in the sink. And once again, no bad odors. Upstairs was the same. The bed was made. A long-sleeve man's shirt had been thrown on top of the pillow.

Nothing to see here.

Fifteen minutes later, he locked up and left the premises just the way he had found it.

TWENTY

Lacey awoke with a start.

Jason was on all fours. He was staring down at her with cold eyes, his hand on the paper bag she'd used as a pillow.

She sat up, clutched her paper bag to her chest. "What are you doing?"

"I couldn't hear you breathing. I wanted to make sure you were okay."

She looked across the space where he'd been sitting since the day she'd dug him out of the box. She could see two wrappers. "Did you already eat both granola bars?"

"I was starved."

"Well, I'm not sharing, so good luck with that. I told you to ration." She looked from her bag to his hand. "Why were you touching my bag when I woke up? Were you going to steal my food?"

"No. I would never do that."

She didn't believe him. "I don't know if you noticed, but I was able to remove two nails from the vent yesterday. It's your turn to do some work."

"What do I get in return?"

"How about you use all that energy from the food you ate and get to work?"

He scratched his jaw.

They didn't have time for this. "One half inch of my granola bar for every two nails you remove," she said.

"I'm a man. I'm bigger and taller than you. I need more calories."

"You've already eaten way more than me. If you want more, that's the deal."

He wasn't happy about it, but he crawled back to the vent, grabbed one of the shoes left on the floor, and began pounding. She'd always known he'd been overly coddled by both his parents, but if someone had asked her, between the two of them, who would take over and be a leader during a traumatic event, she would have said Jason every time.

And she would have been wrong.

He had yet to show an ounce of courage or resolve. He'd already given up.

As he hammered at the nails, she nibbled on a bar and took a sip of water. Her gaze traveled slowly around the space where they had been trapped for a number of days. She'd lost track of time once they had been in the box.

As she looked around, she came to the realization that somebody had designed this room specifically for this purpose, to bury someone alive. How long had it taken the person or persons to dig out an area big enough to not only bury them in a box beneath two feet of dirt but also torment them further by putting that box in a well-sealed cement room? Whoever had done this had wanted them to suffer. He or she had given them just enough water and food to last a few days. A week at best.

If this was someone's idea of a sick game, were they watching them? Listening? She looked around, peering into the semidarkness. They had both examined the walls and the ceiling and found nothing.

Why had he or she left them food?

Nothing made sense.

She thought about that as she made her way into the box and made a hole in the dirt to go to the bathroom. There was no other way. They had agreed to relieve themselves in one particular area and then add a layer of fresh dirt. When she was finished, she pulled her underwear back in place and covered the area with dirt. Something winked at her from the bottom of the soil near her foot. Something shiny. Maybe a coin. Brushing the soil to the side, she noticed the object was a key. It wasn't an average, everyday sort of key. It was bronze and antique. It looked like an upside-down *F*, welded to a flat ring.

She glanced at Jason, who hadn't stopped hammering, intent on getting the job done so she would share her food. She should have kept all the granola bars from him, but at the time she hadn't thought it fair.

After crawling out of the box and propping herself against the wall, she examined the key. She and Jason had checked out every inch of this place but had yet to see a keyhole. She wondered if the vent led to a door that could only be opened with the key. Or maybe there was a box or something they couldn't see inside the vent. It couldn't be to a door inside the vent because air and light were able to enter their space.

As she twirled the key in her hands, she thought about the man she'd married. For most of their marriage she'd always thought of him as very loving. The more she'd thought about it, though, the more she realized she'd always been aware of his self-indulgences. She didn't mind that he drove a Mercedes while she drove a Camry. Material things weren't important to her. Throughout the years, she'd chalked up his difficulty with expressing his feelings as a male thing. Whenever he forgot her birthday or anniversary, she tended to dismiss his acts of selfishness as cluelessness since he always apologized so profusely. Now, though, she recognized his pattern of saying one thing and doing another.

And she couldn't put all the blame on Jason, even knowing he'd betrayed her in the worst way, because she had known the truth. It had been right there, staring her in the face. She'd chosen to put her head in the sand because he was the only family she had. It had been easier to believe in her fantasies than to face reality—a coping mechanism developed during her tormented years with her stepfather.

A tear ran down her cheek as she gently rubbed her stomach. She'd had such high hopes for their small family. She'd been so determined to give her child normalcy and stability, something she'd never had. She wanted her child to wake up every day knowing he or she was loved.

Not even Jason knew of the horrors she'd endured when she was young. She'd been ten when her father had suffered a heart attack and died. Her mother, never doting or overly affectionate, was at the very least always there for her. That was, until Everett Miller came into the picture. In the beginning, Everett had courted her mother, bringing her small gifts or a bouquet of flowers when he visited. He would bring gifts for Lacey, too: a new dress, a pretty doll, something nice to put in her room.

She was too young to know if her mother was playing hard to get or if she really wasn't ready to remarry, but she would never forget overhearing Everett propose to her mom. When she told him she wasn't ready to remarry, he'd cried. But he never gave up. Two years later, Mom gave in and married Everett Miller.

Things had been fine for the first six months. But after Everett lost his job, the change in her stepfather was immediate. Overnight, it seemed, his eyes became those of a predator, and Lacey was his prey.

When she came home from school, he would lock her in her room until her mother returned from work. He often lectured her mother about the importance of disciplining children, especially females.

Lacey tried to talk to her mom, but Everett always interfered. So Lacey climbed out the window and ran away. The police brought her back. And that was when her mother and stepfather told her she would be homeschooled.

A week or so later, Everett told her he'd made her something—chains and cuffs. They were for her own good, he explained. He secured the bed to the floor, and the window to the sill, so that when he chained her to the bed, she couldn't get free. She fought hard, kicking and screaming and grabbing hold of tables and chairs to stop Everett from locking her away, but her efforts were futile. Her mother did nothing to stop him. She worked two jobs to pay the bills and keep a roof over their heads, and Lacey could tell by her cloudy, dull eyes that she'd given up on life. Spending most of her time at work was probably her mother's way of escaping.

Her stepfather took out his frustrations on Lacey every day. He never raped her. But he would rub his crotch while he stood before her, his lusty gaze roaming over every inch of her while he lectured her about staying away from boys.

If Lacey told him she was hungry, he would come into the room with a tray of food and shove it down her throat until she gagged.

Begging and crying didn't help.

Almost every night he would bathe her using a hard-bristled brush, lecturing her about the importance of staying clean. To this day she carried hundreds of tiny, imperceptible scars on her body from that brush.

Lacey's only hope at the time had been that her grandmother on her father's side would visit, see what was happening, and rescue her. It was a long shot, considering the two women had never gotten along when her dad was alive. When Lacey finally had a chance to talk to her mother alone, she asked if she could call her grandmother but was told she'd moved to Europe.

That's when Lacey knew she was on her own.

Every minute of every day for years afterward, Lacey did nothing but dream and plan her escape. And when that day finally came, she was ready.

It happened two days before her sixteenth birthday. Her stepfather had failed to fully clasp the chain around her ankle. In the middle of the night when everyone was asleep, she quietly searched her room for a clean shirt and a pair of pants. Tiptoeing into the kitchen, she grabbed a knife from the counter and slipped it into her back pocket for protection. She also stole money from inside the pages of a cookbook next to the stove where her mother used to hide cash before her father died. Some things never changed.

Minutes felt like hours as she crept across the living room and out the front door, careful not to make even one tiny sound. The cold air hit her face as she darted across the front yard. Prickly weeds scratched her ankles. The night was black and starless, overrun with shadows. Her only fear was of being caught and taken back home. She lucked out when she found an unlocked door to the men's room at a gas station a few miles away. She chopped her hair, changed her clothes, and walked for hours to a bus terminal where she waited until someone arrived to sell tickets. The employee wanted an ID, but he took a crisp ten-dollar bill as a bribe instead. With the money she'd stolen, she got all the way from New Jersey to California.

That was seventeen years ago.

She hadn't seen her mother or stepfather since. She didn't know if they were dead or alive. She didn't care.

And she'd never told anyone what had happened.

Certain that her stepfather would try to find her and bring her back, the first thing she did when she stepped off the bus in Los Angeles was buy a box of cheap hair dye and color her light-brown hair black. During the bus ride, she'd overheard a woman talking about one of her children moving to Sacramento because of the cheaper cost of living compared to LA. She'd said there were lots of job opportunities. So that's where Lacey set her sights. When she got to Sacramento, she used restaurant and hotel bathrooms to clean herself, and every morning she would walk for miles to interview for nanny jobs.

She was sleeping on benches in the park and had run out of money, but everything changed the day she met Mr. and Mrs. Brightman. They had a loving and hectic household. They'd believed her when she said she lost her ID after having her purse stolen—one of many lies she'd told them. They weren't a wealthy family. The only thing that mattered was that their two children instantly fell in love with her and that she was happy and willing to move in and be a nanny full time in exchange for room and board and a small allowance.

Before anyone discovered she wasn't who she said she was, Lacey saved enough money to hire a shady lawyer, who helped her with fake adoption papers. She changed her name from Anne Elizabeth Corrigan to Lacey Page. That was all she needed to take a driver's test and obtain a license.

Overall, it had all been fairly simple.

At the age of twenty-three, she met Jason Geiger. She thought she was the luckiest girl alive. They married two years later, and the rest was history.

Her life had come full circle.

Now, after eight years of marriage, she was trapped, buried deep, with the realization that the only person she could rely on was herself.

The room went silent.

Jason had stopped batting a shoe at the cement. When she glanced up, she saw him looking at her.

"What's in your hand?" he asked.

"A key."

"To what?"

"I don't know." She tossed it his way.

While he examined the key, she went to view the vent cover. Half the nails had been removed. She started toward the food and water she'd given Jason earlier. He'd eaten half a granola bar and finished off another water bottle.

Her shoulders sagged. She went to her side of the room and sat down. "Do you think whoever built this place had the two of us in mind when he designed it?"

Jason had relieved himself in the corner of the box before kicking dirt and making his way to his usual spot where he slumped down. "I have no idea."

"Well, I do. He built this place specifically for us."

"And how do you know that?"

"In one of the bags I found a picture of you and Chaya in our bed. I ripped it up and tossed the pieces in the box, if you don't believe me."

Silence.

"You're not even going to deny it?"

"One time. It meant nothing."

Her stomach tightened. She refused to get upset. It was over. After she escaped, she would leave Jason, never see him again, never waste one second thinking about him. "This place was designed to hold two people," she said. "Assuming the driver is the one who put us here, he is playing with us. He left us just enough food and water to last a specific number of days. I wonder if he's watching us."

"I don't see a hidden camera anywhere." His gaze moved around the room. "How many days do you think he intended to keep us alive?"

"Who knows?" Lacey said. "Now that you've eaten most of the food and drunk nearly all the water, does it really matter?"

He said nothing in response.

"Did you recognize the driver?" she asked.

"No."

"I've been racking my brain, trying to think of anyone you might have pissed off over the years," Lacey said.

"Why?"

She shrugged. "Curiosity more than anything else. Don't you wonder who might have done this?"

Jason was staring at her as if she'd grown two heads. "So you really think this is somehow my fault? What about you?"

She snorted.

"What?" he asked.

"I just told you, he left a picture of you with another woman. Somebody's been following you. Maybe Chaya's husband." She knew Jason didn't have many friends, and she'd always thought that was a reflection of how hard he worked and his devotion to her, but now she was beginning to see things a little differently . . . much differently.

"You've changed," Jason said. "You're feisty," he added. "Gutsy."

"Yeah, well, I guess being buried alive can open a person's eyes. I'm done being Perfect-Fucking-Lacey," she said. "June Cleaver without the pearls. She cooks, bakes, pays the bills, and begs for sex." She wiped her brow in an exaggerated manner. "It must be exhausting, being married to someone like me," she said before changing to a deeper voice in an attempt to mimic Jason: "My wife tries too hard to please me. I want to find a curvy, voluptuous woman who chain-smokes and gambles away my hard-earned money."

He laughed.

It had been so long since she'd heard Jason laugh, the sound was no longer familiar or even amusing, especially since she wasn't trying to be funny. She didn't like the way he was looking at her, staring at her as if they'd only just met.

"You really think we'll get out of here?" he asked.

She shrugged. "I have no idea, but if we do, I want a divorce."

"No."

"If we don't die," she said, "I'm going to leave you."

"I've changed my mind," he said firmly, as if that ended all discussion.

"About what?"

"About us."

Her laughter came out sounding maniacal. "I don't love you, Jason."

"When did you figure that out? Yesterday? Ten minutes ago?"

She ignored the question and instead gestured at the key in his hand, knowing he could easily be swayed to give up any talk of love. "That key goes to something."

On her hands and knees again, she started off in search of something she might have missed. It was much easier to see in the morning when the light coming through the vent was at its brightest. Later on, eerie shadows would envelop them before darkness set in. Every once in a while, she could hear the distant howl of a coyote. She stopped and pointed a finger at him. "Don't you dare touch my granola bar. I will kill you if you do, and I'm serious."

He rolled his eyes.

She wasn't going to die because of his selfishness, she thought as she started at one corner of their cramped space, working her fingers over the floors and walls, looking for anything abnormal.

TWENTY-ONE

It was Saturday morning in New Jersey. Jessie sat in a rental car across the street from Claudia Miller's house. She had arrived at the Newark airport after 6:00 p.m. the night before. She rented a car and drove to her hotel, where she ordered room service and spent the next few hours researching Anne Corrigan's mother and father, Claudia and Jim Corrigan. Two years after Jim passed away, Claudia married Everett Miller, an accountant.

Claudia had received a small sum of money from Jim's life insurance policy, which must have helped, considering she didn't make much money.

Jessie was able to locate pictures online of Everett Miller at an accounting firm where he once worked. He looked like your stereotypical accountant. Neatly combed hair, glasses, button-down shirt, and tie. After high school he attended Middlesex County College, working as an accountant right up until a few months after his marriage to Claudia.

Claudia was born and raised in Hoboken, New Jersey. She took a few college courses after high school but mostly waitressed and later worked as a clerk at a large grocery chain until four and a half years ago when she injured herself on the job.

Neither Claudia nor Everett had any sort of criminal record.

So why had Anne run away?

It was 9:00 a.m. Jessie grabbed her oversize bag and climbed out of the car. Compared to the rest of the homes on the street, the Miller house appeared neglected. A cracked-cement walkway, weeds in place of a lawn, a couple of overgrown hedges.

She knocked on the front door.

Jessie had called and left another message on the Millers' home phone yesterday, and again before she left the hotel this morning. Again, no return calls.

She pushed the ringer and figured it must be broken since she didn't hear anything. Another knock, before she said loud enough for anyone inside to hear, "My name is Jessie Cole, and I need to talk to Claudia Miller. I've come all the way from California to talk about your daughter, Anne Elizabeth Corrigan."

Damn. She hadn't wanted to use the money card, but some things couldn't be helped. "Grant Taylor, an attorney in Arizona, has been trying to get in touch with you. Claudia, if you're in there, it's very important that we locate Anne because her grandmother, Laura Corrigan, has passed away and left her a large sum of money. If you would agree to talk to me and I am able to locate Anne, I will be sure and tell her what a big help you and your husband were. And I would think she might be inclined to share—"

The door opened.

Jessie straightened. The woman standing before her looked nothing like the images Jessie had found on the internet. Claudia Miller looked bloated. Her hair was greasy, pulled back, and wrapped tightly with a rubber band, which made the broken capillaries on her nose and face stand out.

"I'm Anne's mother." Her voice was deep and hoarse. "I wasn't able to find my daughter, so what makes you think you'll be able to?"

"It's my job," Jessie answered. "It's what I do."

"How much did the old woman leave her?"

"If I can't locate Anne within the next few weeks, Anne will get nothing. Otherwise, we're talking over a million."

She whistled through her teeth. "Sounds like Laura's move to another country worked out well for her."

Jessie had nothing to say to that.

"If you promise to tell Anne that I helped . . ." Claudia must have realized she needed to do a better job of playing the grieving mother because she sniffled suddenly and wiped her eyes. She stepped back to give Jessie room to enter. "Why don't you come in so I can tell you whatever you need to know—anything to help my baby."

The air freshener Claudia must have sprayed before answering the door wasn't helping. The place smelled like stale smoke and beer. A layer of dust covered much of the furniture.

"Keep moving," Claudia urged as Jessie walked down the hallway ahead of her. "All the way through to the family room where I watch television."

Jessie did as she was told. The TV was on. A half-smoked cigarette had been snuffed out on a dinner plate.

Claudia sank down into a wicker chair padded with yellow-and-blue pillows. "Okay," she said. "Now what?"

"Is your husband here?"

Her laughter came out, sounding more like wheezing. When she got control of herself, she said, "He left years ago."

"I'm sorry."

"Don't be. I never should have married the schmuck. He's the reason Anne ran off to begin with."

"Why? What did he do?"

She pointed toward the kitchen. "Her room used to be over there— a sharp left after the refrigerator. He kept her locked in her room for years."

For years? "Why would he do that?"

She shrugged. "He grew up with a crazy sister who wouldn't obey her parents. He didn't want the same thing to happen to Anne. Plus," she added, "he was just a mean son of a bitch who needed someone to take his frustrations out on."

"Did you try to stop him?"

"I was working ten-hour days. Hey, don't look at me like that. I didn't do it."

Jessie felt queasy. "Mind if I have a look inside her room?"

"She ran away when she was sixteen. That was seventeen years ago. I don't think you're going to find anything helpful in there. But sure, go ahead," she said when she saw Jessie already heading that way.

The door to Anne's room was ajar, but Jessie had to use her body weight to push it all the way open. The inside was cluttered with junk—piles of it everywhere. A bed frame with a mattress took up most of the room. The carpeted floor was covered with blankets and clothes that looked unwashed.

The room smelled like mold. She walked to the bedside table and opened the drawer. Chewed-on pencils. Gum wrappers. Something sticky. Rusty nail clippers, broken eyeglasses, and mouse droppings. Letters had been etched into the wood beneath all the crap. She reached for a dirty shirt from the floor and used it to push it all aside—Help!

A chill washed over her. *Did Anne write this?*

She tried to imagine being sixteen and locked in a room for hours on end. Through the window she saw a man mowing his lawn across the street. A couple of kids rode their bikes in circles in the middle of the road. She tried to crank open the window until she realized it was stuck. Upon closer examination, she saw that the window had been cemented in place. *Why?*

Like the room, the closet was jam-packed with junk. She searched through a pile of shoes that looked as if they once belonged to a young girl. On the highest shelf was a photo album. She stood on her tiptoes and pulled it down. It was dusty but intact.

When she turned toward the bed, a glint of metal caught her eye. She stepped over stacks of magazines and pushed through plastic bags filled with who knows what to get to whatever was half-hidden beneath piles of clothes. She set the album on the bed and reached for the metal object. It wouldn't budge. On her knees, she tossed the clothes to the side, confused by what was in her grasp—a crudely made metal cuff, soldered to a thick chain. She followed the chain to the leg of the bed. All four legs had been cemented to the floor.

What the hell?

She stood, grabbed the photo album, and made her way back to Claudia, whose attention was focused on a game show. "Anne wasn't just locked in that room," Jessie said. "She was chained to the fucking bed, wasn't she?"

Claudia stubbed out her cigarette, pushed herself to her feet, and gestured toward the front entry. "Get out!"

Jessie stood her ground. No way. She wasn't going anywhere.

"Don't you dare come into my home and judge me," Claudia growled. "I didn't do nothing wrong. If I had tried to help, he might have locked me up, too. He was bigger than me. What was I supposed to do?"

How about take your daughter and run, or maybe call the police? Jessie thought but didn't say. She inhaled, tried to rein in some of her anger. "I'm not leaving until you answer my questions."

"I'll call the police."

Jessie had a feeling she would do no such thing, considering what she'd just found in Anne's old room.

"Go ahead."

Claudia didn't make a move to find a phone.

"Did Everett Miller chain Anne to the bed?"

"Yes!" Claudia said, throwing her arms wide. "He did a lot of things."

"Like what?"

"He laughed at her when she told him she was hungry or needed to go to the bathroom. Every night he used a wire brush to scrub her body with a bucket of vinegar water. He said it was the only way she was going to get clean."

Every word that came out of Claudia's mouth was coated with spittle as she listed the horrors of what Everett had done to her daughter. "He used a fork to poke and prod at Anne as she stood naked before him. If she wanted to eat, she had to stand still with her mouth open while he shoved food down her throat. He called her names and teased her with promises of freedom. Should I go on?"

Jessie shook her head. She couldn't breathe. Her stomach roiled.

A real-life house of horrors. *Jesus.* Anne's own mother had let it happen. The woman could have called the police, could have taken her daughter and left. But stating the facts wouldn't help Jessie find Anne. Forcing herself to calm down, she remembered the album still in her arms.

Claudia hadn't moved. She stared at Jessie, probably trying to decide what to do about her.

Jessie opened the album. Just as she'd hoped, it was filled with pictures of Anne. A little girl with her mother and father. Two candles on a cake as the child closed her eyes before blowing at the flame.

She flipped the page.

Claudia was much younger. She looked beautiful. But she wasn't smiling in any of the pictures. Not a happy woman, it seemed, but neither did she look like a woman who would let someone harm her child.

"Is this Anne?" Jessie asked, pointing to the little girl.

Claudia's face was still red, but she stepped closer for a better look. "That's Anne. I didn't know I still had those."

Standing side by side, they looked through the pictures. By the time they finished, Claudia's eyes were watery with real tears. She sucked in a breath as she walked back to her chair, where she plopped down on the cushions and wiped her face.

Jessie found her purse and pulled out the picture she had of Lacey Geiger in the wedding announcement from eight years ago. She handed it to Claudia. "Is this Anne?"

Claudia's eyes rounded. "That's her! Where did you get that?"

After seeing the metal cuff attached to the bed, Jessie didn't feel like telling her the truth, didn't want the woman to know where her daughter lived. "It was in a newspaper in New York," she lied. "Are you absolutely sure that woman in the picture is your daughter?"

"One hundred percent." Claudia jabbed a finger at the woman in the wedding-announcement photo. "See that scar on the right side of her face? It looks like a dimple, but it's not. Weeks before my first husband's death, she fell off a swing and ended up with that scar. That's Anne."

TWENTY-TWO

Colin had just stepped out of the shower and was drying off when he got a call from Sharon Willis.

"You gave me your business card when we met at the theater in Sacramento. I need to talk to you."

She was rambling. She sounded worried. "What's this about, Mrs. Willis?"

"My husband left early this morning to go kayaking on the American River. He still hasn't returned."

"I'm sure he'll walk through the door at any moment."

"He's not answering his cell. And I have reason to believe I should be worried. Please come."

"Where are you located?"

"Citrus Heights."

That wasn't in his jurisdiction, but it wasn't like he was stepping on any toes. She was merely worried and needed someone to talk to. It wouldn't hurt to give her a few minutes of his time. If it did turn out to be a missing person's case, he would contact the Citrus Heights PD and hand it over to them. "I can be there within the hour."

"Thank you."

After he hung up, he considered the possibility of Willis fleeing bail and accosting another child. Every minute that passed without Sharon calling him back to let him know her husband had returned was a red flag being raised, indicating potential trouble ahead.

Forty minutes later, Colin took the Antelope Road exit off the highway. He called Ren Howe, the rookie detective he'd been training, who was turning out to be a regular Sherlock Holmes, to tell him what was going on and let him know he would be late getting to the gun range.

As he followed the street signs, he recalled that Ben Morrison lived in the same area as the soccer coach. Although he wasn't a fan of Morrison's, he was thankful the crime reporter had been able to locate Jessie's niece, Olivia, after she was abducted. That was the second time since working with Jessie that Morrison had come to her rescue.

Hero or not, Colin didn't trust him.

For as long as Colin had been reading the *Sacramento Tribune*, Morrison had been writing about crime. Colin's relationship with reporters, in general, was strained. But Morrison was especially good at pushing Colin's buttons since his stories often pointed out what he saw as the SPD's flaws. Unfortunately, press involvement could be vital when it came to solving crimes, especially at a local level.

Basically, reporters were just part of the deal.

But that wasn't the only reason he didn't trust Morrison. When Colin pulled him over because of a broken taillight a month or two ago, the man had looked trapped . . . guilty. And that recollection brought Colin back to the reason Morrison had begun working with Jessie in the first place. Morrison had been in the car with Jessie's sister, Sophie, when the accident occurred that left *him* with amnesia and everyone else with more questions. Questions that might never be answered. Like what the hell had Morrison been doing in the car with Sophie to begin with?

Nobody knew.

Colin's instincts lit up with warning signs every time he was around the guy. Morrison was bad news, hiding the truth behind a decade-old diagnosis.

Cranking the steering wheel, he made a left onto Twin Oaks Avenue and a sharp right up ahead. He turned off the navigator when the automated voice told him he'd reached his destination. He was barely out of his car when Sharon Willis stepped out of her house and waited for him on the front porch.

"Thank you for coming," she said. "My girls are playing upstairs. They have no idea how worried I am." She glanced at his unmarked car before looking around the neighborhood as if she wanted to make sure no one was watching. "Why don't you come inside?"

"Sure." He followed her across the tiled entry and into the kitchen. He took a seat at the table where she gestured.

"Can I get you some coffee?"

"No, thanks. I'm good. What time did your husband leave here?"

Sharon sat across from him. She rubbed her hands together as she talked. "Roger hasn't been sleeping well. I was half-asleep when he left, but I think it was well before five a.m."

Colin glanced at his watch. It was 9:30 a.m. Roger Willis had been gone for at least four and a half hours. "Did you call his cell?"

She nodded. "No answer."

"I believe you said he went kayaking."

"Yes."

"In the middle of January? It's cold out there, especially early in the morning."

"I know. Crazy, right? Kayaking is one of his passions. He's always wanted to take part in the New Year's Day paddling outing in Iowa. He has an inflatable kayak that he takes out when he needs time to himself."

"I've never been kayaking," Colin admitted. "Is there a certain spot where he would access the river?"

She nodded. "South Bridge Street in Rancho Cordova."

"Did he mention wanting to run errands while he was out?"

"No. He would have said something."

Colin felt for the woman. She'd obviously been through a lot. Dark shadows circled her eyes. She looked wiped out. Why she stayed with Willis did give him pause. And yet, he knew she could be staying for any number of reasons: economic dependence, to keep the family together, shame, low self-esteem. The list was long. "How about the grocery store?" Colin prodded. "Did you mention needing milk or butter?"

She shook her head, but Colin could tell she wasn't paying attention. She couldn't stop wringing her hands, convinced the worst had happened. "I don't think he's ever kayaked for more than a couple of hours," she said. "And why isn't he answering his phone? Something isn't right."

"What kind of car is he driving? I'll check out the parking lot on South Bridge Street, and if his car isn't there, I'll contact the Citrus Heights PD and see if they'll put out an APB."

Her eyes met Colin's—watery green eyes rimmed with red. "I think someone has hurt him." She swallowed. "He would have been better off staying behind bars. People around here treat him as if he's Frankenstein. A dead rat was left in the mailbox yesterday." She pointed at a crack in one of the windows. "Someone threw a rock the other day. One of our neighbors, Gretchen Sullivan, held a meeting to talk to a group of parents about Roger. Gretchen wanted to warn everyone in the neighborhood to stay vigilant and keep their eyes open. She's spreading rumors, hinting that Roger abuses his own daughters and that he might break into their homes while they sleep."

Tears streamed down both sides of her face. "Fear of the unknown. We all have it. Roger has a disorder, a mental illness, and the laws are failing him. The laws emphasize punishment, not prevention. And now the entire town is out to get him."

It seemed to Colin that there had to be more to this story. "Did something happen—other than the meeting?"

"Paden White, Jane White's father . . . you know . . . the girl at the theater . . . Anyway, Paden attacked Roger when he saw him sitting in his car, waiting to pick up our daughter from indoor soccer practice."

"Attacked him?"

"Yes. Jumped him and brought him to the ground."

"Were the police called?"

She shook her head. "Ben Morrison pulled Paden White off Roger and told Paden not to do anything that might jeopardize the trial. He wants to see Roger locked behind bars. They all do."

"Were you there at the time of the incident?"

"No, but I have a few friends left who still care about me. Morrison told Paden White to lay off my husband and let justice be served accordingly." She exhaled. "I wouldn't be surprised if it was all an act on Morrison's part."

"Meaning?"

"When Ben Morrison stopped Paden White from hurting Roger, I think he knew exactly what he was doing—playing the Good Samaritan so that if and when something happened to Roger, nobody would think to point a finger at the man who saved Roger from taking a beating in the parking lot."

Colin thought about the two young females who had recently come forward with allegations against Roger Willis. He thought of his own daughter. If Piper had been a victim of sexual abuse, his heart would be broken. It would devastate him to know he'd been unable to protect her. Most young victims of abuse blamed themselves, assuming they were somehow the cause. The shame and humiliation often made it difficult for children to heal.

A young girl stepped into the room. It was Paige Willis. He recognized her from the incident at the theater.

"Mom? Why are you crying?"

Sharon quickly wiped the tears away before jumping to her feet and walking to her daughter's side.

As Sharon assured her daughter that everything was all right, Ben recalled that it was Ben's daughter, Abigail, who'd made a scene in the theater to stop Roger Willis from touching her friend and teammate when they were at the movies for a day of team bonding. It appeared that the apple didn't fall far from the tree. Ben's daughter was a hero, too.

Colin's phone buzzed. It was Ren Howe. He looked over at Sharon and pointed to the backyard. "I need to take this call. Mind if I step outside?"

"That's fine," she said, ushering her daughter into the other room.

Colin unlocked the slider, stepped out onto the concrete patio, and said, "What's going on?"

"Glad I caught you," Ren said. "After you called, I received news of a man hanging from a tree close to Howe Avenue, next to the river. I'm there now."

"I'm listening," Colin said when Ren paused.

"Are you with Mrs. Willis?"

Colin could see Sharon looking at him through the glass. "Yes."

"She was right to be concerned. It's Roger Willis. Dead. Looks like suicide."

"I want the scene treated as a crime," Colin said. "Keep the area secured. Don't let anyone touch anything. I don't want any possible evidence destroyed or altered."

"Got it."

"If there are eyewitnesses, keep them separated until I get there. I want to talk to anyone who might have seen someone coming or going. I'll be there shortly." Colin ended the call and clipped his phone onto his belt.

Sharon opened the sliding door, her sixth sense on high alert. "They found him, didn't they?"

He nodded.

"Is he dead?"

"I'm sorry."

Her face reddened. "*They* did this to him. Paden White, Gretchen Sullivan, and Ben Morrison. They were out to get him from the start. Roger didn't stand a chance." She was sobbing as she followed Colin through the house to the front door. "I want to see him. I want to see my husband."

He turned to face her.

Paige ran to her mother's side and wrapped her arms around Sharon's waist, crying.

Sharon Willis had known from the start that something was wrong. His heart went out to her. "Stay with the girls. I'll be in touch." And then he left.

TWENTY-THREE

Zee sat behind the wheel of her car, as she'd been doing for two days now. She wasn't getting paid overtime, but she didn't care about that since she finally had a "real" case to work on.

The mint-green bungalow on Thirty-Eighth was a nice-looking house, set on a well-maintained street lined with lots of leafy green trees. Instead of knocking on the door and trying to get Penny's grandparents to open up, Zee had decided she would wait them out. Whoever left the house first would be her key target.

She'd sat in this same spot all day yesterday. Dorothy Kash had made a trek to the mailbox, but that was it. What did they do inside their home all day?

Zee's seat was pushed back as far as it would go. A portable tray rested on her lap. She'd brought it along so she could do a relationship reading using her tarot cards. If she was going to sit here all day, she might as well try and figure out her life.

Good luck with that, muttered Francis, one of the most outspoken voices in her head.

Leave her alone, Lucy said. *She's in love.*

He's a dork, Francis said. *She can do better.*

Zee ignored the voices and grabbed the deck of cards from the passenger seat. Her plan was to use the tarot cards to gain insight into her relationship with Tobey, which seemed to be going nowhere fast.

Francis moaned. *It's been six weeks, for Christ's sake.*

Do not use the Lord's name in vain.

She'd met Tobey in the coffee shop upstairs from the office she shared with Jessie. Since she didn't have any girlfriends and her experience with boys was severely limited, she really didn't know what to expect. He was a nice guy, and mostly that seemed like enough. But sometimes Tobey appeared to hang on her every word, and other times he made her feel invisible.

She shuffled the cards and set them up in a relationship spread: three on the left, three on the right, and one card in the middle. The three cards on the left represented her. The three on the right represented Tobey. The one in the middle would be the advice card to help her find understanding and harmony.

She flipped the first of three cards on the left.

The Eight of Swords. *Interesting.* That meant she was feeling stuck and powerless, sort of blind to the whole situation. Doom and gloom. Story of her life.

Here comes Ms. Negative, Francis said.

Lucy sighed. *Leave her alone. She's fine.*

If I had the two of you talking inside my head all day, Marion chimed in, *I might want to give up on life, too.*

A bird in flight caught her attention. It landed on a low branch and simply stared at her.

To some, crows were bad omens. She couldn't remember ever seeing many crows in Sacramento. The bird was staring at her, which reminded her of what she'd read about crows.

They never forgot a face.

It was true. They were highly intelligent birds. In fact, if they didn't like your face, they made sure to tell their friends about you. A group of crows was referred to as a "murder." Which turned her thoughts to what she'd read last night about Penny's grandfather, Ellis Kash. Two weeks before Arlene Snyder disappeared thirty years ago, her husband,

Nathaniel, was driving to the store when an SUV ran a red light and hit him. Nathaniel's airbag didn't work. Despite the fact that his car was not drivable, Nathaniel walked away with a few bruises.

There was something about the accident that made Zee dig deeper. And that's when she discovered that the driver had been a good friend of Ellis Kash.

What were the odds?

An old pal happens to hit your son-in-law, whose airbag doesn't work. And two weeks later, your daughter disappears, and you and your wife testify in court that she was afraid of her husband.

She flipped the next card.

The Death card, an armored skeleton riding a majestic horse.

Chills raced up her arms and legs. She didn't like where this was going.

Jessie had suggested Zee talk to Pam Carr, Arlene's good friend at the time of her disappearance. But Zee figured Pam Carr could wait.

Before she had a chance to analyze the Death card, movement caught her eye. The front door to the Kashes' house opened.

There he was. Ellis Kash in the flesh. A big man, tall with rounded shoulders, just as Jessie had described. His hair was white and slicked back from his face with gel. He walked toward his car parked in the driveway.

It might be go time.

She picked up the tray and set it beside her, adjusted her seat, and started the engine. As she waited for Ellis to pull out onto the street, she glanced at the skeleton riding the horse.

It could be worse.

What could be worse than the Death card? Francis asked.

"So many things," Zee said under her breath.

Name one.

A life without meaning or purpose, Zee thought as she watched Ellis drive away.

Twenty-Four

On Sunday morning Jessie woke to the sounds of dishes clattering against the kitchen sink. The clock on the nightstand told her it was 10:00 a.m. She never slept in, but she'd always been a lightweight when it came to travel. She had arrived home last night, just after midnight.

Before she'd left for New Jersey, arrangements were made for Olivia to stay with her friend Friday and Saturday night. They must have dropped her off early this morning.

Jessie climbed out of bed, pulled on her robe, and made her way to the kitchen where she found Olivia cooking at the stove. "Good morning, kiddo."

Higgins greeted her, his stump of a tail wagging.

Cecil fixated his one eye on her, his body rigid. He did not look happy. She bent down and scratched his neck. "Hey, Grumpy Cat."

"Morning," Olivia said. "How was New Jersey?"

"Like a blur. I'm exhausted. I feel as if I visited another country."

"Were you able to locate that Anne woman you're looking for?"

"Not yet. It appears Anne Corrigan ran away from home when she was sixteen, traveled alone to California, and found a way to start a new life under an alias."

"Why did she run away?"

As Jessie started the process of making coffee, she thought about the metal cuff and the chain she'd seen in Anne's bedroom. "Her stepfather and her mother kept her locked away in her bedroom for years. It's too horrible to repeat all that happened to the poor girl."

Olivia scooped scrambled eggs onto two plates and carried them to the table. She returned to the kitchen for napkins and forks. "So you think Anne made her way to California and just picked a new name?"

"Yes."

"But how would she get a license to drive?" Olivia had returned to the table where she took a seat. "Maybe she never drove," she said, answering her own question. "But it's been years, right?"

"Seventeen years since she ran away," Jessie said. "She changed her name to Lacey Page, and after she married, she became Lacey Geiger. She's thirty-three years old now."

"So what do we know about Lacey Page, other than her age?"

Jessie smiled. Olivia had always shown interest in the cases Jessie took on, and her curiosity kept growing. "I did some research while I was sitting at the airport. I did find a Lacey Page who died in a car accident in Sacramento at the age of sixteen. I have no idea why Anne/Lacey chose to live in Sacramento. My theory is she chose a new name and then found someone to help her get an ID. Once she had a birth certificate, she could go to the DMV and apply for a driver's license. One good piece of ID, that's all you need. The rest is easy."

Jessie scooped coffee into the filter, added water, and hit "Brew" before joining Olivia at the table.

Olivia raised her eyebrows. "So, what now? What's your next step?"

"Good question. I'm going to assume Anne Corrigan is now Lacey Geiger and go from there."

"So you're going to concentrate on learning everything you can about Lacey Geiger?" Olivia asked.

"Since I don't have a lot of time, I might focus on her husband, Jason, since they were last seen together."

"Maybe Lacey and her husband decided to be spontaneous and go hiking through the mountains or desert?" Olivia frowned. "When couples go missing, it usually turns out they went off the trail and got lost and couldn't find their way back."

Jessie shook her head. "They were last seen getting into a car that wasn't theirs, supposedly going off to celebrate their eighth wedding anniversary. If they'd decided to go somewhere, I would think they would have taken their own car."

"Have you searched social media?"

"Not thoroughly enough." Jessie went back to the kitchen to see if the coffee was ready. "I need to organize all the information I have on both Lacey and Jason and go from there."

"After I take Higgins on a walk, mind if I help you?"

"What about homework?"

"I'm caught up."

"Great. You've got yourself a deal." Jessie could use the help, and besides, it would give her and Olivia a chance to spend more time together.

TWENTY-FIVE

Ben made it to Abigail's indoor soccer game about five minutes after it began. Melony waved him to where she and Sean were seated high on the bleachers.

"What took you so long?" Melony asked when he sat down next to her and pulled off his coat.

Before he could answer, her eyes grew round. "What happened to your hand?"

He followed her gaze, watched as she pulled his shirtsleeve up to his elbow. He twisted his arm for a better look. He had one long, fairly deep scratch that started at his wrist and ended halfway up his forearm. He tried to recall when and where he might have injured himself.

"Damn it," she said.

"What?"

"There was broken glass inside the garbage you took out last night. Sean broke one of the dishes when he was helping me put away the dishes. I knew I should have taken it straight outside."

"Don't worry about it." He pulled his sleeve back in place.

Applause broke out. One of the girls on Abigail's team had scored a goal.

Ben gestured toward their son, Sean. "I thought we agreed not to let him bring his gaming device to Abigail's games."

She shrugged. "I've been dragging him all over the place this week. I decided to reward him."

Ben sighed.

"You never told me what took you so long," Melony said, her eyes on the game.

"What?"

"I thought you were just stopping by the office to grab something."

"I was, but Ian was there, and we ended up chatting for a while."

"How's Ian doing?"

"Good. He turned seventy recently, and he's healthy as an ox. His words, not mine."

"How does he do it?"

"He swears by his plant-based diet. Says his arteries are like a thirty-year-old's."

She chuckled. "I haven't seen Ian in years. We should invite him and his wife over."

Ben rested a hand on his wife's leg as he watched Abigail anticipate where her teammate was going before passing the ball. Sitting here with Melony, his children nearby, caused him to choke up suddenly. The past six months had been a strain on all of them. He thought about the missing memories and how after his accident he'd been a blank canvas as far as personality. For instance, he hadn't understood sarcasm or how to take a joke. His emotions had deserted him.

But Melony and the kids had changed all of that.

"A penny for your thoughts," Melony said.

He turned to her and smiled. "I was just living in the moment, enjoying being here with you and the kids."

She kissed his cheek. "I love you."

"Pass it!" one of the parents shouted, pulling Ben's attention back to the game. "Be aggressive, Molly. Shoot it!"

"Here they go," Melony said, nudging Ben's arm. "Whatever happened to the notion that the kids should just go out there and have fun?"

"The volume in the crowd always ramps up when the score gets close," Ben whispered. Sadly, he had to admit that it wasn't always easy to stay calm. But listening to the parents giving their kids instructions was always a good reminder for him to stay quiet.

Thirty minutes later, he and Melony were walking to their cars when they were stopped by one of the kids' mothers. "Did you hear the news?" she asked, out of breath.

Melony frowned. "No. What's going on?"

"Roger Willis is dead. He hung himself from a tree somewhere along the banks of the American River."

Ben stiffened, unsure how he felt about hearing the news. The woman looked excited, as if she'd just told his wife about a great sale going on at the mall.

"What is it?" Melony asked.

"I was just thinking about Sharon Willis and their daughters."

"They're better off without him," the woman said. "This might have been the only decent thing Roger Willis ever did . . . saving his kids from having to go through the hassle of a trial."

She shook her head. "I'm just glad I won't have to constantly look over my shoulder to see if he's stalking my child." She raised her hand over her head, flagging down another couple to give them the news before running off.

"I guess the pressure was too much for him," Melony said.

"It seems so."

"What is it? You look pale."

"I'm fine."

Melony rubbed a comforting hand over his back. "You did everything you could to stop people from picking on Roger. You wanted him to have a fair trial. You're a good man."

"I don't know about that," Ben said.

"Stop it," she scolded. "If I were Sharon, I would bury my husband and move out of town to save the kids from having to listen to all the gossip about their father."

Abigail and Sean joined them before he could respond.

"What's wrong?" Abigail wanted to know, sensing their apprehension.

"We'll tell you in the car," Melony said. "Come on. Let's go home."

"You did good today," Ben told his daughter. "Your foot placement and passing skills are excellent. Work on your speed and you'll be the next Hope Solo."

"She was a goalie."

"How about Alex Morgan?"

One corner of Abigail's mouth turned upward. "Thanks, Dad."

Family, Ben thought to himself. *It's all that matters.*

TWENTY-SIX

By the time Colin arrived at the scene, Ren had established the perimeter of what they were calling a crime scene until they could prove otherwise. Better safe than sorry.

Roger Willis lived in Citrus Heights, but his body was found in Sacramento County, thus giving the SPD jurisdiction. Uniformed officers were stationed outside the crime scene, keeping the media and onlookers from entering the area.

Roger Willis's body had been taken down and was now lying faceup on a tarp. A photographer set up his camera on a tripod and adjusted his flash before each picture, taking images from all angles. Once that was done, the medical examiner could inspect the body and give Colin her opinion as to the cause of death.

There were two witnesses, both of whom said they saw a man walking away from the area where Roger was found.

Ren had kept the witnesses separated until Colin arrived. It was best to keep them apart and to talk to each one individually so they didn't feed off each other. Witness number one was a young man, late twenties, out for a run. He didn't have much to say to Colin about the person he'd seen leaving the area, other than "Big shoulders. Didn't see his face. Heavy, dark jacket." The rest of Colin's questions were answered with yes, no, maybe.

Standing in front of Colin was witness number two, a homeless woman. Even with the thick, dirty wool blanket draped over her shoulders, she looked frail. Her naturally curly hair was a mixture of brown and silver. Her skin was leathery from time spent outside. She described the man she'd seen leaving the area as white, tall, and dark-haired. Had she been slightly intoxicated, his chance of getting a truthful account would have been higher. It was a known fact that intoxicated witnesses talked freely and were usually truthful.

Unfortunately, witness number two had dilated pupils and rapid eye movement, and she kept picking at her hair. Colin's guess would be that she was a meth user. And that would mean she probably wasn't a reliable eyewitness. But she was one of only two witnesses at the moment, and therefore he wanted to hear what she had to say.

"How tall would you guess the man was?" Colin asked.

"The man walking away or the dead man?" She used her right hand to slap her left arm as if swatting a mosquito.

"The man walking away," Colin said patiently.

"About as tall as you, maybe." She put a hand to her chin and looked toward the sky. "Maybe he was taller than you, after all. I think he was Latino. Do you have anything to eat with you? Any candy?"

"No. Sorry. Do you recall what the man walking away was wearing?"

She scratched her neck, her fingernails leaving red lines across her flesh. "Dark pants, maybe jeans, and a coat! A thick coat. Puffy and warm-looking." She pulled her blanket tighter around her shoulders and shivered. "Do you want to know what color it was?"

"That would be good."

"Oh. Hmm. Dark," she said. "Maybe blue. Could have been black."

A lot of homeless had left downtown Sacramento for the river. Most of the tents were usually hidden behind thick vines, but every once in a while, you would see a tent set up right on the shore. Piles of trash often surrounded the tents, along with broken bikes and shopping carts.

"Did you see the man climb into a car and drive away?"

She pointed to a heavily wooded area opposite the parking area. "He walked that way."

"You're sure?"

"Yep. Positive."

He thanked her, handed her a ten-dollar bill, and walked back to where Ren was overseeing the collection of evidence.

"How did that go?" Ren asked.

"Tall white male with dark hair and a warm coat," Colin said. "You tell me."

"One of a kind," Ren said in a sarcastic tone. "What makes you think this isn't a suicide?"

"Never a good idea to assume." Together they walked to the edge of the tarp where Brenda Parsons, the medical examiner, was using tweezers to pull something from Willis's hair before sliding it into a plastic bag.

"What is that?" Colin asked.

"Looks just like a flower from a shrub commonly known as the Mexican orange. I have one in my front yard. Drought resistant and shunned by deer. The leaves are narrow and leathery, and the flowers lose much of their luster in the summer, but look at it now. Look around," she said. "Do you see anything so vibrant and pearly white in the vicinity?"

He and Ren took a good long look. Mostly clay banks, oaks, riverside vegetation.

"It's winter," Colin said. "Wouldn't that mean it would have come from a nursery?"

"Not necessarily. They do well in mild winters like the one we've been experiencing."

"And take a look at this." She pointed at the grass stain on the dead man's pants. "Do you see any grass around here?"

Ren shook his head.

"I still have a lot of work to do," she said, "here and in the lab, but from what I've seen thus far, I would say there's a high possibility that someone very effectively staged this scene."

"Strangled at another location and then brought here where he was strung up to make it look like a suicide?" Colin asked.

"Exactly."

Colin's phone buzzed. He picked up the call, listened, then hung up. "Willis's car has been located on South Bridge Street in Rancho Cordova. It's the same area where rafts are rented out in the summer."

"Security cameras?" Ren wondered aloud.

"Doubt it, but I'm going to make my way over there when I'm done here."

"Who kayaks in the dead of winter?"

"His wife told me he was a passionate kayaker. She also gave me three names of people she thinks had it out for Roger: Gretchen Sullivan, Paden White, and Ben Morrison."

"The crime reporter for the *Tribune*?"

"The one and only."

"His name seems to come up a lot."

"Yeah, looks like I'll have to pay him a visit."

TWENTY-SEVEN

Zee waited until her subject, Ellis Kash, was at the end of the block before merging onto the street. She'd never done a moving surveillance before, not really. Well, once, unexpectedly, when Olivia was driving her car for the first time. That didn't work out too well.

He was headed west on Third Avenue. At the first cross street, he made a right. Next came a left onto Stockton Boulevard. She had no idea where he was going. She didn't really care. She never did much on Sundays. Trailing a target was much more exciting than hanging out with Dad and his girlfriend. Fingers tapping against the wheel, she realized she probably should have put a GPS device on his car. That would make things so much easier in the future.

He merged onto US-50 west toward Capital City Freeway and headed east until he hit CA-65. She wondered where he might be going that took him past Rocklin toward Lincoln: the dump, a rodeo, the Sky Zone, a trampoline park—that would be cool.

He knows you're following him, Marion warned.

Francis added, *I hope you brought your pepper spray and brass knuckles, because I'm pretty sure he's leading you right to some old, dilapidated warehouse where he can hack you to pieces and play with your parts.*

Lucy sighed. *Here we go again.*

Usually it was Francis who did all the talking inside her head, but for the past few days, all three of the voices in her head suddenly had opinions on everything she did.

Zee's doctor once told her that dealing with the voices was one of the most difficult challenges people with schizophrenia faced. Voices could lead someone like her to do something stupid or dangerous. Her doctor said the voices were hallucinations, but she knew they were real. She also knew that most "normal" people also heard voices. For instance, her dad heard voices, and he didn't get all bent out of shape over it. Her doctor told her she shouldn't confuse the inner voice with hallucinations. At every appointment, her doctor would lecture and give her advice, and all the while she'd be thinking, *Whatever, Doc. Just write my prescription and hand it over. I have enough problems without listening to you, too.*

She'd met other people with schizophrenia before. One guy said he had one distinct voice that mumbled nonstop. Now *that* would be annoying. At least *her* voices were manageable. In fact, if she didn't hear one of them after a few hours, she worried they might leave her for good. The notion panicked her. She would be lost without them.

Up ahead, Zee noticed her subject slowing down. He drove like an old man, which made sense considering that's what he was. Ellis Kash was three cars ahead of her when he turned onto Industrial Boulevard. A minute later it dawned on her where he was going: Thunder Valley Casino.

Loud music and bright lights, Francis warned. *Turn around.*

The voices knew that too much stimulation could cause confusion and headaches. But there was no way she was turning around. Instead, she followed her subject into the parking garage, making sure to stay far enough away so he didn't see her as she followed him inside.

Ellis Kash headed toward the back of the casino as if he'd been here a zillion times before. For an old man with stooped shoulders, he walked at a pretty good pace. He waited patiently for a seat at a slot machine lit up with an eagle and gold eggs. She found an ATM close by where she could watch him while she withdrew $200 from her checking account.

For the next fifteen minutes or so, she kept her distance and simply watched him. Francis had been wrong about the lights and the noise being a problem. She wasn't a big fan of secondhand smoke, but she was an investigator now and had to deal with it.

An elderly woman sitting next to her subject stood up, shouting at the machine for failing to make her rich. After she walked off, Zee hurried that way, barely beating out another customer for the machine.

"That's a good machine," Ellis told her. "You just have to talk nicely to it if you want it to cooperate."

Cooperate? And people thought *she* was crazy. She pulled out a twenty, slid it into the money slot, and slapped her hand on the button that said "Max Bet." A minute later, her twenty was gone. She stuck in another one and then watched Ellis pet his machine as if it were his beloved dog or something. "Come on, sweetie," he said.

Sure enough, he hit a small jackpot.

"Wow," she said. "That really works."

"Told you so."

Zee petted her machine in the same ridiculous manner and said, "That mean lady left. I won't yell at you like she did. I think you're very attractive." She hit the button. A little green leprechaun began prancing around. He reached his little hand into a pot at the end of a rainbow and tossed gold coins all over the place.

Ding. Ding. Ding.

The little green man danced as the reels spun and music played. People gathered around, and it took her a minute to see that money was being added to her payout. What the heck was going on?

She didn't know what to do other than worry that Ellis Kash would get up and leave and she would have to leave her machine and follow him.

"You hit a big jackpot," Ellis told her. "Seven hundred and fifty dollars."

"You're shitting me! Sorry, I mean, are you joking?"

He chuckled as he explained what all the gold coins and leprechauns meant and how it all added up. After listening attentively, she pointed at his payout, which was close to $900. "Wow, looks like you're going to be leaving a lot of money to your kids."

He chuckled. "She's not getting any of this!"

Zee forced a laugh, wondering if he realized what he'd just said, which he must have, because he sort of blushed and went back to coddling his machine.

The leprechaun stopped dancing. Zee turned to Ellis and said, "Do you ever run out of nice things to say to the machine?"

"Never. It's good karma." He gestured at her slot. "Just tell the leprechaun that he's charming and you would really like to see him dance again."

She said exactly that before hitting the button again. Sure enough, a row of purple-and-gold pots filled the screen. Her audience returned to watch the show. "How much this time?" she asked the old man.

"Three hundred dollars," he said. "I told you. Sweet-talking the machines. It works every time."

"Do you ever bring your daughter gambling with you?"

He frowned, even seemed to think about what he was going to say before he said it. "I don't like to talk about my daughter."

Zee didn't say anything, hoping he would go on, which thankfully he did.

"The truth is, she was murdered by her husband, a much older man who sadly made good on his threat to kill her."

"I'm sorry."

"Don't be. It's been a while now. She'll be fine."

She'll be fine? He did it again. Very strange. Something wasn't right. "What was your daughter like?"

"I don't mean to be rude," he said, "but like I told you, I'd rather not talk about it."

"I understand." Zee played for a while longer and asked him a few more questions, but clearly her subject had shut down. She hit the payout button and grabbed her ticket. She said goodbye and wished him luck. Halfway across the room, she turned to look at him and saw that he was watching her leave.

Chills washed over her. Her heart skipped a beat. She smiled and waved, then hurried off.

She's not getting any of this! She'll be fine.

Listen to your gut. That's what Jessie always told her, over and over again. Zee didn't have that queasy little feeling most people got when they knew something was off. Zee's gut was like a whole person inside of her, his or her fists pounding on her innards, telling her Arlene was alive!

Twenty-Eight

Jessie was home, sitting at the kitchen table, her laptop open, papers scattered about, and her cell phone pressed against her ear.

Until now she hadn't had any reason to research, let alone try to locate, Jason Geiger. But much had changed since her first initial talk with Grant Taylor, the lawyer from Arizona.

Colin had called her while she was in New Jersey and left a message letting her know he'd searched the Geigers' house, inside and out. Nothing appeared out of sorts, no sign of foul play.

While Jessie made phone calls, Olivia helped her organize information she'd found on Jason Geiger. He was thirty-five years old. He'd started his own company, JHG Properties, at the age of twenty-seven, the same year he'd married Lacey Page. The JHG website stated that his company was responsible for the design and construction of new shopping centers. His Sacramento office managed the leasing and property-management activities for the company's portfolio of shopping centers.

"For a company that has only been around for eight years, Jason Geiger has been, and still is, involved in a lot of lawsuits," Olivia said when Jessie put down her phone.

"How many?"

"I've found at least a dozen suits filed by JHG, claiming shoddy work."

Jessie frowned. "That does sound excessive."

"There was an article written about one of the companies he sued."

"Send me the link, will you?"

"Already did."

"Great. Thanks." Jessie called Derek McDowell, the Geigers' neighbor who said he was collecting their mail. Since there was still no sign of Lacey or Jason, the call was short.

Jessie's next call was to Jason's parents, who lived in San Diego. A woman answered on the second ring. Jessie introduced herself before telling the woman her reason for calling.

"You're a private investigator?"

"That's right," Jessie said. "Is Jason Geiger your son?"

"Yes. Why? What's going on?"

"I'm actually trying to locate his wife, Lacey."

"Has she done something wrong?"

"No. It's nothing like that. I need to let her know that her grandmother passed away."

"Next time I talk to my son, I'll let him know."

"I went to their house," Jessie blurted, afraid that the woman was about to hang up on her, "but nobody was home. Jason's car is inside the garage, and Lacey's car is in the driveway. The neighbor across the street has been collecting their mail for about a week. The last time he saw them was last weekend. Apparently, they were headed to a nice restaurant to celebrate their eighth wedding anniversary."

"Oh, yes. Jason did mention something about it being their anniversary."

"The problem," Jessie said, feeling the need to explain since the woman didn't sound the least bit concerned, "is that they haven't been seen since. That was a week ago."

Silence on the other end.

"Did Jason happen to mention going anywhere else? A trip to surprise his wife, maybe?"

"Oh, no. He wouldn't do that."

"Why not?"

"It's complicated."

Were Jason and Lacey having marital problems? Jessie wondered. No, it had to be something else. Why would Jason take his wife out to celebrate a special occasion if he planned to part ways?

Jessie heard muffled voices in the background. "Hold on a minute," she told Jessie. "My husband is going to call Jason's cell."

After a long pause, she said, "He left Jason a message to call us. Why don't you give me your name again and a number where you can be reached? My husband will call you if he hears from him."

"If?"

"Jason is a busy man. He's been known to be unreachable before."

"Really?" Jessie asked. "This isn't the first time your son has disappeared for days without notifying anyone?"

"Well, he went on a business trip once and didn't tell anyone where he was going."

"How long was he gone?"

"For the weekend, I believe."

Before Jessie could ask another question, the woman's husband took the phone and said, "My wife and I our heading out. Next time we talk to Jason, we'll tell him you called."

He hung up.

Olivia looked at her. "Another dead end?"

"Yep."

"Bummer." There was only a short pause before Olivia said, "I haven't seen Zee lately. Is she still hanging out with that boy she brought to dinner over the holidays?"

"Tobey?"

"Yeah, Tobey."

Jessie cocked her head. "You know, I'm not really sure."

"Whenever you get too busy at work, you tend to lose sight of the important stuff, like the people around you, people who care about you and love you."

Jessie crossed her arms. "Spit it out, Olivia. What are you trying to say?"

Olivia shrugged. "Why hasn't Colin been coming for dinner?"

"We've both been busy."

"That's not what I heard."

Jessie smiled. "What did you hear?"

"Piper called. She said her dad is sad because he never gets to see you."

"Now you're just making up stories. I saw Colin at the shooting range, and we talk every day. Everything's fine."

"Aren't you afraid that if you keep putting your work before everything else, you'll end up all alone?"

"No. I'm not afraid of that."

"Well, you should be," Olivia muttered under her breath.

Jessie's phone buzzed before she could say any more on the subject. Saved by the bell.

The number on her cell wasn't anyone she knew. She picked up the call anyhow.

"Is this Jessie Cole?"

"Yes. Who's this?"

"My name is Amanda. I work with Lacey Geiger at the fitness center in Midtown."

"Yes, we met when I stopped in." Jessie hoped she had good news. "Did you hear from Lacey?"

"No, but there's something I think you should know."

Jessie waited.

"It's about Lacey's husband, Jason. Last month I saw him at a dance club with another woman. They were very cozy with each other. I wanted to tell Lacey, but there was never a good time since we're always surrounded by people."

"Any idea who the woman is?"

"Yes. Her name is Chaya Cohen. The only reason I know that is because she works out at our gym. Even worse, she lives in Lacey's neighborhood and has been to their house."

"How can you be sure?"

"Because Lacey invited me. I was there."

Jessie thought about her conversation with Jason's mother. The woman had said that things were "complicated." Did Jason's mother know her son was seeing another woman?

"Anything else you can tell me?" Jessie asked Amanda.

"No—just that I really hope you find Lacey soon. I'm worried about her."

"I won't stop looking. Thanks for letting me know."

After she hung up, she tapped her finger on the table. Jason was having an affair. And yet he'd taken his wife out for dinner to supposedly celebrate their anniversary. Maybe Jason's dinner plans with his wife had pissed off Chaya Cohen and she'd hired someone to pick the couple up? It sounded far-fetched but definitely worth checking out.

Jessie noticed that Olivia had gone to her room. Her niece's speech about Jessie needing to spend time with the people who were important to her made Jessie wonder what was going on inside that head of hers. She was a lot like her mom. She was obviously feeling neglected.

Jessie made a few quick notes before shutting down her computer. She found Olivia on her bed, Higgins and Cecil cuddled close.

"Come on," Jessie said. "Let's go for a walk."

TWENTY-NINE

Ben's van rattled as he pulled into the parking lot of the apartment building off Stockton Boulevard. He listened to the engine for a minute. Whenever he wasn't moving, the rattling stopped. He shut off the motor and climbed out.

The apartment building reminded him of a Motel 6. It was shaped in a U with stairs on both ends. He was looking for Apartment 12B on the top floor. He knew which way to go since he had lived in Apartment 11B before his accident. He and Melony had stopped by many times over the years in hopes of sparking a memory or two, but it had never worked. The place used to be painted blue. Now it was green. Everything else was exactly the same, including the parking lot littered with trash. As he headed for the stairs on the right, he noticed that the surrounding wood fence was ready to topple. The rusty metal stairs creaked as he dodged dead cockroaches on his way up.

He was here to talk to Renee Walker about the cold case he was doing a story on. Her name was scribbled on the notes he'd taken twelve years ago after the death of Jon Eberling. Apparently, at the time of Jon's death, Renee had been his on-again, off-again girlfriend. The only address he had for Renee was this apartment complex. He knocked on the door. The odds against Renee still living here were a million to one.

A woman opened the door but kept the chain latched as she looked at him. "What do you want?"

"Ben Morrison with the *Sacramento Tribune*. I'm looking for Renee Walker."

"What do you want with Renee?"

"I'm doing an update on the Jon Eberling murder, and I believe he was a friend of Renee's."

For a long moment she didn't say a word, merely stared over the chain at him. He'd seen that look before. She knew who he was. They had met before.

"Is Renee here now?"

"You really don't recognize me?"

"I'm sorry," Ben said. "Should I?"

"I read about your accident when it happened. You still don't remember anything?"

"Nothing that happened before the accident, no."

"*I'm* Renee Walker. We used to be neighbors." She undid the chain and invited him inside.

She gestured toward an overstuffed couch. "Have a seat." She closed the door and walked into the living room behind him.

"We have to keep our voices low," she said. "I have a two-month-old who's asleep in the back room."

Ben nodded before he took a seat and readied his notebook and pen.

"I don't usually invite strangers into my house, but in a sense you're not a stranger at all. You might not remember me, but I remember you very well."

Before he could ask her about Jon, she said, "If it weren't for you, I might not be standing here now."

He frowned. "How could that be?"

She put a hand through her hair. "God, I really can't believe you don't remember. That's crazy." She couldn't stop shaking her head as if in wonder. "In a nutshell, Jon was an asshole. No better way to put it.

He used to steal from his own mother just to pay his share of the rent when I let him move in for a couple of months."

Ben thought of Gina Eberling. *Did she know her son stole from her?*

"When I threatened to tell his mother, he hit me." She brushed a hand over her left cheek. "I was shocked. I told him to get out, but he begged and told me how sorry he was until I agreed to let him stay. Every day for a week he brought me flowers and gifts from the mall. The next time we had a disagreement, he pushed me." She sighed. "And it all went downhill fast from there."

His chest tightened, and what felt like a spark of energy shot through him. His shoulder twitched. He took a breath and waited patiently for Renee to go on.

"I would run into you every other day, coming or going from this place. I remember you stopping me in the parking lot once and asking me if I was okay. I told you I was fine. But I knew that you knew what was going on. These walls are thin. You probably heard every argument we ever had." She swallowed hard. "The last time Jon Eberling hit me, he nearly killed me. If you hadn't kicked down my door and pulled him off me, I wouldn't be here. I know it. I could see it in Jon's eyes. That was the day he was going to kill me." She turned her head to show him the scar that ran down the side of her face. "Thirty-nine stitches. Broken cheek, fractured skull, bleeding from my ears."

Shit. Ben could feel it coming before it happened. A sharp pain sliced through his skull. He closed his eyes, squeezing them tight as if doing so would make it stop. He saw it then. A fist slamming into Renee's face. And then again. Blood spurted from her nose. He grabbed hold of Jon, had him in a chokehold as he pulled him off Renee. He dragged the man outside. Ben held the side of his head. Suddenly he was somewhere else, in an alleyway; it was dark, and the only sound was a dog barking in the distance as he wrapped his hands around Jon's throat and squeezed the life out of him.

"Are you okay?" she asked.

Ben's eyes snapped open. "I'm sorry." He rubbed the side of his head. "Since the car accident, I get shooting pains every once in a while. I'm just glad you're okay."

"Thanks." Her smile looked strained. "Not long after the incident, Jon was found murdered. And I've always found it odd that you and I never talked about what happened in my apartment. I thought about knocking on your door or leaving a thank-you card in your mailbox, but I never did. For two years we passed each other without a word said."

"I'm sorry I didn't come by to check on you."

"Are you kidding me?" She waved a hand through the air. "You did enough." There was a short pause, followed by, "I remember you doing a write-up in the *Sacramento Tribune* on Jon's murder."

Ben nodded.

"You wrote about his mother and how a masked intruder broke into her house and killed her cat. Two days later, Jon, her only son, was found dead, strangled to death and left in a dumpster. When I read the part about his mother, I remember thinking I bet the intruder was Jon."

With nothing left to say, Ben put away his notebook and stood. "Thank you for allowing me inside your home and for taking the time to talk to me."

The baby made a noise in the other room.

Ben smiled at her. "It sounds like you've made a good life for yourself."

"I have. Thank you." She followed him to the door. "There is one more thing."

Ben looked at her.

"When I read about Jon's murder in the newspaper all those years ago, I found it strange that you never interviewed me for the story. Even odder, you didn't mention in your write-up what had happened right next door to where you were living. But then I realized that it was just another nice gesture on your part." She smiled at him. "You were protecting my privacy, weren't you?"

He wasn't sure how to answer the question, so he didn't.

"I know you don't remember because of your amnesia, but I want to thank you for keeping my name out of the paper. I was in a bad place at the time. I don't think I could have handled the media attention it might have brought." She kept her gaze locked on his. "You're a good man, Ben Morrison. I'm grateful you came today so I could thank you in person."

Her praise was followed by an awkward embrace. When she pulled away, he gave her a tight smile, thanked her again for talking to him, and started back toward the parking lot.

He had just reached his van when his cell phone buzzed. He picked up the call and said hello.

"Ben Morrison?"

"Yes?"

"This is Ren Howe, investigator with the Sacramento PD. We were wondering if you would mind coming to the station to answer a few questions we have regarding the death of Roger Willis."

"What for? I heard he hung himself near the river."

"Where did you hear that?"

"From one of the parents of a child on my daughter's soccer team."

"When was that?"

"Sunday morning."

"We will need you to come in."

"When?"

"Today. Would one thirty p.m. work?"

Ben rubbed his temple. "I'll see you then." He'd hoped he'd heard the last of Roger Willis for a while. The idea of being dragged into the middle of an investigation didn't sit well with him.

As soon as Ben hung up, his phone rang again. It was Ian Savage, his boss at the *Tribune*. "Yes?"

"Did you get a call from the Sacramento Police Department?"

"I did."

"Why do they want to talk to you?"

"Nothing to worry about. They said they had a few questions. Roger Willis was my daughter's soccer coach. A few months ago, I had a run-in with Willis on the field, in public."

"I heard this was a suicide," Ian said.

"It would be a mistake for them to handle the case as anything other than a homicide," Ben said. "As a professional law enforcement agency, they shouldn't assume any death is a suicide or a natural death. Not unless they want to risk losing crucial evidence."

"So, you're not a suspect?"

"No," Ben said confidently. "I'm sure they want to talk to me and other parents in hopes of getting information that could be pertinent to the crime."

"On the one hand, it's a shame we have to spend resources investigating a guy like that."

"And on the other hand?" Ben asked.

"Pay attention to what's going on when you're there. We might have a big story on our hands."

"I'll keep you updated." Ben hung up, shaking his head at the notion that Ian was more worried about getting the story than the fact that Ben was being sucked into their investigation.

Ben reached his van without further interruption and climbed inside. He had a few hours before he needed to meet with investigators, and he planned to make good use of his time.

THIRTY

Colin walked at a clipped pace down the hallway that ran through the center of the police department and entered one of the conference rooms. He'd just been on the phone with Paden White's neighbor, an elderly woman who happened to know a lot about the comings and goings of the White family. The last to arrive, Colin shut the door. He took a seat at the rectangular table next to Ren Howe and across from Gretchen Sullivan, the woman who apparently had invited neighbors in Roger Willis's area over to talk about Roger.

The room was small, sparsely decorated with a black-and-white framed poster of the Tower Bridge. A one-way mirror took up half of one of the walls. At the moment, nobody was on the other side.

"I have things to do," Gretchen Sullivan said. "Can we get started?"

"Sure," Colin said as he grabbed a pad of paper from a stack of notebooks sitting on the table. "We'd like to know about the meeting you held at your house recently."

"Really? Oh, my God. Is that what this is about?"

Colin nodded. "We were told that a group of people had gathered to talk about how they could get rid of Roger Willis."

"We gathered at my house to talk about bullying. Later on, the conversation turned to the child molester—I mean, Willis, of course—and how we might be able to keep our children safe from him."

"Let me reword the question," Colin said. "Did you or anyone else in the room discuss ways to possibly rid the neighborhood of Roger Willis?"

She rolled her eyes. "Nobody discussed hiring a hit man, if that's what you mean." Her brow puckered. "If you people are going to try to use word trickery to get me to say something I shouldn't, maybe I do need to call a lawyer."

Ren sighed. "That's your call, ma'am."

"Ma'am." She chuckled. "I was assured I was not a person of interest and that there was no reason to bother calling my lawyer. They said you just had a few questions. But now I don't know . . . I don't like the vibe I'm getting in this cramped little space."

"This is not an interrogation," Colin told her. "It's just an interview."

She glanced at her watch. "Nobody said one word about 'getting rid' of Roger Willis. It was more about keeping our eyes wide open and making sure he didn't set foot on school grounds." She looked at Ren. "Do you have kids?"

He shook his head.

"How about you?" she asked Colin.

"I have a daughter."

"Roger Willis was sitting in his car a few feet away from where our girls were playing soccer," she went on, her voice scolding. "After everything that happened, the man was sitting right there in plain view as if he didn't have a care in the world. Let that soak in for a minute."

Colin and Ren waited her out.

Her face reddened. "We, the group of parents at my house, had recently been made aware that other victims accusing Mr. Willis of sexual abuse had come forward. I called the meeting because I wanted everyone in the neighborhood to know what we were dealing with."

She jabbed a finger at the table every time she made a point. "If the soccer coach had made a move on one of *your* daughter's teammates," she said point-blank to Colin, "I bet you would have wanted to make sure everyone in the community was aware that the creep was on the loose."

Again, Colin remained silent.

"Who was at the meeting?" Ren asked.

She exhaled. "Let's see. Hmm. Sunil Rajan, Earle Laredo, Max DeCosta, Ruby Safford, Marlee Mogelson, and her husband, Peter."

"What about Paden White?" Colin asked.

She shook her head. "Paden was the one who gave Roger Willis a piece of his mind in the parking lot outside of the indoor soccer facility."

"Were you there?"

"No. But I wish I had been."

"Why is that?" Ren asked.

She shrugged, looked him squarely in the eye, and said, "No reason."

Ren asked, "Was Ben Morrison the one who pulled Paden White off Roger Willis?"

"That's what I heard."

Colin read over his notes. "You didn't mention Ben Morrison as one of the people at your house on the night of the parent—"

"My bad," she said. "Ben was there. So was his wife, Melony. But they left early."

"Do you know why?"

"Not really. I think Ben was worried we were all jeopardizing the upcoming case against Roger Willis, especially after the altercation between Paden White and Willis in the parking lot."

"Where were you Sunday morning between four a.m. and eight a.m.?"

"I'm a single mother, raising two daughters. I was asleep."

"Anything else you would like to tell us?"

She presented them with a tight-lipped smile. She nodded. "I'm glad he's dead."

"Roger Willis?" Ren asked.

"Yes."

Ten seconds after Gretchen Sullivan left, a uniformed officer entered the room to let them know that Paden White had arrived with a criminal lawyer in tow.

The interview with Paden White went much differently than the one with Gretchen Sullivan.

Paden's answers to their questions were vague, if he answered at all.

"How good of friends were you with Roger Willis?" Ren asked.

"He was my daughter's soccer coach. I think that says it all."

"Not really," Colin cut in. "Did you ever spend time with him and his wife, Sharon, outside of soccer practices and games?"

He shrugged. "Sure, yeah. We spent a day or two on the weekend by their pool."

"With Roger, Sharon, and their kids?" Colin continued.

"Yes."

"Did you know Roger's daily routine?"

"I didn't know he had a routine."

"His hobbies?" Colin provided. "What he enjoyed doing in his free time?"

"I have no idea."

Ren cut in. "Didn't you and Roger run a marathon together?"

Paden scoffed. "It was a half marathon. That was nearly two years ago."

"But you knew he enjoyed running," Colin said. "What about kayaking? Did you ever go kayaking with him?"

"No."

"But you were aware of the fact that he enjoyed the sport."

"Sure. I think it would be safe to say he enjoyed many sports. Unlike Roger, I didn't have the luxury of time."

"What do you do?" Ren asked.

"I'm an investment banker. I work long hours, including many weekends."

"What about yesterday?" Colin asked.

"What about it?"

"Can you tell us where you were between four a.m. and eight a.m. on Sunday?"

"I was asleep."

"Were your wife and kids home?"

"Of course. They were—"

"This interview is done," Paden's lawyer said before Paden could finish answering.

The lawyer stood. Paden followed suit.

Colin thanked Paden for his cooperation. After the door clicked shut, he looked at Ren and said, "He just lied. His wife and kids were in Lake Tahoe."

"How do you know?" Ren asked.

"I left business cards at the homes of neighbors we were unable to catch at home. Paden's wife called me before our meeting. I want to get a warrant to search his home."

THIRTY-ONE

Both Lacey and Jason had spent endless hours either banging nails on the vent cover or looking for a place where the key might go. Although Jason had consumed more than his share of food and water, they both knew she would give in and share her rations.

She'd calculated that they would get two inches of water each for the next three days. They both had one more inch of water left for the day. She didn't trust Jason to take only his share, so she poured his ration into an empty bottle and gave it to him that way.

When nighttime came, the place grew dark, almost as dark as it had been when they were buried in the box. But she could still see shadows, depending on which way she looked. "Don't you think we should talk about the people who may have had grievances with you or your company?"

"*My* enemies?"

"Yes."

"What's the point? We're here, aren't we? Knowing who did this to us isn't going to save the day."

"If we know what we're dealing with, maybe that will help us figure a way out of here. There's nothing else to do. Humor me."

"The list is long."

She frowned. "I'm serious."

"So am I."

"Did you get in a fight with one of your friends?"

"I don't have many friends, Lacey. I'm talking about work."

She tried to recall the last time they'd talked about his work. Whenever she asked him about his day, he said everything was fine. Rinse and repeat. "I don't understand," she went on. "I thought your employees and clients respected you."

"It's not a big deal. It's business. Sometimes you have to trounce the competition to stay in the game."

She wasn't sure why she was surprised, but she was. "Give me an example?"

"Last summer, rumor had it that one of my main competitors was having a tough time. So I quickly announced that I was hiring and that new employees would receive a two-thousand-dollar bonus if they agreed to stay on for at least one year. That's what you call kicking a rival while he's down."

"So the other guy's employees came to work for you?"

"Yes."

"That's horrible."

"No, Lacey. Use your brain. It's business. And it worked out better than expected. With so many experienced laborers, no other builder could match our productivity and quality of work. Earnings skyrocketed."

"You said we were broke."

"Did I say that?"

"Yes."

"Well, we did agree to keep our money separate, didn't we?"

"I see. So *I* was broke, but you've been doing pretty well for yourself."

"Here we go. This is why we can't have a conversation."

"Why is that?"

"Because somehow I always end up being the bad guy."

Another lie, she thought. If anything, she always pumped him up and told him how wonderful he was. If he talked badly about himself, she told him he was talking nonsense. "So what did your competition do? The company that lost their workers?"

"They folded. They no longer exist."

"What about the employees who didn't take you up on your offer? What happened to them?"

"All that was left were the ones either making too much money or were too old. If I worried about every employee, it would defeat the purpose of trouncing the competition."

Lacey wasn't sure why she was shocked, but she was. She'd always known Jason was decisive and strong-minded and sometimes unwilling to compromise when it came to his business, but she'd also thought he had integrity. A heaviness settled within her, tightening her chest, reminding her of that awful time in her life when she realized her mother had married the devil. She'd felt lost and helpless. But everything had changed when she ran away to California, and again when she met Jason.

She had begun to think of her time with her stepfather as an event in her life that had served her well, since it made her appreciate the little things in life. After she'd run away and started a new life, she'd worked hard to wipe out all those incredibly horrific memories. She's done it with kindness and optimism. She'd chosen positivity over negativity and happiness over sadness.

She'd read a lot of self-help books over the years. It never hurt to be reminded that life was precious, every day a miracle to be cherished. And every person walking this earth had a sliver of good inside of them.

What a fucking crock of shit.

"Listen," Jason said, breaking into her realization that life was hard and had a way of fucking you over when you least expected it. "The men who play softball when it comes to business may look good in the press, and they might even show an uptick in earnings for a year or two, but it won't last because they aren't winners. They're losers. Instead of running around playing the game, they're standing on the sidelines watching. And when their business tanks, they get that deer-in-the-headlights expression and wonder what the hell happened."

He was right. His list of enemies must be very long, she realized.

Lacey was more certain than ever that she might die a slow and horrible death all because she had chosen to marry an asshole, maybe the biggest asshole in the history of the universe.

THIRTY-TWO

Jessie was asked to have a seat while the receptionist went to find her manager, Gregg Fisher, second in charge at JHG, since Jason Geiger was out of the office.

The building was impressive. There were lots of windows and gleaming marble floors. Jason Geiger appeared to have made quite a name for himself. His company was responsible for developing more than twenty community shopping centers.

Gregg Fisher approached a few minutes later. He was six feet tall with a lean body, sandy-colored hair, and a deeply dimpled chin. He shook Jessie's hand. "I was told you were looking for Jason Geiger."

"That's right. I'm a private investigator. His wife, Lacey, is the person I've been hired to locate, but it appears neither Jason nor Lacey have been home in over a week."

"Do you mind my asking why you're looking for Lacey?"

"Her grandmother passed away and left her a gift."

He nodded.

Jessie glanced around. "Do you think we could talk in a private setting?"

"Sure. Follow me."

Once they were in his office, he gestured for Jessie to take a seat in front of his desk. While he settled in, she took a few seconds to admire his office—a large mahogany desk, plush carpeting, and floor-to-ceiling windows. Once Gregg was seated, she got right to business. "The inheritance Lacey is set to receive requires my finding her in a matter of weeks. That's why I'm here, and that's why I need to be frank. I need to know if you or anyone in this building might know where Jason and Lacey could be?"

He rubbed his chin in a thoughtful manner. "As the president of JHG, Jason's absence has been a concern."

Jessie was surprised by his statement. Although the Geigers' neighbor and the people Lacey worked with hadn't seen Lacey in days, Jessie kept thinking there would be a simple explanation for their leaving the city and that the search would end here. "So you don't know where he is?"

Gregg Fisher looked toward the door as if to make sure he wouldn't be overheard. "He has a habit of coming and going as he pleases. As far as I know, no one in this building is aware of Jason's sudden disappearance. Most of the people around here have been easily placated when I tell them he'll be back next week."

"When do you plan on telling them the truth?"

"I can't answer that because I don't know what the truth is. I, too, drove by their house and knocked on the door, but as you said, nobody was home."

"Have you called the police?"

He shook his head. "Word would have gotten out quick. I decided it was too early to worry project managers."

"A friend of mine, a detective at the Sacramento PD," Jessie told him, "was able to gain access into the Geigers' house. He said there was no evidence of foul play. The Geigers' neighbor has been collecting their mail. The last time the neighbor saw Lacey and Jason was Friday night before they drove off. Did Jason mention anything about going out to dinner for his anniversary?"

Another shake of the head. "He rarely talks to me about his home life."

Jessie knew she might be overstepping an invisible line in the sand, but she wanted to keep Gregg Fisher talking, hopeful he would recall some little tidbit that might give her a clue to help find Lacey. "I've done some research," Jessie said, keeping her voice low. "And I could be wrong, but I've gotten the impression, based on complaints and lawsuits against Jason Geiger, that the president of JHG is not well liked."

Gregg tugged at his tie. "That would be putting it mildly."

"Can you elaborate?"

"I shouldn't, but since we're being frank, let me sum the man up for you." Gregg leaned forward and said, "Jason Geiger is not a good businessman or leader. He lacks empathy and has zero integrity, taking credit for my work and others' and placing blame where it doesn't belong. Because he doesn't know how to empower others, he is unable to engender loyalty. He is a narcissist, and that, Jessie Cole, is just the beginning."

Jessie nodded. Chills skittered up her back as she reached into her purse for her notebook. The man was angry. His jaw had visibly hardened, and his body tensed when he talked about Jason.

She slid her notebook across the desk so Gregg could look over a list of names she'd compiled.

"What is this?"

"I put together the names of companies and individuals Jason has sued over the years. I was hoping you could put a star, or make a note in the margin, next to any company or person you think might be holding a grudge against Jason."

He chuckled. The tension had left his shoulders. "I take it you don't think Lacey and Jason are off sipping mai tais in the Bahamas?"

"No," she said. "I don't believe that. Not after speaking with Jason's mother."

"Ahh. She's lovely, isn't she?"

His sarcasm was thick. "It sounds as if maybe your name should be added to the list," Jessie said.

His gaze fell to the paper she'd handed him. "Maybe so."

"Why are you still working for the man?"

"That's a good question. Quite honestly, I was going to turn in my resignation on Monday. But Jason was a no-show, and here I was, the only employee at JHG with the authority to sign important documents, including paychecks, to keep the gears turning. There are budgets and schedules to be made, shopping centers being built as we speak, tenants that need guidance, and day-to-day fires to be put out. I couldn't just walk out and leave Sally, Kim, Gary, and all the others to fend for themselves."

———

Jessie and Gregg Fisher spent the next thirty minutes narrowing her list to the top five people who might have it in for Jason Geiger.

By the time Jessie left the building, she knew more about Jason Geiger than she cared to know. He wasn't just a bad boss; he was an awful human being who held no regard for others.

She also had one more name to put on her list: Gregg Fisher.

There was something about his carefully controlled tone and the way he hid his hands whenever he started to get twitchy that made her take notice.

THIRTY-THREE

Zee and Tobey had been sitting in Zee's car across the street from Dorothy and Ellis's house since 8:00 a.m. It was almost 10:00 a.m. Tobey had the day off and had agreed to come with her. She figured he must not have any idea what he was getting himself into; sitting in a car all day could get tedious quickly.

She'd spent the first hour explaining what she did and how the Jessie Cole Agency specialized in finding missing persons, including runaway teenagers and old friends their clients had lost touch with, or helping an individual search for their birth parents. Search engines and databases, some free and some paid for, were just the beginning of the process. The next step was contacting anyone who might be able to give them another piece of the puzzle. In a way, they were in the information business, she'd told him.

The last fifteen minutes had been filled with an awkward silence, so she decided to find out more about him by asking him a list of truth-or-dare questions she'd found on the internet. "Have you had a girlfriend before?" she blurted.

Tobey squirmed uncomfortably in his seat. "Of course."

"How many?"

"I don't know . . . three, maybe four."

He's too experienced for you. Get rid of him.

"Stop it," Zee told the voices. "Leave us alone."

Tobey frowned. "Excuse me?"

"Sorry. I told you about the voices, didn't I? Marion, Lucy, and Francis. I'm pretty much a four-for-the-price-of-one kind of deal." She laughed.

He didn't.

"Have you ever been cheated on?" she asked next.

"Not that I know of."

"Impressive. What is the most expensive thing you've ever stolen?"

This time he looked at her as if she'd lost her marbles, which, of course, she had. "I've never stolen anything. Why would I? Have you?"

"No," she lied. "Never. I was just testing you."

He seemed much different from the guy who served her tea at the coffee shop. Much more confident.

The silence hung in the air again. She couldn't handle it. "Who here would you most like to make out with?" she asked.

"You're the only one in the car," he pointed out with a smile.

"So that means me, right?"

His smile turned into a wide grin. "Do you want me to kiss you?" he finally asked. "Is that what this is all about?"

"Sort of. I mean, I am on the job and everything, but even if we happened to kiss, I could still see out of the corner of my eye if someone left the house." She gestured across the street. "I mean, the house we're watching is right there!"

She was ready to pucker up, but suddenly Tobey had questions of his own.

"What are you going to do if someone walks out that door?" he asked.

"Well," she said, "I'm really hoping they both leave because I want to sneak inside and have a look around."

"Isn't that illegal?"

"I don't know." Another lie. "Maybe. Probably. But definitely not if nobody finds out."

"I don't think you should risk breaking and entering."

"How else am I going to find out for sure if their daughter is alive?"

"What helpful information do you think you'd find inside the house?"

She shrugged. "I don't know. An address in their contact book?"

"If they've kept quiet about her being alive all these years, do you really think they would put their daughter's name and address right with all their other contacts?"

"Point taken," she said.

He's such a downer. Dump his ass.

Not yet, Zee thought. There was something about Tobey that made her insides do funny things. Besides, he hadn't kissed her yet. "Are you going to kiss me or not?" she asked, sounding more exasperated than intended.

He leaned forward and brushed his lips over hers. Much too soon, he pulled back to look at her.

Bummer.

That was it?

It was over before she had any time at all to figure out if she liked the kiss or had a chance to rate it on a scale of one to ten, but she quickly realized he wasn't finished when he leaned forward and kissed her again.

This kiss was firmer, deeper, longer, better.

She melted into him, and for the first time in forever, the voices in her head appeared to have been rendered speechless.

Thirty-Four

Ben walked through the littered alleyway where Jon Eberling had been found strangled to death twelve years ago. Not much noise came from the apartments on both sides. Traffic hummed nearby. He half expected to experience flashbacks after having one while talking to Renee Walker. But nothing happened.

Ben picked up some trash and tossed it into the dumpster.

Renee had thought it odd that Ben hadn't mentioned his altercation with Jon Eberling in the write-up he'd done at the time. Ben agreed. She thought he'd done so to protect her privacy. He might not remember much before his accident, but he'd read enough of his notes and old write-ups to know that he'd never been the kind of reporter to leave out such an important detail. Ian had told him many times over the years that Ben was known for his hard-core, tell-it-like-it-is reporting. So why hadn't he stated that Jon Eberling was responsible for putting his own girlfriend in the hospital? Thirty-nine stitches, broken cheek, fractured skull, bleeding from her ears. *Jesus.*

Ben's jaw hardened, and his fingers curled into fists. He looked down at his hands and forced them to relax. He took a breath. Had he dealt with the problem himself after Jon killed his mother's beloved cat and nearly killed Renee?

The only reason Ben could think of for omitting such an important detail would have been if he'd had something to hide. The thought caused his insides to tumble around like sopping-wet clothes in a dryer.

He glanced at his watch. He still had time before his scheduled meeting with Detective Grayson and Ren Howe. He was hungry. He climbed into his van and drove to a nearby coffee shop. He ordered soup, a sandwich, and water; found a table; and opened the file from twelve years ago. This time he read every word, starting with the police report and ending with the piece he'd written for the *Tribune*.

Apparently, heroin had been found in Jon's pocket. The police had been quick to surmise that Jon's death was a drug deal gone bad. Never mind that the autopsy revealed no sign of drugs in his system.

Ben had used drugs as the theme for the article he'd written back then, meticulously showing how heroin got into the state via a sophisticated distribution system that allowed the criminals to deliver the drug as if it were pizza.

His food was brought to the table. He ate while he read.

Just as Renee Walker had pointed out, there was nothing in the article he'd written about her having a relationship with Jon. Ben had stated that Jon didn't have any enemies. Friends and coworkers claimed that Jon Eberling had a temper, but overall, he was an okay guy.

It was noted on the police report: *"Also found in the victim's pocket was a diamond ring, most likely a wedding ring."*

That specific footnote gave Ben pause. He pulled out the notes he'd taken when he'd recently spoke to Gina Eberling, Jon's mother.

Just as he'd thought: she had told Ben—stated clearly, in fact—that the intruder had taken her wedding ring, left on the counter next to the sink.

Ben searched through the papers at the back of the file, which included the interview he'd done with Gina twelve years ago. No mention of her wedding ring being stolen. At the time she referred to the intruder as a "young man." If she hadn't been able to see his face due to a black mask, how would Gina have known if he was young or old?

She must have recognized something about the intruder and realized it might be her son . . . a certain mannerism? Or maybe she hadn't known for sure until Jon Eberling was found strangled and left in a dumpster with her wedding ring in his pocket. That's when she knew without a doubt that it was her son who had broken into her house and killed her beloved cat, Harry.

When Gina was called down to the morgue to identify her son, she never claimed the ring, and she never told the police or Ben what she knew.

Why?

Because despite what Jon had done, he was her son, and she didn't want anyone to know he'd killed her beloved pet. Maybe she hadn't believed it herself.

Thirty-Five

Again, Colin was the last one to enter the conference room where interviews were being conducted at the station. Ren Howe and Ben Morrison were already seated. "Thank you for coming in," Colin said to Ben.

Ben nodded.

"Can we get you anything?"

"No, thanks. I just ate."

Colin gestured at Ben's hand. "Hurt yourself?"

Ben held his gaze. "Broken glass in the garbage. Just a scratch."

"As you know, we have a few questions we'd like to ask you about Roger Willis."

Another nod.

"How well would you say you knew Roger Willis?"

"Well enough to know I didn't like him."

"You attacked him on the field after a soccer game. Is that right?"

"I grabbed his arm. He fell over. I wouldn't call it an attack."

"Fair enough. Why did you grab his arm?"

"I didn't like the way he was touching my daughter. He had his hand firmly planted on the back of her neck, and he was rubbing his thumb back and forth in what I considered to be an inappropriate manner."

Colin would have done the same thing, but he kept that thought to himself. "So you never attended any functions with Roger Willis outside of soccer?"

"Not a chance in hell."

Colin glanced at the notes he'd brought with him. "It says here that your daughter was good friends with Roger's daughter, Paige."

"I believe they were close."

"Did you ever drop her off at Roger's house?"

"Never. Quite frankly, my wife and I didn't see eye to eye when it came to Roger Willis. If it had been up to me, my daughter wouldn't have been allowed to go to the Willises' home."

"I guess it would be safe for me to assume that your wife was surprised to learn about his arrest?"

"Definitely. She still feels guilty."

"Why would she feel guilty?"

"For allowing Abigail to spend time at the Willises' house. She trusted Roger. She trusted his wife, too."

"Sharon."

Ben nodded.

"Sharon seems to think there are a few of you who held a grudge against Roger."

"I already told you I didn't like him."

"Sharon believes you and other parents would do whatever you must to make sure Roger Willis was never allowed near your daughters again."

"I'm not sure what you're implying."

Something told him that Ben knew exactly what he was implying. Colin scratched his forehead. "Never mind," he said. "Let's move on. Did you attend a meeting held by Gretchen Sullivan?"

"Yes. My wife and I were invited to her house to talk about bullying. As soon as the discussion turned to Roger Willis, we left."

"Why is that?"

"Because I wanted Roger Willis to be locked up for life, and damned if I was going to be a part of anything that might jeopardize that from happening."

"You believe in the justice system?"

"I do."

Ben Morrison was difficult to read. Colin wasn't sure if Ben was trying to purposefully suppress his emotions or if he was simply indifferent to what had happened to Roger Willis. Colin looked at Ren. "Do you have any questions for Mr. Morrison?"

Ren cleared his throat. "Do you mind telling us where you were between four a.m. and eight a.m. on Sunday?"

"My alarm went off at six a.m. I made coffee, ate some breakfast, then went to pick up a file I had left on my desk at work. After chatting with my boss, Ian Savage, I met my wife at eight in Rocklin to watch Abigail play soccer."

"You and your wife didn't drive to the game together?"

"No."

"Your boss works on the weekends?"

"More often than not."

Colin made a note, then looked at Ben. "What did the two of you talk about?"

Ben shrugged. "I don't recall. Weather, family—small talk."

"Is there anything you would like to add?" Colin asked.

"As a matter of fact, there is," Ben said. "What makes you think this wasn't a suicide?"

Ren shifted in his seat.

Colin smiled. "We're not saying it is or it isn't."

Ben had his own pad of paper and pen sitting neatly on the table in front of him. He kept making notes as if he were the one doing the interviewing. "I saw Paden White in the parking lot as I was coming in," Ben noted. "Who else have you talked to?"

Ren cleared his throat.

Colin stood. "I think our interview is over."

Thirty-Six

The short and explosive shrieks pierced her ears, bringing Lacey awake and to her feet so fast she bumped her head against the cement ceiling above.

She saw stars and felt an intense stab of pain pierce her skull. She put both hands to her head. *Fuck!*

What the hell was going on?

Thin lines of daylight coming through the slits in the vent made it possible for her to see Jason inside the dirt box dancing around like a madman.

If he could stop screaming and hold still, she might be able to figure out what was going on. She looked around and spotted two wrappers, torn bits of paper, and a tin can that was a little bigger than a pack of cigarettes. It took a closer look to see that he was covered in red ants.

"Take off your shirt," she told him, "and use it to wipe them off you."

It took forever for Jason to listen to what she was saying. Finally, he removed his shirt and used it to swat the ants as he hopped up and down. He tossed the shirt her way.

Lacey picked up her shoe, which was turning out to be a very useful tool, and smashed the ants that had fallen to the ground with it before shaking out the shirt so she could help slap the insects off him.

By the time all was said and done, Jason had stripped naked. It took a good thirty minutes to remove all the ants, and another twenty to pick them out of his hair. After eliminating every last ant, she shook out his clothes and tossed them to him.

The tin container, she noticed, had a lock on it. The key was gone, but she knew he'd used it to open the box. He must have been surprised to see all those ants.

Karma could be a real bitch, since she was sure he'd thought there must be food inside, and chances were good he hadn't planned on sharing.

She grabbed one of the wrappers that she'd spotted earlier and held it up so Jason could see it. "This looks like a candy wrapper." Her stomach grumbled.

Preoccupied with his wounds, Jason wouldn't make eye contact.

"After I gave you most of my food and water, you found two candy bars and ate them both?"

"I found them a few days ago and hid them. I was going to share them with you, but then you found another bag—"

"Stop," she said, throwing her arms wide. "I don't want to hear it. I don't care."

"I think I know who built this place," he said after a bit of awkward silence.

She said nothing. She no longer cared about his enemies or who had done this to them. He'd been right all along—what good would it do them, knowing the name of the person who had abducted them? Would it help them find a way out?

The answer was no.

Dropping the wrapper, shoulders slumped, she grabbed the shoe and went to work on the remaining nails.

She wanted to get the hell out of here.

He shut his laptop and fell back laughing. The red ants had been genius.

Watching the big-and-mighty president of JHG scream like a fucking hyena and dance like a clown was more enjoyable than he'd thought possible. The only thing that would have been better was if he'd come down hard on a nail and ended up with an infection.

He raked a hand through his hair as he collected himself.

His gaze fell on a wedding picture of him and his wife. When they'd first married, they had talked about having kids someday. Now she was gone.

Crazy, when he thought about it, because his wife was the only one who had tried to warn him about Jason Geiger. It only took one quick introduction for her to say she had a bad feeling about Geiger.

She'd told him to walk away. But he hadn't listened to her. And it was too late to do anything about it now. All because of one asshole named Jason Geiger.

THIRTY-SEVEN

Jessie spent most of Monday evening researching the top five people on the list she had titled "Jason Geiger's Enemies."

It was Tuesday morning. She was in her car, driving east toward Elk Grove. She felt more determined than ever to find Lacey. She felt a strange bond with the woman who had run away at such a young age, changed her name, and somehow managed to make a new life for herself. It broke Jessie's heart to think of Anne/Lacey cuffed and chained to her bed. Meeting her biological mother and seeing the place where she'd been held captive had made Jessie sick to her stomach. She would find Lacey and see that she got the inheritance she had coming to her.

Jessie was also curious to know if Lacey was happy. Did she have any idea that her husband was seeing another woman? Did she know Jason Geiger had a list of enemies a mile long?

So many questions.

She needed more time.

Jessie had been looking for missing persons long enough to know it wouldn't do any good to file a police report. Not unless the person or people missing were considered "vulnerable." That would include the elderly, a child under the age of thirteen, or someone suffering from a mental or physical condition. A victim of a crime would also cause the police to take immediate action, but she had no proof that either Lacey or Jason were in danger. Bottom line: people over the age of eighteen had no legal obligation to return home.

Brody Hoffman was the first person on her list of Jason's enemies. Brody's company, Hoffman Construction, went belly-up after JHG Properties sued Hoffman Construction for breach of contract, stating that the contractor had done work of unacceptably poor quality.

Brody Hoffman lived on what looked like a deserted farm in Elk Grove. The single-story ranch house sat front and center on the property. As she walked to the door, she stopped to listen. No dogs barking or pigs grunting. Just a faint whistling sound as the wind blew through tall rows of corn. In the far distance she saw cows grazing in the fields surrounding the house. She knocked on the door, waited, knocked again. She was about to walk around the side of the house to see if someone might be working in the back when the door opened.

She knew from the research she'd done that he was forty-six years old. He looked closer to fifty-six. He was short and on the stocky side. His hair was gray. Two deep lines made twin rivers between narrow eyes. "Are you Brody Hoffman?"

"Yes, ma'am."

"My name is Jessie Cole. I'm a private investigator looking for Jason Geiger."

He shook his head. "Name doesn't ring any bells."

"Jason Geiger owns JHG Properties. His company sued Hoffman Construction five years ago."

"Ahh . . . JHG Properties. Now that definitely rings a bell or two."

"I thought it might." She tried to look over his shoulder into his house. "If I'm not interrupting anything, I was hoping I could come in and ask you a few questions."

He hesitated.

"It won't take long. I promise."

Reluctantly, he allowed her inside. As she followed him toward the back of the house, she reached into her purse and turned on the recorder she'd put in the front pocket.

He brought her to the kitchen. The Formica counters had seen better days. The sink was filled with dirty dishes. He took a seat at a small, deeply scarred wooden table in the kitchen nook and gestured for her to do the same. He didn't offer her anything to drink, just crossed his arms, making it clear she needed to get on with it.

Jessie pulled out her notebook, skimmed the first page, and said, "It looks like the trial between your company and JHG went on for months."

"It did."

Jessie read on. "The jury agreed with JHG, and it cost you a lot of time and money."

"I'll save you some time. I lost everything: my business, my home in Sacramento, my respect, and my dignity. My wife left me, too. It was all too much for her. But my story probably ends better than most." He gestured through the window toward the fields she'd seen earlier. Beyond the cornfields, she saw a tractor and a backhoe. "I found this place for cheap," he told her. "Fifty acres with hilltop views and lots of small ponds. The cattle keep the roof over my head and food on the table. The equipment out there is what's left over from when I was running Hoffman Construction. I rent it out for a good price, and that keeps the utilities paid."

"Are the cattle used for beef?" she asked, mostly to put him at ease.

"Oh, no. The cattle don't belong to me. I get paid to let them graze. It's a win-win since having them on my land makes for a healthier pasture if I ever decide to grow corn or alfalfa."

While Jessie wrote in her notepad, he asked, "Why are you here?"

She flipped to the next page of her notepad, purposefully displaying the list of names she'd been compiling in hopes of getting a reaction. "Jason and his wife have been missing for a week now and—"

"Yeah, so?" he asked, cutting her off. Leaning forward, he took a closer look at the names. He snorted. "Looks to me like you have a long list of people with grievances against Jason Geiger."

"Does that surprise you?"

"Do I look surprised?"

"No."

"You're grasping for straws, lady."

Her cheeks warmed.

"I don't mean to be rude," he said, "but do you really think I, or any of these people on your list, would tell you if they did something to Jason Geiger?"

That was a very good question, one she didn't plan on answering honestly. Fifty percent of the work she did included talking to people, getting into their heads, reading them. She wanted to see how hard Brody Hoffman would work to deflect any guilt from himself. She sighed. "He doesn't seem to have a lot of friends, so I decided to talk to people like you, people who filed complaints against JHG, people who might be able to tell me more about Jason Geiger."

"He's ruthless. Does that help you?" He glanced at the clock. "Listen, I can't help you."

"You can't, or you won't?"

"Maybe both. I haven't seen that man since I completed his shopping center in Roseville. I don't know where he is or what he does in his free time. I never once saw or met his wife, Lacey." He came to his feet. "I'm going to have to ask you to leave."

She sighed. "Do you mind if I use your restroom?"

Frowning, he gestured to the hallway close to the front door. "Have at it."

Jessie tucked her pad into her purse.

There was a bedroom next to the bathroom. Glancing over her shoulder to make sure he wasn't watching her, she quickly poked her head inside the room. The bed had not been made. A pile of clothes filled an armchair in the corner of the room. The top of the dresser was packed with knickknacks. The closet doors were closed.

Heavy footfalls prompted her to hurry back the way she came. As quietly as possible, she shut the bathroom door, flushed the toilet, and washed her hands. When she came out of the bathroom, he was standing a foot away, his arms crossed.

He followed her to the entryway and held the door open for her, closing it behind her before she had a chance to thank him for his time.

Gravel crunched beneath her shoes as she walked to the car. The air was chilly, prompting her to pull her sweater up close to her ears. Brody Hoffman, she decided, seemed a bit off but not exactly unstable. He was definitely bitter about his interaction with Jason Geiger, but who wouldn't be?

A cat meowed. She spotted the animal huddled beneath a beat-up car with a broken window and a flat tire. Once she was inside her car, she used the navigator to log in the address to an apartment building on Florin Road.

Number two on the list was Ashton Greer. When Jason first started his business, Ashton was Jason's mentor and partner. After the first five years, JHG Properties took off, the money was pouring in, and Jason fired Ashton unexpectedly and without notice, cutting him out of a promised cut of 25 percent of the company.

Ashton sued Jason.

Jason hired a team of experienced lawyers and won.

Forty minutes later, Jessie knocked on the apartment door, hoping to find Ashton at home. The building was small and quaint, with only seven units as far as she could tell.

"Who is it?" a woman asked from inside without opening the door.

Jessie introduced herself, told her why she was there.

The woman who opened the door had a friendly face. She was short with hunched shoulders. She smiled and offered Jessie her hand. "I'm Wendy, Ashton's wife. Did you say Jason Geiger was missing?"

"Yes."

"Come inside."

The apartment was small but tidy. "Is Ashton at home?" Jessie asked.

"Oh, no. He's working."

"What does he do?"

"He's a teacher at Florin High School. The kids love him." She waved Jessie into the kitchen. "What can I get you?"

"I'm fine. Thanks." Jessie followed her into the living room and took a seat, as instructed.

"So, what can I do for you? I'm not sure why you're here, but do you think something bad might have happened to Jason?"

Jessie explained the situation, beginning with her search for Lacey and ending with the fact that nobody had seen Jason or Lacey in more than a week.

"So why come here to see Ashton?" Wendy asked, clearly perplexed. "We haven't seen Jason in years."

"I talked to Jason's parents and the manager at JHG, Gregg Fisher."

She laughed. "Is Gregg still working there?"

"He is," Jessie said. "Nobody has any idea where the Geigers might have gone, so I made a list of anyone who might hold a grudge against Jason and—"

Wendy reached for the paper. "Can I see that?"

Jessie obliged.

Wendy chuckled as she looked over the names. "It's worse than I thought. If someone was going to do away with Jason, I don't think they would drag his wife into it, do you?"

"It depends on how angry they were," Jessie said. "Life is often stranger than fiction."

Wendy handed the list back to Jessie. "If Ashton wanted that man dead, Jason Geiger would have gone missing years ago."

"From everything I've read about Jason, the articles and interviews he did when he was first starting out, I sensed he was closest to Ashton.

I was hoping your husband might be able to tell me more about Jason when they first met. For instance, was he always so ruthless?"

"I don't think so. In my opinion, Jason Geiger made too much money too fast, and it went to his head. Ego can be a real bitch. Money, too. It gave him power, and he didn't know how to handle it. Jason became suspicious of people. He thought everyone was trying to rip him off."

She rubbed her shoulder as if it pained her. "It's that simple, really. After Jason let Ashton go and refused to pay him what he owed, Ashton felt he had no choice but to take him to court. Unfortunately, it was a verbal agreement between the two men, and it only took a few hours for the jury to decide on Jason's behalf."

"So Jason literally transformed because of greed?"

She nodded. "I think so. If you ever get to meet Jason Geiger—a thrill, I'm telling you—you'll see a great con artist in action. He lies, cheats, and fools people into thinking that if they work for him, they'll be making the deal of the century, when in fact Jason is the one who'll be raking in the money. He's good at taking advantage of other people's weaknesses. That man does not have a conscience."

When Jessie left the apartment, she felt confident that Wendy and Ashton Greer knew nothing of Jason's whereabouts and therefore crossed their names off the list.

By the end of the day, Jessie had talked to five people who had all been screwed over royally by Jason Geiger. Not one of them had any clue where Jason and Lacey might have gone. Most of them didn't care.

Tomorrow, she decided, she would change the direction of her investigation, since she was getting nowhere fast. The notion that one of Jason's many enemies might have kidnapped him and his wife, or harmed them in any way, was a bit over the top, but it had been worth a shot.

It was time to talk to Jason's girlfriend, Chaya Cohen.

The problem was, Chaya was married. That wouldn't be too big of a deal if she wasn't married to an officer at the Sacramento PD.

She needed to tread lightly.

Thirty-Eight

Colin entered the medical examiner's lab and talked to the woman at the front desk. He was here to talk to Brenda Parsons about the Willis case. Since it was going to take another day or two, at least, to get a warrant to search Paden White's home, he figured he'd make good use of his time. Ren would be spending the day visiting local hardware stores to watch video footage and see if any person of interest had recently purchased rope.

"Brenda's waiting for you," the woman said. "Go right in."

He didn't need to be told where to go. He and Brenda had been working together for years. He entered the room at the end of the hallway. The unpleasant smell of a refrigerated-yet-decomposed body greeted him. After the first wave passed by, he was fine.

Brenda smiled and pointed at the gloves by the door. "Glad you made it. I want to show you something."

He put on shoe and hair coverings and slipped on disposable gloves as he crossed the room to where she stood next to the corpse lying on the steel table in the center of the room.

Using a tongue depressor, she pointed out two distinct marks that looked like circles, slightly larger than a quarter, both close to the Adam's apple and partially overlapping the distorted and purplish-red ring made by the rope from which he'd hung.

"What are those?" Colin asked.

"Thumbprints. This is the first time since I've been practicing that I was able to develop prints from a dead body."

He perked up. "How is that possible?"

"It rarely is. Humidity is often a factor when it comes to using techniques required to process fingerprints from the skin. In this case, though, I believe it was the rope that helped protect the prints while moving the body. The rope was left in place until the body was taken from the bag. Once the rope was removed, and because I knew you wanted the case handled as a homicide, I used cyanoacrylate—also known as superglue," she said. "After the glue was heated to vapor form, it affixed to the residue of the fingerprint. I was able to get photographs, but the bad news is that these prints are not reliable."

"And the good news?"

"Someone strangled Roger Willis," Brenda said matter-of-factly. "And whoever did it staged the scene to make it look like suicide. In my opinion, you're dealing with a homicide."

Ten minutes later, back in his car, Colin sifted through pictures from the crime scene. Although he was keeping a close eye on the three people Sharon Willis had personally named, he wasn't ruling out the possibility of more names being added to the list of people he might want to talk to.

Gretchen Sullivan, Paden White, and Ben Morrison.

He sat there and stared at the photo of Willis dangling slack-mouthed from the tree. The rope had been wrapped around the tree branch three times before it was knotted.

He looked over the copy of the report Brenda Parsons had just given him. Roger Willis weighed 170 pounds. Gretchen Sullivan was a sturdy woman, to be sure. She had made it clear she didn't want Roger Willis anywhere near her child. But was she capable of strangling the man, hauling him into her car, and hanging him? She would have had to climb a tree with heavy rope in tow and have the strength to pull 170 pounds of deadweight high off the ground.

No way.

As far as he was concerned, Gretchen was not a suspect. But he would leave her on the list of persons of interest for now. She might not be strong enough to pick up Willis, but what was to stop her from getting help from a friend?

And what about Paden White? He worked many hours and had limited free time, but he and his family had spent time with Roger Willis on the weekends, away from the soccer field. Paden White had trusted the soccer coach enough to have allowed his daughter to spend time at his house and a myriad of other places, including a trip to the theater for an afternoon of team bonding.

The notion of having a trusted friend inappropriately touch his eleven-year-old daughter would be a hard pill to swallow.

Paden White definitely had motive.

He was also in good shape. Lifting a 170-pound man would be doable. Paden had also shown his aggressive nature when he attacked Roger Willis in the parking lot in front of plenty of witnesses.

Colin examined the close-up pictures of the thumbprints that looked like two round bruises. It wasn't easy to strangle a man with your bare hands, but Ben Morrison had proved himself quite capable of that when he saved Jessie and others from the Heartless Killer. Why hadn't Ben Morrison stopped before killing the man? He could have found a way to restrain the man as he waited for the police to arrive.

But that was then, and this is now.

Stick to the case at hand, he reminded himself.

Ben had strangled a man before. There was no reason for Colin to think he wouldn't be capable of doing it again.

Ben was a few years older than Paden. Ben was also in pretty good shape. He had attacked Roger Willis on the soccer field in front of many witnesses. But did he have a motive for killing Roger Willis?

Colin scratched the side of his face as he examined the close-up of the pants Roger Willis had been wearing. Both areas around the knees were stained with streaks of grass. And there was the vibrant white blossom found in Willis's hair. It was distinct. He would have to do a drive-by—see if Gretchen, Paden, or Ben had the same shrub growing in their yards.

Next were alibis. Gretchen had said she'd been asleep. She also had two children.

Paden had also said he was asleep, but he'd lied about his family being home.

Ben Morrison had been out and about between four and eight, picking something up from work where he supposedly chatted with his boss.

All worth checking out.

THIRTY-NINE

Jessie spent the morning sitting in her car, waiting for Chaya Cohen's husband to leave for work so she could ring the doorbell and hopefully have a chance to chat with Chaya in private. If she *was* having an affair with Jason, the odds were against her wanting to talk to Jessie. Maybe the woman had known that Jason was taking Lacey to dinner for their anniversary, so she followed them. Seeing the two of them together could have flipped a switch, prompting Chaya to kill them both. Jealousy could be a very dangerous emotion.

The front door opened at nine o'clock. Officer Cohen walked out the door, jumped into his cruiser, and left the house. Before Jessie could get out of the car, the door opened again, and Chaya emerged. She was tall and slender with long, wavy hair and a perfect hourglass shape.

Jessie considered jumping out of the car and approaching Chaya, but something niggled at her, stopping her from making a move. Where was the woman off to? Maybe Chaya Cohen would lead Jessie straight to Jason Geiger.

It wasn't long before Jessie merged onto the street behind Chaya, careful to stay far enough back so as not to be seen.

Thirty-five minutes later, Jessie pulled into the Nordstrom parking lot at the Westfield Galleria mall in Roseville and let out a groan. Unless Jason was hiding out in a dressing room inside, this wasn't the place she wanted to be right now. Just in case Chaya and Jason had set up a place to rendezvous, Jessie followed Chaya across the parking lot and inside the building. The department store had opened at 10:00 a.m. And they were having a big sale, which meant more people. Not a bad thing, since it meant Jessie might not stand out.

As she watched the woman, it became clear right away that this wasn't about meeting up with Jason Geiger. This was about doing some serious shopping. While Chaya tried on designer clothes, Jessie hung out in the lingerie department where she could keep an eye on the woman.

If Jessie had known she would be going to the mall, she might have worn something other than sneakers, jeans, and a plaid button-down shirt. It was comfortable but not exactly an outfit suited for high-end clothes shopping.

"Can I help you?"

Jessie looked at the employee and smiled. "No, thanks. I'm just browsing." She thought of Colin. Maybe she should surprise him.

"We have a great sale on shapewear and loungewear today."

"What about something a little more risqué?" Jessie asked.

"I've got just the thing."

After the sales clerk ran off, Jessie turned back the other way. *Damn.* Chaya was no longer in the same area where Jessie had last seen her.

Jessie crossed the wide aisle between the two departments and walked through the area where Chaya had just been. Another employee asked her if she needed help. Jessie politely turned her down and continued on.

After a quick stroll through the other departments, she started back to the parking lot. Chaya's car was still there. Go back inside the mall, or wait in the car? She opted for the latter.

An hour and a half later, Chaya was putting her bags in the trunk of her car when Jessie approached her. "My name is Jessie Cole. I'm a private investigator, and I was told that you might know where I can find Jason Geiger."

"Who told you that?"

"I don't recall."

Chaya slid her Prada sunglasses down her nose so she could get a better look at Jessie. Her brown-eyed gaze roamed over her, starting at the top of Jessie's head and working its way down to her sneakers. Sunglasses back in place, she asked, "Did you go to his house and knock on his door?"

"I did. Nobody has seen Jason or Lacey in over a week. The neighbor across the street is collecting their mail. I also went to his work. Same thing. Nobody has seen him. I wouldn't bother you if it wasn't urgent that I locate him and his wife, Lacey."

She didn't look concerned. "What could possibly be so urgent?"

"Lacey's grandmother passed away and left her something."

"Oh," she said as she pushed the button that prompted the trunk to close automatically. "I'm sure she'll be thrilled to find out whenever they return." She left Jessie's side and opened her car door.

Her grandmother died, Jessie thought but didn't say. Most people would be saddened by the news, not thrilled. Regardless, Jessie closed the distance between them and pressed on. "Jason isn't answering his phone. Doesn't that worry you?"

"Why would it?"

Damn. Jessie hadn't wanted to spell it out, but her hand was being forced. "I was told that you and Jason were spending time alone with each other. If there is any truth to that, if you care about him at all, I would think you might want to help me find him. I'm afraid Jason and Lacey could be in danger."

Chaya stiffened. "In danger? Why?"

"Because Jason has pissed a few people off over the years." Jessie tilted her head in wonder. "Maybe someone's husband got wind of an affair. Or maybe you were upset after discovering that Jason was taking his wife out to dinner to celebrate their anniversary?"

"Oh, please," she said in a bored drawl.

"Did you know Jason was taking his wife out last Friday night?"

Chaya glanced around as if to make sure nobody was close enough to hear what she was going to say. "I don't think you realize how much trouble you could be in . . . stalking me . . . accusing me of adultery. Jason and Lacey are my neighbors, nothing more. Now get away from me before I call the police and have you arrested."

Jessie watched her climb into her car, start the engine, and drive away.

Shit.

FORTY

Zee hated hospitals. They smelled funny. Too many sick people. She stopped at the information desk in the lobby and asked the woman sitting there where she could find Penny Snyder's father, Nathaniel Snyder.

After that, she went to the gift shop and bought him a cactus and a stuffed animal—a kitty with wiry whiskers and stripes.

She checked in at the nurses' station, told them she was a good friend, and headed straight for his room. She had no idea it would be that easy.

Nathaniel Snyder did not look well. There were tubes running from his arms to the machines behind the hospital bed. He also had tubes in his nose. His skin was yellow, and his breathing was shallow. His eyes were closed. The machines beeped softly around him. There were tubes running from his arms to machines.

She had been reading up on the man, digging deep and using every database she could get her hands on to find information on him. She knew he once had loving parents who had died in a car crash when he turned eighteen. Leaving his two brothers with an aunt, he joined the army. When he returned home, he'd moved into an apartment with his youngest brother and cared for him until he died of AIDS. Two years later, he'd lost his other brother to cancer. He'd gotten a job at a food market, and over the years he worked his way up from checker to produce manager and finally, head manager of the entire store.

It was in the bakery where he'd met Arlene and fallen in love, madly in love.

But sometimes love could be fleeting.

Or dangerous. Or just plain fucked-up. After his wife disappeared, Nathaniel's in-laws had testified that he'd beaten Arlene, and she'd been afraid for her life.

Arlene had never reported domestic violence to the police. Neighbors never called 9-1-1. But it was the bloodstain in the trunk that most believed was the reason Nathaniel was found guilty.

Nathaniel stirred.

Zee set the cactus and the stuffed animal on the windowsill, then went to stand at the side of his bed. His eyes were still closed, but she decided to talk to him anyway. "I'm sorry to bother you, Mr. Snyder, but I'm trying to find Arlene Snyder, and I thought maybe, just maybe, you know more than you've been letting on."

His finger twitched.

You were right! He knows something.

His finger hardly moved. Don't be stupid. If he knew where his wife was, he would have told the jury in the courtroom and saved himself all those years in the slammer.

Ignoring the voices, Zee said, "I work for a well-known private investigator, and this is my first missing person's case. I've been reading up on you. Does your daughter have any idea what an amazing man you are? You have sacrificed so much. Even before I started my research on you, I sort of knew you didn't do it—you know—kill your wife."

All five fingers moved this time. He looked as if he was heavily medicated, but he could hear her.

"Penny loves you very much. She found your love letters and pictures, and she thinks you're innocent, too. She wants to find her mom and prove you didn't kill her."

His head moved just enough to make Zee think he was trying to shake his head no.

"I just don't get it. You told everyone you didn't kill her, but why didn't you get on that stand and tell everyone what you knew?"

Deafening silence.

"I hope you don't die in this place. It smells. Get better so you can come home and let Penny take care of you, just as you took care of your brothers. Maybe then you could tell her the truth and tell me why you allowed them to take you away." Zee started toward the exit. She was at the door when she heard him say something. Zee hurried back to the side of his bed where she stared at him for a long moment. "I asked you why you let them take you away and lock you up, and you answered me, didn't you?"

She waited.

More silence.

Again she turned, walking back to the door. There it was again. Only this time she heard it loud and clear. He'd said one word. *Love.* He'd done it for love.

As Zee made her way to the elevator and out of the hospital, she tried to figure out what Nathaniel had been trying to say. Did he know where his wife had run off to? Zee couldn't help but think he loved her so much he didn't want the world to find her and judge her. Had he been willing to give up his daughter and waste away in a cell in the name of love?

It made no sense, and yet Zee knew that her dad would do something stupid like that if he thought it would save her in any way. He would sacrifice his life and his happiness for her. It was a parent thing. She was pretty lucky, now that she thought about it.

FORTY-ONE

Jessie glanced at the time as she drove slowly by the house belonging to Olof Hagnevik in North Natomas. It was 2:33 p.m. After the debacle with Chaya Cohen, Jessie had returned to her office to continue research-ing the list of names of people who might have it out for Jason Geiger.

One name stood out above all the others: Olof Hagnevik.

Like Brody Hoffman, Olof Hagnevik owned a construction com-pany that had done the majority of work on a shopping center in the city of Lincoln. That was only two years ago. Upon completion, Olof submitted the final bill and never got paid. He was owed more than $200,000.

That had begun the demise of the Olof Hagnevik Company and a beautiful friendship.

Confident he could recover the money owed him, Olof Hagnevik took Jason to court. By then JHG and its plethora of lawyers were like a well-oiled machine when it came to defending themselves in court and getting away with not paying people they owed.

After reading the court transcript, *Hagnevik vs. JHG*, Jessie had gone back to other cases where JHG had refused to pay. To date, dozens of suits had been filed against Jason Geiger and his company. There were also liens and judgments against JHG because of failure to pay. It was becoming clear to Jessie that JHG had a system. Jason's team of lawyers would finan-cially overpower smaller companies, keeping them in court and draining their resources until the people or the company that was owed money either settled for much less or gave up getting paid altogether.

Jessie pulled to the curb and shut off the engine. Sitting in the middle of a big lot, at least five acres, was a one-story house. The front window was cracked. Shingles were missing from the roof.

She grabbed her purse and case file and climbed out of the car. The stairs to the porch creaked under her weight. Seconds after rapping her knuckles against the door, it opened.

He looked just like the photos she'd seen online. Olof Hagnevik had a smooth, hairless scalp. More than six feet tall, he towered over her. If he wasn't built like a boxer, she might have felt a little more at ease.

Much like Chaya Cohen had done, he let his gaze wander. Chaya had looked her over as if to demean and humiliate her. This guy was just plain intimidating. Unlike Chaya, he appeared to like what he saw despite her casual wear.

"My name is Jessie Cole. I'm a private investigator, and I'm looking for Jason Geiger and his wife."

"Jason Geiger," he said in a voice so deep it vibrated. "I was sort of hoping I would never hear that name again."

"His wife, Lacey Geiger, is actually the person I need to find. The last time she was seen, she was with Jason, so I'm talking to friends, family, people who—"

"Who were fucked in the ass by him?"

She swallowed the lump in her throat. "Sorry about what happened. I read the transcript from the hearing. You and Jason used to be good friends, is that right?"

He said nothing. Just stared at her.

"You knew him back in college, spent time with him before his business took off. He's not well liked—"

That got a laugh.

"I've talked to his neighbor, and mother, and people at his work, but I'm getting nowhere fast. I thought maybe—"

"Maybe I had something to do with his disappearance?"

She blushed. He was right about that, but it was in her best interest to play it cool. "No. Actually, I was hoping you would know things about Jason that might help me find him. For instance, did he have a favorite place he liked to go to unwind?"

His silence made her one-sided conversation awkward. "Like I said, he was with his wife." Jessie plodded along. "They were seen leaving for dinner, but that was it. Nobody has seen either one of them since. I figured it wouldn't hurt to talk to you."

He opened the door wider and gestured for her to come inside. His hands and work boots were caked with dirt.

It was in that moment she realized she'd left her gun in the glove compartment.

Damn. She looked over her shoulder toward her car parked at the curb. She still hadn't gotten used to keeping her gun with her at all times.

"Coming in, or not?"

It wasn't his obvious strength that intimidated her. It was his calm, emotionless demeanor that made her feel as if he were daring her to enter his lair.

She took the dare and stepped inside.

Not only did he shut the door, he also locked it. "That way," he said, gesturing to a room she couldn't yet see. She could feel his breath on the top of her head as she walked through a narrow hall. The place was cluttered, dirty.

She thought about making an excuse along with a quick exit. Instead, she entered the family room and took a seat when he pointed to the couch. Beer cans were scattered across the tables and floor.

She pulled out her notebook and pen, relieved when he took a seat in his recliner. "So, what do you want to know?" he asked.

"Years ago," Jessie said, "you and Jason were friends. If he had gone missing at that time, I am assuming you would have wanted him to be found. Is there anywhere—a cabin, a camping ground, a friend's house—that you would think he might have gone to?"

"Nope. All he cared about was making money."

"He didn't play poker with the guys or meet you at a bar for drinks?"

"Nope." Olof rubbed his forehead. "I don't think you understand. Nobody wanted to be around the guy. Jason is an asshole. Period."

"Can you elaborate?"

Olof chuckled. "Sure. Jason never made any effort to understand or empathize with others. He acted only in his own self-interest. He was cruel. He liked to demean people. He only dated women with low self-esteem so he could easily control them. He never cared about anyone but himself."

"So why did you remain friends for so long?"

"Because we were pals. No matter how he treated others, I never for a second thought he would pull that shit on me." He rubbed a large hand over his smooth, shiny head. "He fucked me over good, though. I never saw it coming."

"Did you know Lacey?" she asked next.

"Yeah, sure. Seemed like a nice enough girl. She fit the bill, as I just described."

"Low self-esteem?"

"That's right. A people pleaser with no confidence." Olof's jaw hardened. "If Jason was standing here right now," he said, "do you know what I would do?"

She shook her head. "What?"

"I would kill him."

Jessie's stomach quivered.

A dog barked.

Jessie jumped to her feet.

Olof stood and walked around his chair to the sliding door, opening it wide. The backyard was nothing but a wide expanse of tall green grass and foxtail.

The German shepherd rushed inside and gave Jessie a good sniffing before trotting back to Olof.

Jessie gestured toward the piles of dirt outside. "Looks like I caught you in the middle of a project."

"Yep. I'm fixing a failed septic system." He scratched his jaw. "I don't know what to say about Jason and Lacey. If I knew where he might have gone off to, I would tell you."

Jessie nodded.

"My guess," he added, "is that Jason is either running from the law or he finally pissed off the wrong guy."

"Meaning?"

"I think you know what I mean." He gave her a tight smile. "I should get back to work. You can let yourself out?"

"Sure. Thanks."

He shut the slider and then trudged through the grass, his dog at his side. She didn't know what to think about Olof Hagnevik. Was he the "wrong guy" who Jason had pissed off?

Had Olof learned from the best and finally gotten his revenge?

On the drive back to her office, something gnawed at Jessie. It wasn't her talk with Olof Hagnevik that replayed over and over in her mind. Instead, she kept thinking about her conversation with Brody Hoffman, top man on Jason's list of enemies. Although there was nothing particularly threatening about Hoffman, not at all intimidating like Olof Hagnevik, Hoffman had an unnatural stillness about him. But that wasn't the only thing that bothered her. He was no longer married, and yet she was certain she'd seen a purse sticking out from under a pile of clothes on the chair in the bedroom when she'd poked her head inside.

It was never a good thing to assume, though. He could have a sister or a girlfriend.

And yet nothing in the house had hinted at even a touch of femininity.

She pulled to the side of the road, dug around inside her purse for her recorder that she'd had playing during her visit with Brody

Hoffman. She rewound the tape to the beginning, hit "Play," then merged back onto the main road, listening while she drove.

She was nearing Sacramento when she heard him say, "I never once saw or met his wife, Lacey. I'm going to have to ask you to leave."

Her heart skipped a beat.

Again, she pulled over and rewound the tape.

"I never once saw or met his wife, Lacey. I'm going to have to ask you to leave."

How did he know her name was Lacey if he'd never met her? Maybe Jason had talked about Lacey when they worked together. But that was years ago.

She looked through previous addresses on her navigator and tapped the one in Elk Grove. It would take her thirty-five minutes to get to Brody Hoffman's residence.

As she merged back onto the road, she considered all her options. Talk to him again—press him for answers, find a way to get back into that bedroom and see if the purse was still there—or call for help.

She sighed. It was too soon to call the police since she had zero proof that Brody Hoffman had anything at all to do with Jason and Lacey's disappearance. They would shrug her off if she tried.

No missing person's report.

No worried friends or family members.

One worried neighbor and an investigator with news for Lacey Geiger wouldn't cut it. She would go with her first option and talk to Brody Hoffman a second time, see if she could get him to squirm.

With time to spare on the long drive, she called Zee to get an update on the Arlene Snyder case.

No answer.

Next, she tried Colin. She hadn't heard from him in days.

Again, no answer.

Where was everyone?

Forty-Two

Fuck! He couldn't stop thinking about the nosy investigator.

What was her name?

Pushing himself from the couch, he started looking around the house. There it was. On the kitchen counter. Her business card: Jessie Cole Detective Agency.

Back at his computer in the family room, next to his gaming video, he plopped down on the couch and entered the address to her website. It popped up right away. Clean and simple. Easy to navigate. Apparently, her specialty was finding missing persons.

On his feet again, he paced the floor. His mind swirled with speculation. His head throbbed.

After a while he picked up the remote, turned on the television, and flipped through the local news channels. Not one anchor mentioned anything about Jason Geiger and his wife being missing.

If they had been reported missing, wouldn't it be on the news?

No way. Ridiculous. It wasn't as if Jason Geiger was the mayor or anything. Nobody even liked the guy.

He'd been planning his revenge on Jason Geiger for years. No fucking way was he going to let a stupid little investigator like Jessie Cole screw everything up for him.

Nothing made any sense. Her list of names had been long. She'd simply lucked out in coming to see him. That had to be it. He couldn't think of any reason why he would have been singled out of so many disgruntled people.

Was Jessie Cole lucky? Or incredibly clever?

Back in front of his computer, he did a search on her name. *Jesus.* She was everywhere. Fucking pain in the ass. "Ahh," he said when he realized she was the investigator who had identified and helped take down the Heartless Killer. He tapped away at the keyboard. She had also shot a lawyer in a public park in Midtown. She was trigger-happy, and because of it, her gun license had been revoked. Good to know.

His leg bounced up and down as he tried to think.

He should have gotten rid of her while he had the chance.

What had he been thinking, allowing her inside?

She was pushy. She hadn't given him a chance to say no.

A thought struck him, and he jumped up. His heart raced as he ran around the house, looking underneath lampshades and tables, searching for listening devices or cameras.

Investigators could be tricky. He should know. He'd spent years doing his own investigative work on Jason Geiger. He was exhausted by the time he'd searched the entire house. He sat down. It took him a few minutes to calm himself.

Wait a minute, he thought to himself. He got up, walked across the room, and opened the front door. The cops would have come already if the investigator had been onto him.

He was fine. Everything was fine.

FORTY-THREE

The building that housed the *Sacramento Tribune* looked to Colin like nothing more than a cement block with windows. He wondered how much longer the newspaper would last in the growing digital age.

Ian Savage, the publisher, had agreed to meet with him this morning to talk about the death of Roger Willis. Savage hadn't pressed for details. If he had, Colin wanted to be sure his bias toward Ian's top crime reporter was not apparent.

As far as Colin was concerned, there was a good chance Ben Morrison had killed Roger Willis. For now, though, he'd keep that tidbit to himself. Even if Morrison admitted he'd killed Roger Willis, Colin would still need solid physical evidence to support his confession. It was imperative that Colin kept his dislike for Morrison in check while he weighed the facts. They had a pool of potential suspects, and each needed to be looked at closely. A lot of the work Colin did was not particularly exciting, let alone interesting, but no matter what, it was his responsibility to make sure his team was on the right side of the law all the way to the end.

He climbed out from behind the wheel of his car, shut the door, and headed across the parking lot. Up ahead, he spotted Ben Morrison getting out of his van. He had a parking spot up front, closer to the building. Ben saw him coming and waited for him to approach. Together they walked side by side toward the main entrance.

"What are you doing here?" Ben asked.

"Just dotting the *i*'s and crossing the *t*'s."

"Checking my alibi, are you?"

"It's all part of the process."

"Let's be straight with one another," Ben said as they walked. "You had a problem with me even before I contacted Jessie about her sister."

Colin stopped a few steps away from the entry door. "Okay, since you've gone there. Why were you in the car with Sophie on the night she died?"

"I wish I knew."

"I bet you do."

"That's the problem with you, Grayson. You can't handle the truth even when it's staring right at you. Whether you want to believe it or not, I don't remember anything before the accident. I don't know why I was in that car with Sophie Cole." There was a short pause before Ben added, "I get it, though. In your attempt to protect Jessie, you've pegged me as the bad guy. Bottom line: I think you have a tendency to take everything I do personally."

For Jessie's sake, Colin had been trying to see Ben Morrison in a different light—an innocent, guiltless light. But it wasn't easy for Colin to do. What Ben didn't understand was that his estimation of Ben was a gut feeling, a vibration, good old intuition. And Colin felt it every single time he was around him. "What about the write-up you did about police becoming more concerned about drugs than homicides?" Colin asked. "I shouldn't take that personally?"

"I stand by what I wrote. The war on drugs hurt everyone. It became so easy for police officers to meet their arrest quota by busting people for possession and earning overtime by making all those court appearances. How can you investigate a crime if you're making a drug bust or stuck in court?" Ben exhaled. "And I get that homicides are expensive and time consuming. That's life and that's the truth, so no, it's not personal."

Colin started walking again, heading for the entrance.

"So you really are here to check on me?" Ben asked as he opened the door and held it there.

"I thought we cleared that up two minutes ago. It's nothing personal, Ben. Just like you, I'm only doing my job." Colin walked off. He could feel Morrison's eyes burning a hole in the back of his head as he continued on toward Ian Savage's office.

Colin's meeting with Ian was short and sweet. Ian was an affable man with a dry sense of humor. Colin wasn't too surprised by how quick Ian was to defend his best reporter. But he was taken aback by Ian's fondness for the man. In a matter of minutes, he made it clear that Ben Morrison was not only a brilliant reporter but also like a son to him.

On his way out of the building, his phone buzzed. He picked up the call.

"Ren here. Good news. I'm holding the warrant to search Paden White's house in my hot little hand. What are you doing right now?"

"Meet me at White's residence in ten minutes," Colin told him.

"See you there."

Colin ended the call. As much as he didn't like Morrison, by no means did he want to arrest the wrong man. He would follow the evidence and see where it led him.

FORTY-FOUR

Once again Zee found herself parked across the street from Arlene Snyder's parents' home. Her original plan for today was to have a chat with Pam Carr, one of Arlene's friends from way back. But she couldn't stop thinking about what Ellis Kash had said about his daughter when they were at the casino: *She's not getting any of this!* And later, *She'll be fine.*

Arlene was alive. Zee felt it in her core. But she needed proof. And the only way to know for sure would be to take a look inside Dorothy and Ellis Kash's home. If Arlene was alive, the answer was inside that house. There would be some sort of correspondence, a note on a calendar, something.

As she stared at their front door, willing it to open, she found her mind wandering, thinking about the kiss.

She had read about first kisses before. Fluttering stomachs, the heart skipping a beat, warmth flooding through the body. Describing a kiss that way sounded silly and cliché. But that's exactly what she'd experienced, along with a rushing sound in her ears that had drowned out the rest of the world.

The kiss had been wonderful.

And yet she hadn't heard from Tobey since. She'd read about that part of the deal, too. Every article she'd come across said that if a guy didn't call after the first kiss or the first date, then he just wasn't into you. It was that simple. And so she hadn't been to the coffee shop since.

At least now she knew why she'd turned over the Death card the other day. It stood for the death of their relationship. She released a heavy sigh just as the door to the Kash's house opened and both Dorothy and Ellis walked outside together. Ellis turned back to the door and locked it.

Without making any sudden movements, she slid low in her seat, out of sight. Her pulse picked up a notch at the thought that her perseverance might just pay off.

It felt like forever before they climbed into the car and drove off.

Her insides vibrated as she reached for her bag on the passenger seat. She had packed everything she could possibly need, including tools that would help her break into their house. Breaking and entering. A felony? Not if she didn't get caught.

Don't do it. Your dad will be so disappointed in you.

He'll never talk to you again.

Do it, Zee. Hurry up before they come back. You're wasting time.

Unlike Francis, Lucy and Marion tended to get uptight in these types of situations. Zee ignored the voices and headed out. She didn't bother checking for a key under the mat on the porch. Instead, she made a beeline for the side yard, slid her hand over the fence, and unlatched the gate.

Nothing to see here, folks.

A dog barked in the neighbor's backyard. The dog spotted her and was trying to stuff his nose through a loose board in the fence. It was a small dog. Looked like a miniature schnauzer. Small but loud. She reached inside her bag for the veggie wrap she'd brought in case she got hungry.

Hurry. Hurry.

The voices in her head weren't helping matters. She was removing the foil wrapper as quickly as possible, but the dog was getting louder, its bark sharp and piercing. Finally, she was able to toss her snack over the fence. She prayed the animal liked pesto and hummus spread over a spinach tortilla.

It worked. No more barking. Thank God.

She ran around the house, looking for the sliding glass door she'd seen on a real estate site on the internet when the house had been up for sale years ago.

There it was. An outside slider. *Perfect.* Again, she reached into her bag. This time she pulled out a pry bar.

About six inches from the corner, diagonal from the latch, she inserted the pry bar between the door and the doorframe. Using a bit of muscle, she tilted the door and heard a click. That one movement lowered the latch, releasing it from the bracket.

She put her tool away and opened the door.

Way too easy, and a good reminder to tell her dad he better make sure their sliding doors had an inside slider instead of an outside one.

She stepped inside. It smelled like apple pie and cinnamon. The floors were so clean she was sure she could eat off them. The interior of the house was much bigger than she'd expected—high ceilings and wide-open spaces. She headed straight for the kitchen, which was massive. Lots of granite countertops and a large island in the middle of the room. Her plan was to start in the kitchen and work her way to the bedrooms.

As expected, she found an address book in one of many kitchen drawers. She skimmed through the contacts, looking for any clue at all that Arlene was still in their lives—maybe they used a nickname for their daughter or had written a cryptic note in the margin. When she realized she'd taken fifteen minutes just to go through the address book, she picked up her pace, opening and closing drawers: silverware, knives, junk drawer, buttons, and tape. *Nothing to see here,* she thought as she searched the bottom drawer that was filled with drying towels. And that's when she found something very interesting. Beneath the towels were two phones. Burner phones. The type you buy prepaid at Walmart. Burner phones weren't just for criminals. They were for people who wanted to maintain privacy. People like Dorothy and Ellis Kash.

Thinking she heard something, she put the phones back where she'd found them and ran to the front window to take a look outside. Nobody was coming up the walkway. No cars pulling into the driveway.

The burner phones were a sign she was on the right track, but they weren't proof. She turned around and ran up the wide-planked wooden stairs. The master bedroom was on the right. They had one of those cool, motorized, adjustable beds that you could move up and down with the push of a button. She was dying to give it a try but didn't dare waste an extra second.

There were stacks of boxes in the closet, mostly shoes and hats. She felt around in coat pockets and purses. No luck there. She checked under the bed, in between the mattresses, in every nightstand drawer. There had to be a note, a phone number, a picture. Something to indicate Penny was right and her mother was still alive.

Zee opened books lying around, searched the bathroom, and every cabinet and piece of furniture she came across. She searched linen closets and felt behind stacks of fluffy towels in hopes of finding a secret compartment.

When she was finished with the upstairs, she headed back down to an extra room near the kitchen. She set her bag on a twin bed with no headboard. An old Singer sewing machine sat in the far corner. Stacks of magazines and books filled two plastic bins. It looked like a guest room, sewing room, and junk room all in one.

She was searching the closet in the same manner she'd done upstairs when she heard the main door open and close.

Shit!

She rushed to the bed, grabbed her bag from where she'd left it, then ran back to the closet and stepped inside. As quietly as possible, she shut the wooden, double-slatted doors. Hunkered down, she made her way to the darkest corner, sank to the floor, and pulled her cell phone from her purse.

She had been inside the house for two hours.

Dumb. Dumb. Dumb. She should have known they wouldn't stay out very long. Heck, they rarely left their house to begin with.

Now what was she going to do? It would be days before they went out again and hours before they headed for bed.

She could hear Dorothy and Ellis talking in the other room. This was the second time since working for Jessie that she'd found herself stuck in a closet of a home she shouldn't be in. She was in big trouble.

Her phone vibrated.

Tobey had just texted her: WHAT'S UP? WHERE ARE YOU?

At first she considered ignoring him. He was a jerk. He hadn't even bothered to call her after the big kiss.

He thinks he's Romeo.

Don't waste your love on somebody who doesn't value it.

Thus, with a kiss I die.

You sort of forced him to kiss you. If I were him, I wouldn't have called you, either.

Zee lasted less than two minutes before giving in. She texted: I'M HIDING IN A CLOSET AT THE KASHES' HOUSE.

Tobey: WHAT?! ARE THEY HOME?

Zee: YES. IN THE KITCHEN. I DIDN'T HEAR THE CAR PULL UP. I NEED HELP, BUT I MIGHT NEED TO CALL MY OTHER BOYFRIEND SINCE I'M MAD AT YOU.

Tobey: YOU HAVE ANOTHER BOYFRIEND?

Zee: OF COURSE.

After a minute of silence, she typed: NO. BAD JOKE. WHY HAVEN'T YOU CALLED ME?

Tobey: I WAS WAITING FOR YOU TO COME TO THE COFFEE SHOP. I WENT TO YOUR OFFICE, BUT YOU AND JESSIE HAVE BOTH BEEN GONE.

Zee: WHY DIDN'T YOU TEXT ME?

Tobey: I DON'T KNOW. YOU MAKE ME NERVOUS.

Zee: I MAKE MYSELF NERVOUS. PLEASE COME TO THE HOUSE AND KNOCK ON THE DOOR.

Tobey: WHAT WOULD I SAY?

Zee: YOU'RE SELLING BOY SCOUT COOKIES, I DON'T KNOW?!

Tobey: BOY SCOUTS DON'T SELL COOKIES.

Zee: REALLY? THAT'S DUMB.

Zee froze when she heard voices. Not the usual voices, but real voices right outside the door.

"Pick up the phone!" she heard a woman she assumed to be Dorothy shout.

Zee heard footsteps and drawers opening. "Where did you put the phone this time?"

It was Ellis Kash talking. She recognized his voice. Cupboards were being opened and closed. Cups rattled. There must have been a phone stashed within the dishes.

"Got it!" Ellis said. A minute later, "Hello? Arlene, is that you?"

"Give me that," Dorothy ordered.

"Leave me be," Ellis said. "I want to talk to my daughter."

A whoosh of silence followed by Ellis talking again. The one-sided conversation was filled with normal things that Zee guessed most parents would talk about with their adult children: How are the kids? How's the weather over there in New England? Blah, blah, blah. Except there was nothing normal or blah about this conversation. *Kids? New England? What the hell?*

After further badgering by Dorothy, he must have handed the phone over to his wife, because it was the woman's voice Zee heard now.

"We delivered the package, just as you asked. Yes, we used the post office in Auburn this time. I know. I know. There is something I need to tell you. It's about Penny. She's looking for you."

Silence.

"Nathaniel is sick. It doesn't sound good. Maybe it's time for you to come home."

Tobey: ARE YOU THERE?

Zee: ARLENE IS ALIVE. I NEED YOU TO COME. HURRY!

Zee sneezed. Loud. Then she froze. She could no longer hear anyone talking in the kitchen. The phrase "up shit creek without a paddle" came to mind.

Good job, Bright Eyes.

Unsure of what to do next, she did nothing at all.

FORTY-FIVE

Lacey was nodding off to the sound of Jason's endless chatter.

For months she'd been hoping he would open up to her, but now that he was talking, she didn't care what he had to say. She only wished he would shut up.

She'd learned more about her husband in the short time they'd been living underground than she had in the eight years they'd been married.

She'd learned even more about herself. She was no longer the pathetic little girl chained to the bed. If they somehow made it through this ordeal, she would leave Jason and make a new life for herself. She was strong. She could do anything she put her mind to.

Jason finally stopped talking and went back to pounding nails around the vent. *Thank you, Jesus.* There were only a few nails left, but the vent cover still wouldn't budge.

The constant banging was in perfect rhythm to the pounding inside her head. She was dehydrated. She knew the signs: headaches, irritability, inability to think clearly, dry mouth, cracked lips and hands.

She put a hand to her abdomen. "I'm so sorry, little one." She had been so desperate to conceive, so eager to become a mother. Every thought of late had been about her unborn baby. He or she was eight weeks old. Her baby had fingers and toes, but it would be weeks before she felt him or her move.

A loud clatter drew her attention.

Lacey crossed the distance between them to see what had happened, which wasn't easy considering the ceilings were so low. Had their captor purposely made it so they couldn't stand up tall? She rubbed her back. The vent cover was on the ground. Light spilled through. "Oh, my God! You did it!"

"I told you I would get us out of here."

She groaned. "You are a piece of work."

"Did I say something wrong?"

Ignoring him, Lacey slipped her head up into the vent where she could stand a little straighter. It felt so good to straighten her spine and stretch.

The vent was about two feet by two feet. It was lined with aluminum and stretched out six feet to the right before it appeared to lead straight up again. Her heart thumped against her ribs. Feeling suffocated, she closed her eyes and concentrated on breathing. After a moment, her body relaxed, and she was able to check out the space. The light coming through was bright. She listened for any sounds coming from above, but the silence was deafening. The smell of sweet, tall grass filled her senses. If they got out of here, she swore she'd never take something so simple as the smell of grass for granted.

"What's in there?" Jason asked, nudging her from behind. "What do you see?"

She ducked down and moved aside to give him a chance to look for himself. In such a short time, he'd lost at least fifteen pounds. He fit right inside, but he was tall and awkward, and she noticed his legs wobbling.

Coughing and sputtering, he fell to his knees and then took a seat on the floor.

"What's wrong?"

"I think I heard a rat scurrying around."

A rat was the least of their worries. "It could be our way out of here," she said excitedly. "All you have to do is slide your body to the end, where the vent curves upward, and then twist around until you're on your feet."

The taste of freedom made her giddy. "Once you're on your feet, Jason, I'm guessing it's straight up from there, and you can just pull yourself right out!"

"I'm sorry."

Lacey didn't understand. "About what?"

"I can't do it."

Her shoulders tensed. "Of course you can."

His gaze was directed at his feet as he shook his head.

"What if I reminded you of the baby—*your* baby?"

He looked at her then, his eyes narrowed. "That would be just like you to try and guilt me into doing something I can't possibly do. I'm much too tall and broad shouldered to fit in there."

"When have I ever, in all the years I've known you, tried to guilt you into doing anything you didn't want to do?"

"You guilted me into asking you to marry me."

Her stomach turned. "You're insane."

"It's true. You were so fragile and innocent. You had no family or friends. After the Brightmans' children were old enough to attend school, you told me you didn't know what you would do with yourself because you would be all alone."

She started laughing then—a deep, hearty belly laugh that she couldn't control. She nearly buckled over in hysterics, especially after she started to hiccup.

"You're the one who is insane. Not me," Jason said. He merely stood there, watching her as if she'd lost her mind, which maybe she had.

"So that's why you asked me to marry you, huh?"

"Yes."

"It's funny," Lacey said, "because I remember it all so differently. I had worked for the Brightmans for ten years when I met you. They paid me well, and I had saved every penny I earned. The minute we were married, you told me you needed thirty thousand dollars to start your business." She poked him in the chest. Hard. "You married me for money." Lacey shook her head in wonder. "All this time I couldn't bring myself to believe it could be true, but it is, isn't it?"

He didn't say a word.

A hiccup was followed by "I can't believe it took being buried alive with you to see what a slimy, worthless scumball you truly are."

"Not now, Lacey. Don't say things you might regret. We're both hungry and thirsty, exhausted by our ordeal."

"Yes, that's true, but I'm not ready to give up. I'm getting out of here." There was no water or food left. Nothing to do but give this a shot. She ducked her head under and into the vent.

"Here," she heard Jason say. "Let me give you a boost."

She didn't need his help. Determined to get out of there, she used her elbows to pull herself high enough to where she could half crawl, half slither through the vent. It was a narrow space, but she had nothing to lose and everything to gain. There would have been no point in waiting another day, let alone another minute.

"Are you okay?" Jason asked, his voice sounding farther away than it was. "Can you breathe?"

She ignored his false concern as she inched along on her belly like a snake. It only took her a couple of minutes to make her way to the end, where the vent turned upward just as she'd thought.

As she pulled herself forward and up, she had to contort her body just a bit so that she could make the turn. The metal siding scraped against her back as she planted her hands on the wall, palms flat, and pulled, grunting and moaning, as she made the turn before finally pushing herself to her feet.

Elation flooded through her.

Swallowing, she tried not to think about being trapped or stuck in such a small, confined space. She wasn't the same person who had been buried deep. She was better, stronger, and nobody was ever going to fuck with her again.

Perspiration dripped down her face and neck.

She looked up, the sun shining so bright it nearly blinded her. The very top of the vent looked as if it was covered with a wire grate. It was hard to tell how thick the wire was or if it was fastened to anything. Even if she jumped as high as she could, there was no way she would reach the top.

"Did you find a way out?"

It sounded as if Jason was talking to her through a wall.

Again, she ignored him. He could have done this if he'd had the will or the drive to save his family. He might have been able to use his height to his advantage. As it was, she would have to climb at least eight feet from where she stood.

With her feet planted on the walls on both sides, she attempted to Spider-Man her way up the vent, but her feet and the palms of her hands were clammy, and she kept slipping back down to the ground.

Light-headedness threatened to overtake her.

She looked up again.

So far away.

No sooner had the thought floated through her mind than she rested a hand on her belly and massaged her baby bump. She imagined holding her baby in her arms for the first time. Boy or girl, it didn't matter.

She swallowed hard. A tear ran down her cheek.

She needed to save her baby.

Think, she told herself. *Think.*

Her gaze fell on her sleeve. She had ripped it when she'd pulled herself up out of what she assumed was to be her grave.

An idea came to her. The hem and the sleeves of her dress were made of faux leather. Adrenaline coursed through her as she ripped the rest of the right sleeve off her arm and pressed it against the aluminum siding. It didn't slip. Maybe if she wrapped the leather around her feet, she could make the climb.

It might work. Definitely worth a shot.

There wasn't enough room for her to bend forward, so she lifted her right leg as high as possible, just past her knee, then blindly reached down, her face pressed against the aluminum siding as she tied the strip of cloth around her foot. She repeated the process with her left foot.

Then she just stood there. "You are strong," she told herself. "You can do this."

Straightening, she wiped her hands over the dried dirt caked on her dress for better friction.

She sucked in a deep breath.

This was it.

She was as ready as she'd ever be. With the palms of her hands planted against the siding, she then pressed her right foot against the wall before doing the same with the left foot.

Pushing the palms of her hands and the balls of her feet against the walls, she focused on climbing upward. One inch at a time.

It was working! Her heart raced. She was doing it. *Slow and steady.*

Her legs shook, calves quivering by the time she drew close to the top. Every muscle tense, she reached up and pushed on the grate.

Nothing happened. It wouldn't budge.

No. No. No.

Breathe. Just breathe. She pushed again, harder this time. Sweat ran down her face and back. She gritted her teeth, determined to give herself more time.

The wire bent upward. Not much, but it was something. She used her fingers to circle the outer edge of the grate, looking for wires or metal clasps that might be keeping it from budging. Nothing but dirt and grass.

Jason called out from below.

Every muscle in her body burned.

It sounded as if Jason had stuck his head into the vent again. He was practically screaming, his voice panicked. "You're not going to leave me in here to die, are you?"

Her legs quivered. She wouldn't last much longer before falling back to where she'd started.

Concentrate! You can do this!

If she didn't find a way to push through the grate, she wasn't sure she'd have the strength to make it to the top again. She closed her eyes, counted to three, and let out a roar as she thought about everything she'd been through. She thought of her stepdad and the driver and Jason, and she pushed with every bit of strength left inside of her.

The grate sprang free, toppling over on its side, out of sight.

A feeling of weightlessness flooded through her as she inched her way upward until her head poked out into open air and she was able to prop her elbows on the tall grassy weeds and hold herself in place. She took a few seconds to catch her breath and regain some strength.

Pain shot through her arms and legs a minute later when she pushed and pulled her way through the top. She inhaled the scent of soil and wet grass.

She smiled, then fell backward in exhaustion.

She closed her eyes. Tears rolled down the side of her face. Again, she rested her hands on her stomach. *We made it. We're free.*

Forty-Six

Until Jessie Cole came snooping around, he'd spent his time watching and listening to Jason and Lacey, surprised they hadn't noticed the miniature camera stuffed inside a small hole in the corner of the cement room. They never even found the screwdriver he'd buried with them to help break through the particleboard. Lacey Geiger was a clever girl, though, and she'd found a way. She was much smarter than her husband.

Anxiety was setting in. His insides wouldn't stop quivering, and his legs bounced whenever he sat down. He needed to stay calm. He would call a tow truck and have the car he'd been driving that night hauled away. He shook his head. Never in a million years had he thought anyone would come here looking for Jason Geiger. It was inconceivable.

Hot tea with lemon might help.

Just as he stepped into the kitchen, he glanced out into the backyard and thought he saw something move. The cattle weren't anywhere near the underground room. Maybe it was a coyote?

He stood there for a few minutes longer, straining his eyes.

A head popped up.

He grabbed his binoculars from the kitchen drawer and looked again.

There it was again. *No fucking way.*

She had done it. Lacey Geiger had somehow managed to climb out of the fucking vent. He couldn't believe what he was seeing. He ran to the couch where he'd left his boots and tugged them on, didn't bother tying the laces. His heart raced, making him feel as if he were going to have a heart attack.

Before he could get to the door leading to the backyard, he heard gravel crunching and popping under tires.

Someone was here. *Fuck. Fuck. Fuck.*

He tried to remember if he'd ordered anything from Amazon. His mind went blank.

He rushed over to the front door and peeked through the viewer.

It was her—Jessie Cole had returned. His chest tightened. He knew what needed to be done. It was her fault. She never should have come.

FORTY-SEVEN

The first thing Jessie noticed when she pulled into Brody Hoffman's driveway was the car she'd seen the last time she visited. She pulled up close to the vehicle and turned off the engine. Something didn't feel right. Despite the dented back bumper and broken window, the car looked fairly new. There was no rust or other signs that would signal that the vehicle had been sitting in the driveway for very long.

Her senses on high alert, she grabbed her gun from the glove compartment and slid it into the holster at her waist. She then readied the tape recorder inside her purse, climbed out of the car, and walked to the door.

Before she could knock a third time, Brody Hoffman opened the door. Unlike the last time she'd come to visit, this time he appeared to be all smiles.

Either he was guilty as sin, or she was paranoid.

"I'm glad you're here," he said, out of breath.

She lifted a brow in question.

"I was going to call you. After you left, I-I thought about it for a while, and I came up with a few places Jason might have gone to get away from it all."

"That's great."

He nodded. "Come in."

She stepped inside. From the looks of it, he'd spruced the place up a bit. Swept the floors and dusted the tables, but still no female touches such as flowers or decorative pillows on the couch.

They both took a seat at the same table in the kitchen where they had sat last time.

A sheen of sweat covered his forehead. He glanced over his shoulder toward the fields where cattle grazed. She followed his gaze, trying to see what he was looking at, but all she saw was a field of tall green grass, a few trees, and a bunch of cows in the far distance.

"Is everything okay?" Jessie asked.

"I've been having problems with the waterline. I thought I saw water gushing earlier. I should probably make sure there are no major leaks before we get started. It won't take me long."

Perfect. That would give her time to check the bedroom. She nodded. "I'll wait right here."

As soon as he was out the door and had walked far enough away, Jessie popped up out of the chair and rushed to the bedroom.

The chair was still in the corner, but the clothes and the purse were gone. She took a quick look under the bed. She checked the closet next.

Her eyes widened when her gaze fell on what she was looking for. There it was! He'd tossed everything into a heap.

Her heart raced as she grabbed the purse, unzipped the middle section, and reached inside. She found a wallet. Her hands shook as she opened it and looked inside. There was thirty-two dollars in cash, plus credit cards and a driver's license. Lacey Geiger.

Brody Hoffman had kidnapped the Geigers. Had he picked them up under the guise of being a transportation service?

No time to think about that now. She needed to find Lacey.

The wood floor creaked behind her.

A shadow fell over her.

She glanced over her shoulder as she reached for the gun tucked into her waistband. Brody Hoffman stood over her, holding a bat, ready to take a swing. She twisted the other way just as it connected with her skull.

A bright white light exploded behind her eyes.

She felt dizzy, disoriented. Her stomach roiled.

By the time her senses returned and she knew what was happening, he had dragged her into the main room.

She reached for the top of her head where he'd hit her. She was lucky he hadn't bashed her head in. If she hadn't seen him coming, she'd be dead. Her fingers brushed against something wet and sticky. When she looked at her hands, they were covered in blood.

A rushing sound filled her ears, like waves crashing against the shore.

Fuck.

Her blood phobia was kicking in. She was going to faint.

Don't do it. Don't you dare pass out now.

Her head fell back to the floor, and the room spun and turned black.

FORTY-EIGHT

Lacey lay on the damp grass catching her breath when she heard a rustling in the grass nearby. A twig snapped. She opened her eyes.

A man stood above her, looking down at her with the same flat, expressionless eyes as the driver.

It was *him*.

The man with the mask. Their driver. A bloody baseball bat dangled from his hand.

She sat up, scooting away from him.

"Stop right there. You're not going anywhere."

She should have run the moment she climbed out of the hole. She took in the vast fields of tall grass and the slope of a hill past a wood fence. Behind him, she saw a one-story house. Was anyone inside? Would they call for help if she screamed? "Why are you doing this?" she asked, trying to buy time.

He smirked. "Because your husband needed to be stopped. He's a ruthless bastard who cares only about himself. I used to be a decent guy, married, looking forward to having children. Ring a bell? Jason Geiger ruined my life. I thought it was time I did the same for him."

Escape. Get away. She put a hand on her belly. "I'm pregnant. Please don't hurt my baby."

"I've been listening to the two of you down there. How could you be so stupid? Eight long years, and you know nothing about your husband."

"I saw what he wanted me to see." Her fingers dug into the soil, gathering dirt.

He snorted. "I think you saw what *you* wanted to see."

Lacey was about to make her move when he turned and walked toward the garden hose a few feet away.

She jumped to her feet and ran, stumbling through clods of dirt. Jason shouted from below, but she didn't dare stop.

Every muscle burned as she ran toward the fence. Her pulse raced. It wasn't until he grunted that she knew he was close behind her. Suddenly, a hand grabbed a fistful of hair and yanked her backward. She gasped for air and then let out a primal scream. Someone would hear her. They had to.

He jerked her back. A sharp pain sliced through her head. She twisted around and kicked his leg, but he was unaffected. "You're too weak to fight me," he told her.

She screamed again and tossed dirt in his face.

He sputtered, then dragged her back to the spot where he'd left the nozzle. "Do that again and I'll kill you right now and drop you down that hole so you and your husband can be reunited."

Her chest rose and fell with each breath she took as she watched the man drop the hose into the hole.

"What's going on?" Jason shouted up at them. "Who is there with you?"

The man laughed. "God, listening to him, you wouldn't know Jason Geiger was such a brutally coldhearted man, would you?"

His gaze remained on hers while he sent more and more hose down the vent. "I bet this experience has opened your eyes, huh?"

Lacey didn't want to anger him, so she nodded. She needed a plan. If she could get more space between them, she could make another run for it. Head for the house and hope for the best.

"So tell me, what do you think of your husband now?"

She swallowed, afraid to answer and say the wrong thing.

His face contorted. "I'll tell you what he is. He's self-centered, impulsive, callous, and manipulative. He'll trample on anyone he has to if it means making a buck." He marched back to the faucet and turned the water on full blast.

She'd come too far to die now. She jumped to her feet and took off running again. This time toward the house. The dirt was more compact, easier to run on. There was no way she was going to stop.

She heard water rushing. Jason was shouting, his voice lined with panic. And two seconds later, the bat slammed against the back of her knees. A searing, white-hot pain shot through her as she went down, hitting the dirt hard.

"You dumb bitch."

She could hardly move. One of her legs was broken, she was certain of it. Pain rattled her brain as he grabbed her arm and hauled her back to the vent opening she'd just crawled out of. He dropped his hold on her. Gritting her teeth, the pain agonizing, she let her head fall back on the grass. *Fuck.* Her right leg was useless, the pain excruciating.

It was over. She'd tried.

She inwardly apologized to her unborn child. She never meant to put the baby in harm's way. But that was what she'd done. She'd wanted the perfect marriage so badly that she'd allowed herself to be blinded by all else. She wasn't afraid to die. But she was distraught to think she would never hold her baby in her arms.

From where Lacey lay, she watched as he made his way to a stack of bins. He set the bat to the side, slipped on thick gloves, and then grabbed the top bin. It had air holes on the sides. He carried it to the vent opening, pulled off the lid, then dumped a pile of wriggling snakes into the opening.

Down in the hole, Jason began to scream.

The man pulled off his gloves and dropped them where he stood. He then grabbed her arm again and dragged her along with him across the field toward the house. *The house,* she thought. If she could find a weapon to use against him, there might still be hope.

"Help me!" Jason called out.

"Help me!" the man imitated in a chilling voice.

Forty-Nine

Jessie awoke to the sight of blood on the floor and all over her hands.

She broke out in a cold sweat, and again the room began to spin.

No. No. No.

She tensed the muscles in her arms, legs, and body for as long as she could manage, just as her therapist had her do in his office to stop from fainting. He'd made her watch countless videos of people having blood drawn while she tensed her muscles. As she took her next breath, she felt her body relax.

It was working.

Ignoring the throbbing pain in her head, she reached for her gun just as the door to the backyard opened. Jessie fell limp, pretending to be unconscious.

She heard footsteps as he came into the room. He jabbed her in the side with his booted foot, and when she didn't respond, he turned and walked back toward the kitchen. He was talking to someone now, rambling on about Jason Geiger.

Jessie pushed herself to her feet, legs wobbling as she hid within a small alcove by the TV. From where she stood, she could see a woman on the floor near the kitchen table. Brody Hoffman hovered over her.

The woman sat up and reached for her leg. That was when Jessie saw her face. It was Lacey.

"It's too bad I'm forced to harm innocent people," she heard Brody say as he opened a drawer in the kitchen. "But this isn't my fault. Jason had to be dealt with, and I was the only one willing to make him pay for all the lives he's ruined."

"You've gotten your revenge," Lacey told him. "Jason is scared to death. He's learned his lesson."

"Still defending that man after all he's done to you?"

"If you kill either of us, you'll spend the rest of your life in prison. That doesn't sound like a satisfying resolution to me."

He snorted. "Well, you're not me." He bent down and grabbed her arm, dragging her along with him as he said, "Come on. Let's go watch Jason fight off those poisonous snakes. I want to see him suffer a slow and horrifying death. I think you'll enjoy it, too."

His boots thumped against the floor as he started toward the living room. When he stepped into the main living area, Jessie noticed his gaze fall to the spot on the floor where she'd been lying unconscious only moments ago. He pulled Lacey upward, hard and fast, and held her tight against his chest as if using her as a shield to protect himself. "Where did you go, Jessie Cole?"

Jessie's gaze fell to the weapon in his hand. He'd replaced the bat for a knife and held the blade at Lacey's throat.

"Come out of hiding," Brody said, "or I'll cut her throat right now."

Jessie stepped out into the middle of the room, her arms straight in front of her, both hands on the gun, finger on the trigger, aiming for his head. The room began to spin.

Inhale. Exhale. The dizziness passed.

"Well, look at you," he said, his voice eerily calm. "I don't believe you're supposed to have a gun in your possession. Isn't that right? Do you really want to get in trouble with the authorities again?"

"Put the knife down," she said, hoping the quiver in her voice went undetected. "And then I want you to get down on the floor, facedown, hands on your back."

His eyes pierced hers. The corners of his mouth turned upward in a malicious grin.

Refusing to let him intimidate her, Jessie held her ground. "Get down on the floor now," she stated firmly.

"After all I've been through, all the years of planning, you think I'm going to spend the rest of my life in jail?"

"I know what Jason Geiger did to you. It wasn't right. You're not the only one whose life was ruined by the man. Don't give him the power. You can put a stop to all of this right now."

"I lost everything because of that man."

"You can start over," Jessie told him.

"I lost my business, my pride, my wife."

Jessie didn't know why, but she felt strangely connected to this man. It probably had something to do with all the people she'd talked to who despised Jason. Brody Hoffman had been dealt a hard blow by a selfish man, and it was obvious the burning hatred he had for Jason Geiger had turned into a wildfire. "If you let Lacey go, they'll be lenient on you. You haven't killed anyone, Brody. I'll make sure you get the help you need to turn your life—"

"Shut up! You have no idea what it's like to be shamed and humiliated in front of friends and family. For nearly a year I felt naked, on display for all to see. It's over. For all of you. I'm done talking."

Lacey jabbed an elbow into his side, then lowered her head and bit his arm, catching him off guard.

He cursed, pushed her away.

Lacey dropped to the floor, but she wasn't done. The wild expression on her face gave Jessie chills as she watched Lacey grab hold of his leg and bite into his calf. Brody shook her off and turned toward Jessie.

Remembering what Colin had told her at the gun range, Jessie forced herself to relax as she took the slack off the trigger, aimed for his shoulder, and pressed, but Brody shifted his body suddenly and the bullet struck him in the chest.

He didn't crumple to the floor or stagger backward. He merely stood there and stared at Jessie and mouthed, *Thank you.*

Lacey scrambled away, dragging her injured leg behind her.

Brody Hoffman wanted to die, but Jessie wanted him to live. With the gun still aimed in his direction, Jessie said, "Drop the knife, Brody. Please."

Instead, he pointed the tip of the blade at her, his hand shaking.

Jessie felt desperate to find a way to put a stop to all this. He was in a dark place. If she could only find a way to make him see that in any given situation there was always a way out. Always.

The hand gripping the knife shook as he squared his shoulders. His eyes. The rage had left him, leaving in its wake a dull, empty stare.

Jessie took a step toward him, pleading for him to give it up.

He twisted the knife in his hand and plunged the blade deep into his chest above his heart.

Jessie gasped.

He fell to his knees, relief softening his face before he toppled over.

She rushed to his side. Blood gushed from his wounds. He wouldn't last long.

Jessie slid her gun into her holster, grabbed her phone, and called for help.

"Jason is still out there," Lacey said, pointing toward the field. "We were buried underground."

"How did you get out?"

"Through a vent. I'm not sure how long Jason will be able to survive. That man dropped a hose into the vent and turned it on full blast. It won't be long before—"

Jessie ran out the back door before Lacey could finish.

FIFTY

Colin and Ren stood on the welcome mat in front of Paden White's home. Colin rang the bell. A dog barked. It sounded as if a dozen kids were running around inside. A woman, most likely Paden's wife, opened the door.

"Hello," Colin said. "I am Detective Grayson, and this is Detective Howe. Are you Mrs. White?"

She nodded.

"We have a search warrant to check your property."

Ren handed her the paper in his hand.

"Why?" She ran a hand through her hair. "What's going on?" She skimmed over the warrant, then called out for Paden.

When he came to the door, he looked from Colin to the paper in his wife's hand, snatched it from her, and read it over. "This is nuts. What are you hoping to find?"

"We'll need you to open the garage door," Ren told him.

Paden glared. "You need to leave."

"It won't take long," Colin promised. "We just need to take a quick look around your backyard and then do a thorough search of the garage."

"Come inside and let's get this over with," his wife said. "My husband has nothing to hide."

"Thank you," Colin said. He looked at Ren. "I'll search the backyard—you start in the garage."

Ren nodded.

Paden hadn't moved. His wife nudged him with a hand to his arm. "Open the garage, Paden. It's going to be all right. Please. I want these men to do what they need to and leave as soon as possible."

"This is madness!" Paden growled.

Colin left Ren to deal with Paden and followed Mrs. White to the French doors leading to the backyard. She opened the doors wide and said, "What exactly are you looking for?"

One small child ran up to her side and clutched the hem of her blouse.

"I'm sorry. I can't say." He stepped outside. The back fence was half covered with nicely trimmed shrubs. He walked over to the pergola that lent shade to a wood deck and furniture. There were a couple of seating areas for reading or enjoying the day. He looked around, his gaze settling on a plant with white blooms. As he stepped off the deck, he reached into his pocket and pulled out a pair of disposable gloves and slipped them on. He walked across a small patch of grass to the plant that was growing from a large terra-cotta pot. He pulled out a paper bag. Inside were smaller plastic bags. He used one to collect pieces of the foliage. He was almost finished when he heard shouting coming from inside the house. He pulled off the gloves and tucked everything inside the zippered pocket in his coat.

Colin rushed through the French doors. The commotion was coming from the garage. He followed the sound, running through the kitchen and laundry room. By the time he was inside the garage, Ren had Paden White pinned facedown to the cement floor next to the family car.

"He fucking hit me," Ren said when Colin appeared.

Colin exhaled. One of Ren's knees was jammed into the middle of Paden's back. "What's going on?" Colin asked. "What are you hiding, Mr. White?"

"God damn it," the man answered, his voice muffled until Colin gestured for Ren to lighten up. "I'm not hiding anything," Paden said.

"Then why did you hit Detective Howe?"

"Because he was asking for it . . . pushing my buttons . . . getting in my face."

Colin looked at Ren, who lifted his shoulders.

"I had nothing to do with Roger Willis hanging himself," Paden said. "I don't know why you two are here. You're scaring my wife and kids and making the neighbors nervous. I didn't do whatever the hell you think I did."

"Listen," Colin told him. "If Detective Howe decides that it's safe to let you go, you're going to have to stand to the side and let us do our jobs."

Silence.

"If you don't cooperate, we're going to have to stick you in the back of the cruiser and take you to the station."

"This is bullshit," Paden spat out.

Colin exhaled. "What's it going to be?"

"Let me up," Paden finally said. "I'm not going to hurt anyone."

Ren looked at Colin, and he nodded.

Half of Paden's face was marked with angry red lines after being pressed against the hard cement floor.

Paden straightened his shirt as he found an area near the corner of the garage where he could stare at Ren. His arms were folded tightly across his chest. The twisted mouth and sour expression said it all. He wanted to punch something.

When they left the house an hour later, Colin and Ren walked away with two items: the white bloom from the backyard and a piece of rope that looked similar to the rope used in the hanging of Roger Willis.

"So, what do you think?" Ren asked as they crossed the road.

"I think you need to put some ice on that shiner."

"Yeah," Ren said. "If I thought he was guilty, I would be thinking about pressing charges about now."

"What makes you think he's innocent?"

"Forget it. It's nothing."

"Just say it," Colin urged. "I won't judge."

Ren stopped at his car. Colin waited.

"Research shows that our accuracy of detecting a lie is about fifty-three percent, which means you might as well toss a coin. But the real key is to watch a person's reactions to a question rather than just listen."

"So, if I tell you I hate your outfit," Colin said, "am I lying or telling the truth?"

Ren smiled. "You never shifted from your baseline. Nothing changed in eye movement, et cetera. Definitely the truth."

Colin chuckled. "Okay, so Paden White stuck to his baseline?"

Ren nodded. "I started asking him questions about his friendship with Roger Willis. I pushed and prodded and stepped over the line. If he'd been lying, I would have seen some physical shifts that would have clued me in to his discomfort. Instead, he threw a punch."

"Intuition and creative skills like yours can be helpful in detective work," Colin said, "but science and evidence are crucial."

"Noted," Ren said as he opened the door and climbed in behind the wheel. When Colin headed for his own car, Ren asked, "Where are you off to?"

"I'm going to drop what we found off at the lab so forensics can examine it. How about you?"

"I'm heading back to the spot near the river where we found Willis. I want to take a look around, see if we missed anything."

"Okay," Colin said with a nod. "We'll touch base later."

The rookie had already driven off by the time Colin slid into the front seat of his car. A movement caught his attention. He looked back at Paden's house. Somebody was peeking through the curtain covering the front window.

A kid? A nervous wife? An angry man?

Homicide investigations made people leery. There were times when Colin thought everyone looked guilty, even the dog. But the thing he'd learned over the years was never to rush an investigation.

As he drove off, he thought of Jessie. The same rules often applied to their relationship. Don't rush things. Stay focused. And communication was key to success.

FIFTY-ONE

"Who are you?" Mrs. Kash shouted at Zee when Zee poked her head out of her hiding place inside the guest room closet.

"You're the woman I met at the casino," Ellis Kash said, pointing a gun at her.

Zee nodded. Now that he recognized her, she hoped maybe he would put the gun away.

"Keep your hands up where I can see them," he said, waving the gun around.

Zee thought about trying to wrestle the firearm from the old man.

Don't you dare!

Do it. Do it!

"Not now," Zee pleaded with the voices. She needed to keep her wits about her if she wanted to get through this in one piece.

"Who are you talking to?" Ellis asked.

"Nobody."

He leaned forward and peeked inside the closet and saw no one but Zee. That was Zee's chance to grab the gun, but she didn't. A part of her didn't think Ellis had it in him to shoot her dead. He was old. In his case, life really was short.

"What are we going to do?" the woman asked her husband, wringing her hands.

"Calm down, Dorothy. Just give me a minute to think."

"Your daughter is still alive, isn't she?" Zee asked.

Francis gasped.

Dorothy gasped, too.

Are you trying to get yourself killed? Lucy wanted to know.

"I told you in the casino she was murdered," Ellis said, the menacing look on his face making her a little nervous.

Zee shook her head. "When you won that jackpot, I said your kids are going to be getting a lot of money and you said, 'She's not getting any of this!'"

Dorothy groaned, clearly unhappy with her husband.

What about the two of them talking to their daughter on the phone? Francis reminded Zee.

That's right, Zee thought. She'd almost forgotten. "I just heard you both talking to Arlene on the phone. She lives in New England, and she has kids. Why didn't you ever tell Penny that her mother was alive?"

"Because Penny's father would have gone after her," Ellis said angrily. "He would have killed Arlene. He's a violent man."

"That's not true. He's never hurt a flea, never been in a fistfight, and he never hit his wife. I'm an investigator," Zee stated proudly, "and I'm good at it."

Lucy groaned. *Her ego is the size of Mount Everest.*

Yeah, well, Francis said. *Some things never change. She's definitely going to get herself shot.*

Zee ignored the voices. "There was never even one report filed against Nathaniel, either by neighbors or by your daughter. The worst thing Nathaniel Snyder did was love Arlene too much. He wanted her to be happy."

Dorothy looked at Ellis. "You saw bruises—isn't that right? When I came back from seeing my sister in New York, you said Arlene had a black eye and that he'd hit her, and that that wasn't the first time. He beat her on more than one occasion. That's what you told me, Ellis."

Her husband said nothing.

"Please tell me you didn't lie about the bruises and the black eye," Dorothy pressed.

"She wanted out of the marriage," Ellis explained. "Nathaniel was too old for Arlene. She was so young and free-spirited. She didn't want to be tied down. She was too weak to do it on her own, so I said I would help her, and that's what I did."

Dorothy paled. "From the first moment you met Nathaniel, you didn't like him."

"I told Arlene not to marry him, but she didn't listen."

"She could have divorced him, Ellis."

Ellis grunted.

Zee felt sort of bad for Dorothy, but she really just wished Ellis would put the gun down. Instead, his hands were shaking now, his finger on the trigger, the weapon pointed right at her.

"Please put the gun away," Zee said.

Nobody paid her any mind.

"How could you do that to us?" Dorothy asked Ellis. "We've spent what should have been the best part of our lives worrying about Arlene, afraid Nathaniel would find her and finish her off for good. Why?"

There was a knock on the door.

Everyone froze.

This was her chance. "Help!" Zee shouted.

The doorbell buzzed repeatedly, a grating sound that couldn't possibly be ignored.

With gun still in hand, raised and pointed, Ellis exited the bedroom.

Dorothy looked at Zee, then quickly followed her husband out of the room. "What are you doing?" she asked him. "Don't answer the door!"

Zee stepped out of the closet and ran to the window. Tobey was at the door. She didn't want to knock on the glass or shout and call attention to herself. She tried to open the window, but the latch wouldn't budge.

The doorbell continued to buzz.

Her heart was beating fast. Not sure what to do, she rushed out of the room and headed straight for the sliding door.

"Stop or I'll shoot!"

Zee froze at the sound of Ellis's voice.

"Get over here where I can see you!" he shouted.

He hadn't asked Zee to hold her hands in the air, but she held both arms straight above her head just in case as she moved slowly toward the front door.

Dorothy's gaze was watery as Zee walked past. Clearly distraught, the elderly woman's hands were clasped.

Ellis took his eyes off Zee long enough to look through the peephole.

"Who is it?" Dorothy asked.

"I'm not sure," Ellis said, his voice wavering. When he glanced over his shoulder at his wife, Zee noticed a sheen of sweat covering his forehead.

Ellis glared at Zee. "Get some duct tape from the laundry room," he told his wife.

Zee didn't like the sound of that, but thankfully Dorothy didn't budge.

Zee ran through her options. Run for the sliding door and pray Ellis missed if he took a shot at her. Try to knock the old man over and open the door. Or beg for Ellis to listen to reason. She opted for number three. "Just let me go," she pleaded.

"What's going on in there?" Tobey shouted from outside.

Ellis turned that way, and Zee didn't hesitate to grab a decorative vase from the coffee table. She raised it over her head and was about to hit Ellis with it when Dorothy used all her weight to push Zee to the floor.

Zee toppled over. The vase hit the floor and exploded into pieces. Glass scraped against her arms when she reached for Dorothy's ankle and pulled her to the ground with her.

Ellis paled but stood firm, determined to stop anyone from coming or going.

Tobey knocked on the door and shouted for someone to let him in, prompting Ellis to turn back to the door.

Zee figured this might be her last chance. If she didn't get that door open, she would be back to square one—trapped, maybe killed. She jumped to her feet, rushed toward Ellis, and pushed him out of the way so she could unlock and open the door.

Ellis wrestled with her as she tried to escape.

The gun went off.

The blast was deafening.

Ears ringing, eyes wide, Zee watched Tobey clutch his arm. Blood seeped through his shirt and onto his fingers as he sank to his knees.

Dorothy let out a piercing screech.

"No!" Zee shouted.

FIFTY-TWO

Jessie ran across the field, following a trail of flattened weeds and grass that Brody Hoffman must have made when he dragged Lacey to the house. The path ended at the hole in the ground where the hose disappeared, just as Lacey had said. Jessie located the valve a few feet away and shut off the water.

Looking down the opening, she asked, "Is anyone down there?"

She could hear water sloshing, and then a voice, a small, squeaky voice. "Help me," he said as if he were afraid he might wake someone.

She poked her head inside the vent and leaned in as far as she could. "Help is on the way. Can you make it through the vent? If so, you might be able to use the hose to climb out of there."

"Snakes," he said. "I can't move."

"There are snakes in the water?"

"Yes. There are two large black snakes swimming around."

Shit.

"Are they poisonous?" he asked.

Jessie pulled out her cell and searched the internet for large black snakes. "Is the body of the snake slender?"

"No. Thick and large. Get me out of here!"

It looked to Jessie like he might be dealing with water moccasins. The snakes were deadly. The venom was toxic and would probably kill him if he was bitten. "Do they have a blocky, triangular head?"

"Yes."

"Okay." She needed to tell him the truth. "They are dangerous," she told him. "But they are not easily provoked. Don't make any sudden moves, and whatever you do, don't try to corner the snakes."

"Help me!" he said, his voice quivery and hoarse.

"I hear sirens," she told him. "I need to go and tell them what's going on. I'll be back."

"Don't leave. Help me!"

She pushed herself to her feet and ran back to the house.

Thirty minutes later, emergency workers were trying to find the right people to begin the process of widening the vent area so they could reach Jason Geiger and pull him out.

As medics examined Lacey, Jessie stayed at her side. The EMT had Lacey take small sips of water while they waited for news about her husband. If the emergency workers could free him, they would take both Lacey and Jason to the hospital together.

"He buried us alive," Lacey said, obviously trying to wrap her mind around what had happened. "He trapped us inside a small, windowless room where he planned to watch us die."

The EMT took her blood pressure.

Lacey met Jessie's gaze. "How did you know we were missing?"

"I didn't. I had no idea where you were or if foul play was involved when I first went to your house to talk to you."

"What did you want to talk to me about?"

Jessie frowned. "Your grandmother Laura passed away and named you in her will. I'm sorry about your loss."

A funny look crossed over Lacey's face.

"Don't worry," Jessie told her. "I'm not going to tell anyone."

"Thank you."

Lacey knew what she meant. Jessie could see it in her eyes. Nobody needed to know her real identity.

"I haven't seen my grandmother in years," Lacey said. "I do remember her, though. How did you get the news?"

"An attorney in charge of your grandmother's trust couldn't find you, but he had reason to believe you were in the Sacramento area, so he called me." Jessie smiled. "I'm a private investigator. Nobody had seen you or Jason since you went to dinner for your anniversary. I had a limited number of days to find you."

"In about five minutes," the medic said to Jessie after talking to someone over his two-way radio, "we're going to have to take your friend to the hospital."

"What about Jason?" Lacey asked.

"Looks like it might take a while to get him out."

Jessie wrote down the name of the hospital. "We'll talk later when you're feeling better."

Lacey placed her hand on Jessie's arm. "How did you find us?"

Jessie didn't know how Lacey felt about her husband, but she decided it was best to be up front. "I made a list of Jason's enemies and went after the people he'd hurt the most."

Lacey winced. "Were there many?"

Jessie nodded.

"I had no idea who I was married to until I was trapped underground with him. I'm leaving him."

"It's better that you know the truth," Jessie said. "After all you've been through, I hope you can find peace now."

"Thank you," Lacey said. "I'll be fine." She sipped her water and licked her dry, cracked lips.

"Please don't leave town before we have a chance to talk again." Jessie wrote her number on a piece of paper and closed Lacey's hand around it.

Lacey smiled. "I have a feeling you would find me."

Jessie watched as Lacey was carried off on a gurney. The assistant medic packed his equipment and told Jessie that Lacey had a broken leg and was dehydrated, but that the baby was doing well, and the cooler weather had probably helped keep Lacey alive.

The baby was doing well. *Interesting.*

While crime scene technicians gathered in the house to collect and analyze evidence, Jessie made her way to the backyard, where the detective was sitting on a lawn chair, waiting to get her account of what happened.

It was getting dark by the time the detective finished writing his report. He told her she was free to go, but Jessie asked for permission to see Brody Hoffman's bedroom.

She wasn't allowed through the door, but she could see inside. Notes and drawings covered every wall. Some of the drawings resembled the artwork of a five-year-old. She listened as the detective talked to technicians about the notebooks. Apparently, Brody Hoffman had wanted to play cat and mouse with Jason while he watched from his computer screen. The red ants and venomous snakes were only the beginning. He'd written a lot about being smarter than Jason Geiger, certain Jason would die a slow, agonizing death.

Jessie wondered if, at any point, Brody had realized what he'd done by bringing Lacey along for the ride. The detective had already determined that it took a special kind of person to carry out a plan like this without detection. Brody Hoffman's obsession, meticulous planning, and most likely psychopathic personality had enabled him to bring his plan to fruition.

Nothing more to see there, she decided. Hearing about Brody's obsession with Jason and seeing his irrational thoughts put to paper made her sad. Instead of making her way to the front of the house and heading home, she returned to the backyard. She wanted to wait and see if Jason Geiger got out safely.

As she stepped outside, she thought of the metal cuffs and the hardships Lacey had survived at a young age. Now older, wiser, pregnant, and off to celebrate eight years of marriage, Lacey had been buried alive with a man she'd thought she could trust to be there for her.

Jessie shook her head at the thought of there being so much wickedness in the world. Without war, disease, suffering, and death, would the good—love, laughter, health—not be as meaningful? Did it take the depravity of humankind for people to appreciate everything else?

Exhaustion threatened to weigh her down as it suddenly dawned on her that she hadn't had a chance to tell Lacey how much her grandmother had left her. Lacey hadn't even asked. It could wait another day or two. Her phone buzzed. It was Zee. Jessie hadn't seen her in days. She picked up the call and said hello.

"Are you in your office?" Zee asked, her tone sharp.

"No. I'm in Elk Grove. You sound agitated. Is everything okay?"

"Nothing is okay. Ellis Kash shot Tobey."

Jessie felt as if she'd been punched in the gut. Why would Ellis Kash shoot a young boy? "I don't understand. Did he kill him?"

"No. Tobey is alive, but I'll get to that in a minute. It all started when Ellis Kash pointed a gun at me and—"

"He had a gun pointed at you when you were doing surveillance?"

"No, actually when I was hiding in their closet. I sneezed and blew my cover. No pun intended."

Jessie closed her eyes and pinched the bridge of her nose. "Please don't tell me you broke into their house when they were out."

"I broke into their house when they were out."

Jessie took a deep breath.

"Don't worry. The bullet just grazed Tobey's arm. He's okay now, but after he was shot, he passed out. I gave him mouth-to-mouth, which turned out to be completely unnecessary. While I was trying to save Tobey's life, Dorothy was yelling at Ellis for lying to her all these years. She was so angry I thought for sure she was going to have a heart attack."

"What did Ellis lie about?"

"Oh, I didn't tell you that part?"

"No. You didn't."

"Arlene Snyder, Penny's mother, is alive!"

Jessie took in the news slowly. "Are you sure?"

"Yes. She's married and has two kids and is living in New England."

"So what did Ellis lie about?"

"Listen carefully," Zee said, prompting Jessie to roll her eyes. "They both knew that their daughter was alive, and as you know, it was their testimony that put Nathaniel Snyder, Penny's father, in prison all those years ago. But it was Ellis Kash who told his wife, Dorothy, that Nathaniel was beating Arlene."

"But he wasn't?" Jessie asked.

"No, he wasn't. I met him. The guy wouldn't hurt a flea."

"Why would Ellis lie in the courtroom under oath?"

"Because he wanted his daughter to be free to start her life over—his words, not mine. He thought Nathaniel was much too old for Arlene. And he thought she was too sweet, or maybe too weak-minded, to ever leave him, so he and his daughter made a plan."

Jessie's jaw hardened. "Didn't he stop to think about how all of this would affect Penny?"

"I think that was a big part of his plan—to take Penny in and raise her as their own." Jessie heard muffled voices. "I'll be right there!" Zee said. "I've gotta go. Tobey is milking this for all its worth."

"Does Penny know what's going on?"

"You bet. I called her right after I realized Tobey was going to make it. She came over to the house. You should have been there. It was utter and complete pandemonium."

There was no goodbye before the call was disconnected. Jessie shook her head, then looked up when she heard the emergency crew clap and cheer.

A few minutes later, Jason was on a gurney, being carried to the ambulance waiting out front. "Is he going to be okay?" Jessie asked the EMT.

"Unlike the woman, he's showing no signs of dehydration. Healthy as an ox, but we'll let the doctors examine him just in case."

Jessie made the walk across the field one more time so that she could take a look inside the hole. Bright fluorescent lights had been set up around the perimeter, making it easy to see things clearly: the box where Lacey and Jason had been buried, and the small, cramped quarters where they had been stuck for days, was half covered with water.

The idea of finding a way out after being buried alive, only to realize you were trapped in a small, dark hole, made her shiver.

One thing was certain—Anne Elizabeth Corrigan was a survivor.

Fifty-Three

Penny Snyder stood motionless, closed her eyes, and breathed in the fresh, earthy smell of the river behind the house she was facing.

A long moment passed before she opened her eyes again.

The house in Maine was a charming Cape Cod–style home with a farmer's porch wrapped around the front. Even from the sidewalk, it was easy to see that the oversize windows provided lots of light. The fence surrounding the yard wasn't tall enough to hide views of the river.

The idea of possibly seeing her mother after all these years did not make Penny nervous.

The truth was, she didn't know how she felt. There were too many emotions running through her to pick just one or two. Two weeks ago, she might have been ecstatic at finding her mother alive and well.

But this woman, whom she'd thought about every single day without fail for the past thirty years, had abandoned her. This woman had allowed Penny's father, an innocent man whom Penny had come to love despite her distrust of him, to spend ten years of his life in prison.

Abandoning her daughter was one thing. But allowing an innocent man to go to prison was quite another.

It was Friday. She'd given Dorothy and Ellis no choice but to answer all her questions in detail, threatening to go to the police if they didn't talk. And when she ran out of things to ask them, she said goodbye. She didn't want anything to do with Dorothy or Ellis Kash.

If they came anywhere near her, she told them, she would get a restraining order. She refused to listen to Dorothy's assurance that she knew nothing about Ellis and Arlene's plans. Penny didn't care about either one of them. They were evil, spiteful people who didn't deserve her love.

Dorothy told Penny that her mother had remarried. Arlene's husband, Bob, was a banker. Arlene and Bob had twin fifteen-year-old girls. Penny also learned that Arlene worked at the school the girls attended but took Fridays off to paint or do whatever might strike her fancy, as Dorothy had so fondly put it.

No, Penny decided. She wasn't nervous. She was livid. She pressed the ringer.

"Who is it?" a female voice asked from within.

"Penny Snyder. Your daughter."

The door opened. The woman was tall and blonde, with hardly any worry lines to mark her fifty-nine years. Penny's breath caught in her throat. She felt as if she were looking into a mirror. Her first inclination was to fall into her mother's arms, hold her close, and breathe her in, something she'd dreamed of doing for so long. But the flat look in Arlene's eyes stopped her. "Are you going to invite me inside?"

It was obvious that Arlene had been alerted to the possibility that she might get a visit from Penny. It took Arlene a moment to respond to her question.

"Yes. Of course," she finally said.

Penny stepped inside. Arlene left the door open as Penny walked toward the kitchen, which was wide open and lit up by the sunlight pouring through the windows. The home reminded her of Dorothy's house. How many times, she wondered, had Ellis and Dorothy visited their daughter? How many barbecues and family gatherings had they enjoyed without Penny?

"What do you want?" Arlene asked.

A deep ache settled in her heart as Penny turned to face Arlene, her mother, the woman she'd thought about nearly every day of her life and said, "Absolutely nothing."

"Then why are you here?"

"I wanted to give you this." Penny handed her the aged and sagging cardboard box. The one filled with letters and pictures that her father had collected and saved for all these years. "You can burn the box along with its contents, but I want you to know that I scanned every single memento of your time with Dad."

"I never should have left you with him."

Penny looked into her mother's eyes. Arlene's tone wasn't sad or regretful—it was unemotional. Penny's vision blurred, and she wiped at her eyes, then adamantly began to shake her head. "I'm glad you left me with Dad. If you had an ounce of morality or compassion, or any of those normal human feelings, you would have left Dad and me without resorting to lies and using your weakness to get your father to do your dirty work. I feel sorry for your children."

Arlene's face reddened. "I think you should leave. And take this with you."

Penny stiffened. "I have been here for two minutes, and you're already sending me away?"

There was no response as they stared one another down.

"Do you have any idea how many nights I cried for you after you were gone?" Penny asked. "For years I hated Dad for something he didn't do." A tear slid down her cheek. "I loved you. Dad loved you. What sort of person allows another to go to prison for something he didn't do?"

Arlene raised her chin a notch. The blank look on her face failed to hide the fact that she was nervous. The subtle facial tics gave her away.

Penny wiped her cheek. "Did you ever once think about me? Wonder what sort of person I had become?"

"Of course."

Silence hovered between them, hot and heavy, as Penny waited, hoping for more. It was difficult for her to imagine what sort of person could do what Arlene had done. But it was clear that Arlene had moved on and had never looked back. "I wanted you to have those letters and mementos and tell you that I'm going to write a book."

Arlene exhaled.

"I'm going to tell the world the truth. If you try to stop me, I will hire the best lawyers, and I will do everything in my power to make sure your parents go to jail for lying under oath."

"It's time for you to go," Arlene said flatly.

Penny walked to the door and rested her hand on the handle as she looked over her shoulder at Arlene. "In three years, on your twin daughters' eighteenth birthdays, I will be returning here to tell my half sisters everything I know about their mother. I think they deserve to know the person who has raised them, don't you?"

Jessie sat in the front row listening to Penny talk about her father. Zee sat to her right. The funeral for Nathaniel Snyder was taking place outdoors in the chill of a February afternoon. The burial service was small, with no more than fifteen people in attendance.

Nathaniel Snyder had passed away a week after Penny saw her mother for the first time in thirty years. It was a sad, sad story. Arlene could have divorced her husband but instead had allowed her father to make elaborate plans that included sending Nathaniel to prison.

After her visit to Maine, Penny had stopped by the office to let Jessie and Zee know that her father had passed away. She'd been at her father's side when he took his last breath. Although he couldn't respond, she told Dad she'd found Arlene, and that she knew he was innocent. She held his hand and made sure he knew how much she loved him, letting him know he was the best father a girl could ask for.

Nathaniel Snyder would not be forgotten.

Standing at the podium, Penny spoke about all the great memories she'd shared with her father: how they nearly burned the house down when he taught her to cook, how he would try to impress her friends by standing on his head, and how he spent long hours taking videos when she played sports so he could watch the games again at home.

"He taught me how to use power tools," Penny said, smiling. "And how to climb onto the roof, change a tire, and install a new electrical outlet—all in one afternoon."

Zee chuckled.

"My dad taught me to always wait until the morning to solve a problem." Penny used a tissue to wipe her eyes. "Mostly, my dad, Nathaniel James Snyder, taught me that real love makes you strong and gives you courage and is always, absolutely, without a doubt, unconditional."

Jessie felt a tightening in her chest. She was proud of Zee for solving her first case. She was also happy for Penny. She would finally have closure and hopefully some newfound peace.

There would be no reception after the ceremony.

As Jessie and Zee waited their turn to talk to Penny, Zee gestured to her right. "See that dark sedan down the road? The one parked behind the white Camry?"

Jessie glanced that way. "Looks like someone is inside. Do you know who it is?"

"I think it's Dorothy."

"Why would she come here? Do you really think she was gullible enough to believe everything her husband said about Nathaniel abusing their daughter?"

"Definitely," Zee said. "I did a tarot reading to confirm."

Jessie smiled.

"I did a good job on my first case, didn't I?" Zee asked.

"You broke into another house," Jessie reprimanded. "That's two in less than six months."

"So, I guess that means I won't be getting a raise?"

"You can't just break into people's homes whenever you want, Zee. Your actions are jeopardizing everything I've worked so hard for."

"Breaking and entering worked both times, but I'm sorry. I won't do it again."

"How am I going to trust you, moving forward?"

"I'll never break into another house for as long as I live. I swear on my mother's grave."

"I'll give you one more chance, Zee, but that's it. I won't have any choice but to let you go if it happens again."

Zee opened her mouth, but then shut it after Jessie said, "No raise."

Zee sighed. "Want to see a cool shirt I found online?"

"Sure." It was difficult to stay mad at the girl.

Zee held open her jacket so Jessie could see it, whether or not she wanted to. The shirt was black with bold lettering and read: LISTEN TO THE VOICES IN YOUR HEAD. "Pretty cool, right?"

"Are the voices referring to Marion, Lucy, and Francis?"

"Duh."

Jessie smiled. "Do you listen to them?"

"Do I have a choice?"

They shared a laugh.

Zee zipped her jacket closed. "I've finally come to terms with the voices. They make me laugh and keep me from getting lonely."

Jessie nodded. "How's Tobey?"

"He's a little dramatic. Pretends like he can't use his arm. It's a little annoying, but he did ask me if I wanted to help him find an apartment and move in with him."

"Wow! That was fast. How do you feel about that?"

"I'm really not sure. I think it's too soon. I want him to work a little harder at this relationship, sort of like you and Colin."

"What do you mean?"

"Are you kidding me?" Zee asked. "Look how hard he has to work it just to get you to look at the house he wants to share with you, Olivia, and Piper."

"What are you talking about?"

Zee's eyes widened. "Nothing. I didn't say a word. Except that it has a huge backyard and lots of windows." She zipped her lips closed.

Jessie wondered if it were true. Did Colin want to move in together? Coming home to Colin and the girls every night made her heart race in a good way. She and Colin knew each other's habits, good and bad. They respected and trusted each other. It could work.

Before she could try to get more details out of Zee, Penny joined them. "Thank you for coming," she said.

"Sorry for your loss," Jessie told her.

"He was a cool dude," Zee added. "You were lucky to have him in your life."

Penny smiled. "Thank you both for everything."

"Do you think you'll ever see your mom again?" Zee asked.

"I don't think so," Penny said.

"You were right about Arlene being alive," Zee said, her tone reflective as if she didn't expect a response.

"Yes, I was," Penny said, "but I definitely didn't think it all through. I knew my grandfather didn't like my dad, but I had no idea his hatred for him ran so deep."

The three of them started walking toward the parking lot. Penny looked over her shoulder, blew a kiss toward the casket, and said, "Goodbye, Dad." If she'd been looking ahead, she would have seen Zee wave to the woman in the dark sedan before the car sped off.

FIFTY-FOUR

That evening as Jessie was setting the table, she heard a knock at the door. "Come in!"

Higgins barked until he saw Colin appear at the top of the stairs. The dog sniffed his hand and then began the dance of happiness. The man who had carried him off the street after a hit-and-run and taken him to the vet was here.

Jessie laughed as she tried to squeeze her way between them so she could get a proper greeting from the man she'd come to realize meant everything to her. Colin understood her. He challenged her and listened to her. Her life was better with him in it.

"Wow!" Colin said as she squeezed him tight. "Why do I get the feeling you've missed me?"

"Because I have." She gestured toward the kitchen. "I made lasagna."

"You do love me," he said, smiling. "Where's Olivia?"

"She'll be back soon. She's doing some filing at the office." Jessie looked him over. "You look exhausted."

"I'm tired. I'm not going to lie."

"The Willis case?"

"Yeah. I thought I had our man, but I was wrong."

"Who?"

"Paden White, the father of the girl who was sitting next to the coach at the movie theater."

"Oh."

"The man lied about his alibi, so we got a search warrant. I found a certain bloom in the backyard. White, vibrant. Mexican orange, it's called." He shook his head. "We also found rope that looked similar to the rope used to hang Willis."

"But?" Jessie prodded.

"It wasn't a match. Just got the call a few minutes ago."

"I'm sorry."

"I'm not giving up. I don't want this to end up being just another unsolved homicide to add to the growing pile."

"This case has really gotten to you, hasn't it?"

He said nothing.

"There's something else, isn't there?"

"It's nothing."

"No, tell me."

"In two words, Ben Morrison."

Without Ben she was certain she never would have found her sister, and she and Olivia would still be unable to move forward with their lives. Ben had been a positive force in her life, and it frustrated her that he couldn't see that. "Why does it always come full circle back to Ben?"

Colin exhaled. "Don't you think it's odd how comfortable Morrison is around homicide scenes?"

"You're comfortable, aren't you?"

"Not like that. I go home. I eat dinner, and then I try to go to sleep. But sleep doesn't come. Instead, I toss and turn because all I can see is the face of the victim. Some of these crime scenes are unthinkable displays of a monster's whim—psychopaths who show no mercy. Blood and crushed bones . . . but Morrison never flinches. It's as if he has nerves of steel, or maybe no nerves at all."

"You don't know whether he sleeps at night," Jessie told him.

"True." Colin chuckled.

"What?"

"The truth is, he'd probably make a good homicide detective. I've been reading the cases he's written about over the past few decades. Do you know how many times he's managed to show up before the police?"

"No. How many?"

"At least a dozen times. I couldn't find one other crime reporter who was able to beat the cops one time, let alone twelve."

Jessie went back to setting the table.

"Everywhere I go . . . Morrison seems to appear out of the blue. I still haven't forgotten the guilty look on his face when I pulled him over for a broken taillight. He got out of the car and was walking to the back of his van as if to show me something."

"What are you trying to say?"

"I think he was going to make a confession, show me what he had back there. If I hadn't stopped it, told him it was just a broken taillight, I would have found out."

"But you didn't," Jessie said. "You've had a long day. You're tired. And I think your bias against Ben Morrison is rearing its ugly head again."

He wrapped an arm around her waist and pulled her close. "Maybe you're right."

She smiled. "Did you bring the car?"

"I did. It's parked across the street."

"Is there something else you want to talk to me about?" Jessie asked.

He frowned.

"Zee told me about the house you found."

"How would Zee know?"

"She heard it through the grapevine . . . Piper told Olivia, and Olivia told Zee. It's pretty simple the way that works."

"I don't think I thought this through," Colin said.

"So it's true?"

"Are you interested?"

She stepped back from his embrace and looked around the house. So much laughter, so many tears shed under this roof. She knew every creak in the floor, every scratch, every flaw. How many times had she come through the door, grateful to be home? Looking at Colin, she met his gaze and smiled, thinking about living together and breathing life into a new place. "I think it's time to make new memories—you and me and the girls. Together."

He wrapped his arms around her, his laughter cut off with a kiss as she melted into his arms.

"Get a room," Olivia said as she walked in.

Jessie pulled away from Colin. "Why do you always tiptoe up the stairs?"

"So I can catch you guys making out like a couple of high school kids."

Jessie felt the heat rise to her face.

Colin took a seat on the couch.

Olivia wagged a finger at Colin. "I think it's time for you, young man, to go home." She pointed to the stairs leading to the door.

Colin smirked. "What would you say if I told you I think I could change your mind about sending me away?"

Jessie headed for the kitchen, leaving them to tease each other. She grabbed the pot holders from the drawer and pulled the lasagna from the oven. Her stomach growled.

Olivia snorted. "I would say you've been drinking."

Colin lifted his hands as if to show her he was clean. "No beer or wine in hand."

"You two have fun," Olivia said as she started off toward her bedroom.

Both Jessie and Olivia turned toward Colin when they heard keys jangling.

"Now?" Jessie asked Colin. She knew he had a surprise for Olivia, but she'd assumed he was going to wait until after dinner. The thought that maybe the anticipation was too much for him caused a warm, fuzzy feeling to radiate through her chest.

Olivia brightened. "I can drive your car?"

"No," Colin said. "It's better than that. I found a car—with Jessie's permission, of course. A great deal. It's used, but the engine is clean, and it has low mileage. And it's all yours."

Olivia looked at Jessie. "Is he serious?"

Jessie nodded. Moments like this, knowing how close the two of them had gotten over the years, was exactly the type of thing that made life good. Olivia respected Colin, maybe even loved him. He was a good man, and she felt grateful to have him in her life.

"Are you serious?" Olivia asked Colin.

He jangled the keys again. "I have never been more serious. It's all yours, kiddo."

Olivia screamed.

Higgins barked.

And they all ran outside together to see the new member of the Cole family. A 2010 Ford Fusion. Colin told them to climb in—even Higgins—and they drove a few miles away to their new house.

It was perfect.

That night, hours after Olivia fell asleep in her room and Colin left to get some much-needed sleep, Jessie lay in bed staring up at the ceiling. Remnants of their happy night prompted her to think of Sophie. She usually thought of her sister at times like this. Olivia was getting older. And it was events such as this when Jessie wished Sophie could be here.

She grabbed her Kindle from the bedside table, read a couple of pages, and then gave up and put the device back on the table.

Instead, she thought of Ben.

Colin was a good man, and he had good instincts. He was an amazing detective. What evil signs did he see in Ben Morrison that she didn't?

It was sort of ironic, Jessie thought, that Colin had brought him up tonight, since Jessie had only today called and left Ben a message just to say hello. She liked Ben Morrison. He was a big part of her life, and yet she hadn't seen him since he and his family were over for a holiday feast.

More important, she'd never talked to Ben and told him what she'd heard about the death of Aly Scheer, the woman found buried in the backyard of Ben's childhood home in Clarksburg. Ben's father was found guilty for her murder, and yet Jessie had talked to a woman who said she saw Ben strangle the young woman to death.

Why hadn't she mentioned the news to Ben? Was it because the woman was an alcoholic and not a credible witness? Was it because his father was dead and telling him wouldn't change anything, or was it because Ben had not only saved her life but also Olivia's?

Like Colin, Jessie had put a lot of thought into how and why Ben Morrison seemed to show up at the most opportune of times. Not too many people would deny that there was something off about Ben Morrison. Jessie usually ended up blaming his amnesia for any oddities in his personality.

Would she ever know why he was with her sister on the night of his tragic car accident? Or whether or not he was responsible for the death of Aly Scheer?

The answer came to her then—she didn't need to know.

It was that simple.

Her sister, Sophie, was never coming back. Friends and family had gathered at the memorial service to say goodbye. Jessie and Olivia had spent a decade mourning Sophie's absence. They had closure now.

The truth of what happened the night Sophie disappeared was buried deep within the recesses of Ben Morrison's mind.

Before falling asleep, Jessie envisioned living with Colin, Olivia, and Piper in the house Colin had found. It wasn't the house she was excited about, but the family she and Colin would be building. The four of them would be a strong family unit, giving each other emotional security. They would all be there for one another, supporting each other during the inevitable ups and downs life had to offer.

It was a loving family that made a perfect home.

With that thought at the forefront of her mind, a feeling of weightlessness overcame her as she reached over and turned off the lamp.

FIFTY-FIVE

One week later . . .

After Melony and the kids left to do some shopping, Ben decided that now would be a good time to take a look at his van. It had been making a strange rattling sound.

He flipped on the light switch in the garage, then pushed the button. The garage door rolled open, giving him light.

The first thing he did was check the air pressure in all four tires. Then he made sure there weren't any loose lug nuts. Worn mounts wouldn't hold the engine or transmission tight against the frame, and that could lead to vibrations or possibly a rattling sound.

Next, he went in search of his trusty mechanic's creeper with rollers. He'd been diagnosing and repairing problems with his van for as long as he could remember. He found the creeper in one of the garage cabinets, unfolded it, then got down on all fours and lay down on top of it, faceup. He grabbed a few tools and a flashlight and pushed himself under the chassis. With the flashlight in one hand, he used his other to examine the undercarriage and see if anything might be loose. As he searched, he reached up, his fingers feeling around in an area near the suspension, a spot that he couldn't quite see into, even with his flashlight.

Something rattled. He moved around a bit, using the light to try and see what he was dealing with. Again, he felt around. This time he was able to determine that six-inch metal hooks were holding the object in place. If he lifted the hook high enough, he determined that he might be able to unfasten it from the chassis. It wasn't until he'd removed six hooks total that he was able to slide the object to a spot where he could see that it was a metal box about the size of a small paperback novel.

It took some doing, but he wasn't one to give up easily, and after fifteen minutes of pushing and pulling, he was able to turn the box just so and slide it out of its hiding place. Whatever was inside clinked against the metal interior. It wasn't very heavy. He chuckled at the idea that he might have found a long-lost treasure, valuables once hidden by whoever had owned the van before him.

He set the box on his stomach and then rolled out from under the vehicle. It wasn't until he was back on his feet and holding the box in front of him that he saw that there was a lock on it, a miniature padlock like the kind that kept a diary safe from prying eyes. Since he didn't have a key, he took the box to his work area and grabbed a hammer. Before he could break the lock off, somebody said his name.

Turning toward the driveway, he was surprised to see Colin Grayson. He knew the detective was just doing his job, but at the same time, he sensed something more. Colin didn't like him. Never had.

Ben set the hammer down and walked toward him. "Go ahead," Ben said. "Search my house. Search the backyard, the garage, my underwear drawers, I give up. Just get it over with."

Ben walked to the kitchen door and held it open for him.

"I deserve that. Thanks for the offer, but I'll stay right where I am, thanks."

Ben headed back his way, wiped greasy hands on his already dirty jeans. "Melony would never forgive me if I wasn't a good host. Can I get you water? Hot tea?"

Colin rolled his eyes. "I came here to apologize."

"Why would you do that?" Ben asked. "As you've reminded me on more than one occasion, you were just doing your job. We're all just doing our jobs. And besides," Ben added, "I'm sure Jessie put you up to this. Love can make us do crazy things."

"She's not the reason I'm here."

Ben remained silent. He had nothing left to say.

"I haven't given you a fair shake, and I'm sorry for that." Colin gestured toward the house. "I take it Melony isn't home since you invited me inside?"

"She and the kids went shopping."

"Tell her I'm sorry for causing her undue stress, will you?"

Ben nodded, still not sure what to make of Grayson's visit. With nothing left to say, Ben watched Grayson pivot on his feet and make his way back to his car. He opened the car door and then sort of froze, staring at Ben's next-door neighbor's house or front yard, he couldn't be sure. It seemed like an interminably long time to stare into the horizon, but finally he slipped in behind the wheel of his car and drove off.

Ben walked to where Grayson had been staring, trying to figure out what he might have been looking at. The only thing that stood out were the magnificent little white flowers that had bloomed on the shrubs in front of their house.

Scratching the side of his neck, he went back to where he'd left the box. One smack of the hammer busted the lock right off. The lid was rusty, and he had to put a little muscle into it to get it off.

At first he wasn't sure what he was looking at. He turned the box over, dumping its contents onto his worktable. He picked up one of the cards, but it wasn't a card at all. It was a driver's license. A woman named June Emerson. She didn't look familiar. Unable to comprehend what he was seeing, he focused on a pair of earrings—sterling silver wrapped around blue stones. He scooped up the gold necklace and let it dangle between his fingers before setting it back on the table. There was also a ring with a tiny circle of diamonds.

He picked up a different ID, and when he saw her picture, a wave of dizziness washed over him. Aly Scheer. Female. Green eyes. Blonde hair. Her address in Clarksburg, California.

His stomach knotted.

He turned over all the IDs, placing them in a row so that he could see names and faces.

DJ Stumm. Aly Scheer. June Emerson. Jon Eberling.

For a split second, he stopped breathing.

Feeling numb, he shoved everything back into the box and went inside the house. He took the stairs two at a time. Inside his bedroom, he grabbed his laptop and turned it on.

After a moment, he searched the internet for June Emerson. The same woman on the driver's license popped right up. June Emerson, a day care worker, who had fatally tortured an infant and harmed dozens of children in her care. Police found her inside her apartment with a plastic bag over her head and a rope tied tight around her neck. He shut his computer.

Dazed, he stood up and went to the closet, where he reached into the pocket of a jacket he seldom wore. There was a hole. He dug around inside the lining until he found what he was looking for—another driver's license. This one belonged to Roger Willis.

Ben's heart was beating fast, making it difficult to breathe.

Although he couldn't recall how or when, he knew he'd killed them all: Aly Scheer, DJ Stumm, June Emerson, Jon Eberling, Roger Willis, maybe others. Strangling the Heartless Killer had been a different story . . . he'd killed the man in self-defense . . . or had he? He could still remember the rush of euphoria he'd experienced when he'd wrapped his hands around the serial killer's neck.

And what about Roger Willis?

Roger Willis wasn't a serial killer, nor was he someone from Ben's past. It wasn't until Ben confronted him early Sunday morning and found him clutching a one-way ticket to Miami that he'd realized Willis had planned to simultaneously escape the country and justice. Once Willis left the state, the odds would have been against a warrant being entered into the NCIC. Local law enforcement wouldn't have had the funds to pay the cost or jump through the legal hoops required for Willis to be extradited.

In that moment, Ben had known what needed to be done. But there was more to it than that. Hadn't he been feeling an underlying urge to take the man's life, to kill again?

DJ Stumm had killed his family. June Emerson had killed an infant and tortured children; Jon Eberling had stolen from his mother and killed her beloved pet. Had he killed those people in his own selfish pursuit of justice? If so, why Aly Scheer? As far as he knew, she'd done nothing more than break his heart.

He looked down at his hands, curled and uncurled his fingers. Were these the hands of a killer?

In a state of shock, he made his way back down the stairs. A framed photo hanging on the wall caught his attention. He stopped to look at the recent family picture Melony had enlarged, then framed and hung with the others. His gaze roamed lovingly over his wife and kids, his beautiful family.

His chest tightened.

He took a breath as he realized his sister had known who and what he was all along.

His father, too.

His legs wobbled. He sat on the step behind him, let his head fall into the palms of his hands, and let it all out, emotions weaved tightly together like a ball of yarn. He cried tears of anguish, regret, and shame.

It was a while before he made his way back into the garage.

He added Roger Willis's ID to the others in the box. Sophie Cole's ID was not among the others, which was a relief. She had been driving the car the night of the accident that left him with amnesia. He might never know what their plans had been that night, and now, suddenly, he was glad for it. He and Jessie Cole had become friends in the truest sense, and he hoped to keep it that way.

He set about gathering the tools he would need to reattach the metal case to the undercarriage and got to work.

When he was finished and his dark secret was well hidden and no longer loose, he rolled out from under the van. For now, until he had time to give the situation further consideration, he would leave things be. Destroying the contents of the case would be a wise choice, but he couldn't bring himself to do it.

He was still cleaning up and putting away his tools when Melony and the kids pulled into the driveway. Abigail and Sean jumped out of the car and said hello as they ran past him into the house.

Melony smiled at Ben as she approached. She wrapped her arms around his waist and leaned her head against his chest.

"I'm dirty," he warned.

"I don't care. I'm just glad this whole Roger Willis business is finally over and that you're home where you belong and everything is back to normal." She pulled back so she could look up at him. "Are you okay?"

"Never been better."

She gave him a quizzical look.

"I've finally come to terms with my past," he explained. "I'm done searching. I'm ready to let it all go."

She rested a hand on her chest, over her heart. "This makes me so happy. I've been worried about you for a while now."

"No more worrying, okay? Things are going to change around here. Ben is back."

She laughed. "I'm going to go get dinner started. I'll make spaghetti, and then we'll celebrate with a glass of wine." She got to the door leading to the house and then stopped and gestured toward the van. "Did you find the problem?"

"I did. No more rattle," he said proudly. "It's all fixed and good as new."

"Just like you," she said with a smile before disappearing inside.

"Yeah," he said to no one. "Just like me."

ACKNOWLEDGMENTS

When the idea for the Jessie Cole series popped into my head years ago, it was Ben Morrison's character I saw so clearly. I knew he'd been in a tragic car crash that left him unable to recall any details of his life prior to the accident. Ben was a wonderful husband and father to two young children. He was a good, compassionate, and caring man. The working title for my book was *Family Man*. Ben was the kind of neighbor, friend, and coworker you would invite to dinner at your house. But what nobody knew, including Ben, was the person he used to be before the accident. I soon realized Ben would need help discovering his past, someone strong and equally kindhearted, someone who carried his or her own demons within. That's when Jessie Cole came into the picture and quickly came to life!

Once again, I would like to thank Liz Pearsons, Charlotte Herscher, Amy Tannenbaum, Sarah Shaw, and everyone at Amazon who helped me see another story come to fruition. Additional thanks to Brian McDougle, Cathy Katz, and Morgan and Brittany Ragan.

About the Author

Photo © 2014 Morgan Ragan

New York Times, Wall Street Journal, and *USA Today* bestselling author T.R. Ragan has sold more than two million books since her debut novel appeared in 2011. She is the author of the Faith McMann Trilogy (*Furious, Outrage,* and *Wrath*); six Lizzy Gardner novels (*Abducted, Dead Weight, A Dark Mind, Obsessed, Almost Dead,* and *Evil Never Dies*); and the four novels in the Jessie Cole series (*Her Last Day, Deadly Recall, Deranged,* and *Buried Deep*). In addition to thrillers, she writes medieval time-travel tales, contemporary romance, and romantic suspense as Theresa Ragan. An avid traveler, her wanderings have led her to China, Thailand, and Nepal. Theresa and her husband, Joe, have four children and live in Sacramento, California. To learn more, visit her website at www.theresaragan.com.